Destiny at Cracker Creek

Destiny

at

Cracker Creek

by
Dorothy Lindsay
(1901-1983)
and
Steele Lindsay

THE NATIONAL WRITERS PRESS

Published in the United States of America by
The National Writers Press
1450 South Havana
Aurora, CO 80012

International Standard Book Number: 0-88100-047-7
Library of Congress Catalog Card No. 84-61590

Dedication

This book is dedicated to my beloved Dorothy. I would never have know her had not the ticket office in Boston's Colonial Theatre given us, Harvard's 47 Workshop stage crew (four men and a girl), six tickets instead of five. We did not discover this until we were having dinner.

"Let's get another woman," someone said.

Billy Knight, stage manager, said, "I'll call *Cry*."

He found her a little woebegone. Her three apartment mates were out on the town, but she had refused to join them. It was Ash Wednesday, 1924. Too late for her to join us at dinner, she broke down and met us at the Colonial.

From that moment we were committed for life, though our first date wasn't until April Fool's Day. Dinner deluxe at eighty-five cents each.

Sated, I asked her would she like to go to a movie. She opted for a walk in the Fenway.

We never knew how it came about on that walk, but I was suddenly kissing her, then asked her to marry me. She caught her breath a couple of times and said, "Yes!"

We were married on June 3, 1925. She gave me 59 years of idyllic love until I lost her August 23, 1983, after her second major stroke.

STEELE LINDSAY

1

Mary Meakin left the severe austerity of Mrs. Swenson's boarding house and headed down Schoolhouse Hill for Cracker Creek's distinctive boardwalk. She never missed showing up on weekends, when the Blue Mountains of Eastern Oregon emptied three cornucopias of mountain men—miners, sheepmen and lumberjacks—onto the boardwalk for a 48-hour carouse of its bars and overhead massage parlors. Tourists from near and far came to sample this re-creation of a turn-of-the-century goldboom town, which had been wiped out by fire sixty years ago.

The boardwalk never ceased to fascinate Mary Meakin because of its tremendous range of exotic sounds. She liked to hear the bellicose cadence of miners in calked boots, the bass staccato of a sheepman's prancing pony, the cacophony of a Saturday night; it sent chills up and down her spine.

On this Saturday night in June, the boardwalk was overrun with men, a sight of which she never tired, despite the fact that she was the only woman among Mrs. Swenson's eight boarders. The trouble was, they treated her like a sister. Seven young men, all but one gifted with good looks, and full of life. Yet how many times had she groaned to herself, "Not one of them has ever made a pass at me!"

The seventh man among them, Bill Saxon, was an enigma. Most likely in his mid-thirties. A little man with a bald head too big for the rest of him; he reminded her of a Jack o' Lantern set atop a beanpole. An old smoothie with women. Obsequious and fawning. He would go for the jugular without hesitation if winning were important. An attorney and town councilman.

As for the rest of her tablemates, it did no good to come to meals wearing something sweet and girlish. At 31, she had the figure of a 12-year-old boy: flat as a pancake upstairs and the hips of a rattlesnake. In short, she was nothing but a little runt.

Yet her eyes, which she thought her best asset, apparently failed to make any impression on them. She had only to look in her mirror, which she did quite often, to realize why—if she were honest. They reminded her of a great, mournful Newfoundland dog, looking up at her as if she, at least, understood the depth of its sadness. The only difference was that her eyes were hazel.

She had no shame whatsoever in practicing the same wiles on a man, whenever she found one worth the effort. Usually men were considerably taller than she, hence they had to look down into her eyes to speak to her. Her mirror and the Newfoundland dog told her how to respond. She knew instantly if she had hit home. He would draw back suddenly . . . blink a couple of times . . . then open his eyes wider to take a second look and grin sheepishly upon realizing she had been taking it all in.

She took a deep breath, shaking her head. Of course, it never happened that way. As always on a Saturday night, she had been daydreaming. Men were men and women were what men made of them, and not one of them had as yet been moved to make something of her.

But she no longer had any need of daydreaming. She had reached the bottom of Schoolhouse Hill. Her nose told her where she was. These mountain men had the smell of pine and fir and tamarack about them, and the freshness that comes of dunking themselves in the tumbling waters of creeks that cascaded by their cabin doors.

With them, water was not something to drink, but to revel in and to wash away the honest sweat that men in store clothes never raise, except in passion. They abhorred the use of witch hazel and bay rum to tell the world they had freshly shaved. In fact, not too many of them shaved at all. Whiskers were in style.

Mary took one look at the swirling eddies of humanity on the boardwalk and decided she would be better off if she scooted inside the hitching rail instead, though it meant threading through jams of men outside the swinging half-doors of several bars on that side of the boardwalk.

She was always fascinated by the bar doors, relics of the Old West, louvered like window shutters, hung halfway up, double-hinged so they swung both in and out . . . effectively hiding what goes on inside, as well as those who don't wish to be seen there.

Suddenly she and all those around her were showered with chicken feathers. Looking up quickly, she caught sight of one of the girls in an overhead massage parlor leaning out to shake the stuffing out of a bed pillow and waving the empty case at the crowd below, like the prostitutes did eight years earlier, flaunting the banners of their profession.

"Know any better way to advertise?" said a familiar voice behind her. She knew at once it was the Grizzly when he put his arms around her in a tremendous bear hug.

"Griz!" she exulted, twisting around so she could look up at him. He towered at least a foot above her.

A stray feather settled on her turned-up nose. She stuck her lower lip out, trying to blow it away. Griz playfully flicked it off and found himself looking down once more into the depths of her big hazel eyes. It was not lost on her that he, like the rest, blinked and took a second look.

"I had heard," Mary said, "that this is one of the stunts they pull here on the boardwalk to impress tourists this was typical of the Old West in Cracker Creek, but it's the first time they snared me."

"They're meant for men only," he snickered. "Not for little girls."

She caught another feather and fluttered it around, as if it were a pretty flower to admire, but sneezed violently when it accidentally brushed her nose.

"Cheap perfume!" she snorted when she caught her breath. "Isn't that going too far when they scent pillows, too?"

He grinned. "I wouldn't know about that."

Griz got his nickname on Labor Day the Year before, when, stripped to the waist in Cracker Creek's rock-drilling championship, women learned he had a mattress of brown fur from his eyeballs to the pit of his stomach. The sight of his terrific physique, at six-feet-four and 240 pounds, caused a singer at the Nugget bar, known only as the Redhead, to dub him the Grizzly. When she learned his real name was Quigley, she said, "Ugh! What's your first name?"

"There's no more."

"Not even a first name?"

"Not that I know of."

"Cut it out!" she cried. "Everybody's got to have at least two names."

"How about you?" he retorted.

"I've *got* two—Red Head. Simple as that."

"Miss or Mrs.?"

"Ex-Mrs.," she said, with a toss of her head.

"That's good enough for me. I'll call you Ex-Missus."

"You'll do nothing of the sort! You'll call me Red like everyone else does. What's more, I'm going to give you a moniker that will settle your hash. *You* don't want people to just call you Quigley."

"They always have."

"But it doesn't make sense. First thing you know they'll be calling you Quig."

"They've done that too."

"For one, I don't like it. Do you know what you remind me of?"

"Your ex-husband."

For a moment she was stunned. "You knew him?"

He shook his head. "It was just a stab in the dark."

"I thought you might have seen us in New Orleans. We had a song-and-dance act in a nightclub there.'"

"Sorry, Red. I didn't mean to stir up old memories. You were going to tell me what I reminded you of."

"Yes." She blew her nose gently and turned back to him. The old smile was back in place agin. "I was in Yellowstone on the way here—maybe you're not going to like this . . . "

She pushed him away because he seemed to be bearing in on her.

"Keep going," he insisted.

"Anyway, when I saw you bared to the waist at the rock-drilling, all I could think of was one of those tremendous grizzly bears in Yellowstone . . . especially when you stood up, I mean, like they do, with your arms outstretched, with a god-awful steel drill in one hand and a sledge hammer in the other, looking so almighty big and tall . . . "

She ran out of breath, eyeing him fearfully, lest he turn on

4

his heel and walk out on her.

He rubbed his chin whiskers. "That's not bad . . . no, not half bad. I sort of like it." He tried it on his tongue. "Grizzly . . . Grizzly! Yes, it fits."

"Better than Quigley." She made a sour face.

"I'll still settle for Griz," he beamed happily. "I'm obliged to you, Red, for giving me a new moniker, as you say. I like those fancy words you come up with."

"Oh, pshaw!" Half embarrassed by the compliment, she rubbed her cheek against the whiskers masking his face and came away with a chuckle. "You smell like a grizzly, too!"

"That's tobacco juice," he grinned.

"You must come up and try my tub sometime." She pointed up to her quarters overhead, off the narrow balcony running around three sides of the Nugget. "That's where we women who work here live. Handy enough for you?"

"I kind of like the creek, myself," he grinned.

"My tub comes with hot water and an optional shower," she added persuasively.

He hedged. "Might give it a try sometime."

Of all the eligible men in Cracker Creek, Mary thought Griz was the most desirable, even though she was sure he slept with the Redhead regularly. But this didn't bother her after that big bear hug he had just given her, setting her on fire once more. But she wanted to be accepted by him as a woman, not as a little runt; a red-blooded woman nonetheless, as plagued by desire and a need for love as much as the Redhead must be. She wished she could see this charmer at close hand to determine what made her so desirable. So she took the oblique approach.

"I suppose you're headed for the Nugget?" she suggested.

He looked at her suspiciously before admitting, "I was."

She took his arm and fell in stride with him. "Since you are going my way . . . " She left that thought hanging, then abruptly stopped him. "How'd you like to take me to the Opera House dance instead?" That's where she was actually headed.

"I don't dance."

"You won't even try?"

A shake of his head.

She saw that they had reached the Nugget's threshold. She sought desperately to think of something that would dissuade him from deserting her there.

A terrific jam at the Nugget's swinging half-doors gave her a chance to succeed. They were stoppered wide open by the press of men stuck there who craned their necks to see over and around the heads of those in front of them. The electrifying sound of the Redhead's voice came to them clear and vibrant. She was tearing men's hearts out with the tearful plaint of a drunkard's daughter in the ancient ballad, "Father, Dear Father, Come Home With Me Now."

"Lift me up, Griz," Mary begged. "Ive got to see her."

He put an arm around her knees and sat her on one shoulder. She kept her balance by clinging to his head, wiggling with delight. "This is terrific!" she bubbled.

The Redhead had just swung into the tear-jerking chorus.

Father, dear Father, come home with me now,
The clock in the steeple strikes one;
You said you were coming right home from the shop,
As soon as your day's work was done;
Our fire has gone out, our house is all dark . . .

But even as she sat enthralled on a shoulder of the man she adored, instinct told Mary this was the woman who would be first in his heart. She could read it in the faces of the men now held spellbound by her voice. She was the woman they had left behind when they came to Oregon, or the girl they were always going to marry, but didn't. She was the face on the calendar they saw first thing in the morning and the last one to catch their eye before going to bed at night.

"What's going on up there?" Griz asked, wriggling both shoulders. "You've suddenly become becalmed."

She flinched, realizing he had sensed the change in her mood. "She's much prettier than I expected," Mary admitted quickly.

He laughed. "Or you hoped."

"Let me down now," she said quietly. Gone was the earlier exuberance. She was sober-faced when he put her down.

Griz mentally kicked himself for being so glib with the quick quip. It beat him why women were so easily deflated by one look at Red in action. Offstage, she wasn't even sexy. Just a woman who was cut out to be a homebody, forced to earn a living when she lost her husband. Until then, she had told him, she had never realized she had a voice that would wring tears out of men in an area like the Creek, where most mountain men only had a chance to see her on weekends.

And she was damned good company for a lonesome man like Griz, who wanted no part of a woman on the prowl. Nevertheless, he liked the little runt. All waif and no woman. In her own way she was good for him, too.

The Redhead had ended her song stint and the crowd blocking the Nugget's entrance was breaking up. Griz and Mary stood aside for those coming out, only to be caught in a new scramble of others trying to get inside.

A big lumberjack looked down at Mary's woebegone face and decided he'd better do something about helping her get inside. He tapped two men ahead of him, grumbling: "Let the little lady by." When they saw the size of him, the pair who had been tapped made room for her to squeeze by and passed the word ahead. If she hadn't reached back and grabbed Griz's hand to pull him after her, he would have been swallowed up in the crush.

The magic words caught on. "Let the little lady by!" Before she really understood what was happening, she found she was not only inside, but standing ahead of the pack for all those sitting at tables to see and recognize, if they knew her.

She would have passed out from the shock had she not been holding Griz's hand. She wheeled around, frightened, scanning faces, scared she would see someone she knew.

Reading her fears, Griz assured her there couldn't possibly be anyone there who would report her to the school board or her principal.

"Now that you are inside," he suggested, "why not look around and decide for yourself whether it's half as bad as you expected it to be?"

As an afterthought, he added, with a sly grin, "And, of course, you want to meet Red."

She bobbed her head up and down like a child. He was such a comfort. Her heart stopped racing wildly. Her eyes were never so large. The place was jam-packed, yet nobody seemed to be interested in her. They probably figured she was someone's daughter.

Then she discovered the long mahogany bar, with men three and four deep jostling for position to get refills, their legs almost obscuring the glistening brass rail on which some men liked to put a foot while they nursed a stand-up drink. Long-necked brass spittoons were set at intervals for those who sought to test or even show off their marksmanship.

But she caught her breath when she spotted the massive, carved back bar, festooned with naked little boy babies, flaunting their sex over the tops of huge wall mirrors. Not that she was embarrassed by nudity per se. As a child she went skinny-dipping with any and all kids in the neighborhood, in a pond on her family's farm in the Umatilla district. And she never hesitated after she grew up, during threshing time, to join the crews going skinny at day's end, making a mad dash for the same pond to rid themselves of the dust, dirt and straw caked on their bodies by pure sweat in the hundred-degree heat.

Griz caught the curiosity reflected in her eyes as she noted the walkway overhead and doors opening off it at frequent intervals. "That's where the women who work here live," he explained. "Barmaids and such."

She grinned. "I suppose the Redhead is among those classified as 'such'?"

He pointed to the quarters directly overhead. "That's where she lives. Front and center, with a view of the boardwalk. She gets the best, you know."

"How nice!" she laughed. "For both of you."

He let it pass.

This way she knew what the score was.

There was a movement in the standees behind them. Mary looked around and ducked back quickly, hiding her face against Griz. "That man in the black suit with the bow tie," she whispered. "Tall and cadaverous. I'd swear he's a parson."

Griz turned. "You mean Leckenby?"

"I don't know his name but I've seen him on the walk."

"He fits the description. Evangelist of some sort."

"Don't let him see me," she begged.

He sniffed. "Pay no attention to him. He'd never know you were here if he was standing right alongside. He's got eyes for only one woman."

"Does Red know?"

"Of course. He's harmless. Comes in every Saturday night. Pretends he's getting ideas for his Sunday sermon, if you tax him with it, but he never takes his eyes off her."

When Red started a new ballad, Mary turned around boldly and stared at the Reverend Jeremiah Leckenby. Griz was right. The man was in a trance, or else in love. It showed in his eyes. Her heart went out to him, poor benighted man! Like herself, enamored of someone he dared not tell of his love.

Griz nudged her. "Red's coming our way."

Moving in and out among the tables as she sang, Red had swung into the final chorus of the tear-jerker, "My Mother Was A Lady," and she had them hanging on every word:

My mother was a lady—like yours you will allow,
And you may have a sister, who needs protection now.
I've come to this great city to find a brother dear,
And you wouldn't dare insult me, sir, if Jack were
only here.

Mary chuckled. It was amazing that these oafs treated Red like a lady, too. They had only to put a hand out to touch her, but none did. Tonight she was a Floradora girl from that era Cracker Creek was now re-creating, lacking only one of the ostrich-feathered hats that famous stage sextet always wore. On the golden side of being purely redheaded, fair of face with a touch of rouge, and tall enough to satisfy a man, Red wore an off-the-shoulder burgundy satin dress that showed her bosom to good advantage and fell in graceful folds to the floor from hips that would have been the envy of any woman half her age. Mary guessed she was nearing forty.

She stretched out both hands to greet Mary. "We meet at last," she bubbled. "I had a pretty good idea who you might be. He talks about you a lot."

Mary blushed. "And I didn't know your name, other than 'Red' and 'the Redhead'."

"That's good enough. The real one's sort of private-like, but if you really want to know, honey, it's the same as yours."

"You mean it's 'Mary'?"

"It sure is."

"How nice," Mary Meakin said, clapping her hands. Then to Griz: "Why didn't you say she was Mary, too?"

The Redhead cut in. "I like what you called me." She turned to Griz. "She's Mary and I'm Mary Too. T-double-O. Get it, Griz?" She dug him in the ribs.

He threw up his hands and shook his head. "I'm not going to have any part of two Marys. One of you is bad enough without having double talk. She's Mary and you're Red! Get that!"

The two women looked at each other and giggled.

"I'm Mary," said the Meakin.

"And I'm Mary, too," mimicked the Redhead.

Griz got up, shook his head and turned on his heel to walk out of the Nugget.

"Come back here," shouted Red at his retreating figure. He stopped when everyone at the surrounding tables turned to listen in on something that promised be be interesting. "You brought her in here," Red continued to shout. "Now you do the proper thing and escort her out, when the time comes."

Reluctantly, Griz returned to his seat.

Red wanted to know why he brought Mary into the Nugget in the first place.

"He didn't," Mary spoke up. "We were caught up in the mob at the doors and the first thing we knew we were carried inside by the tide."

"She didn't fight against it." Griz winked at Red. "There she was, sitting on my shoulder . . . "

"Wait a minute," Red broke in. "Why was she sitting on your shoulder?"

"A very unladylike posture, I assure you."

Mary protested. "The only way I could see you, Red, was to ask him to lift me up so I could see inside over the crowd."

"Still very unladylike," growled Griz.

"No, it wasn't. I was sitting sidesaddle."

The Redhead giggled at the picture. "But I still wonder why you wanted to see what I looked like."

"I don't know whether you have ever seen a magazine called the *Police Gazette.* "

"Sure thing," said Red and Griz nodded too. "Used to be the hottest thing going," he recalled, "back when Cracker Creek was booming. It went bust for awhile, but it's back in business now and being imported and sold here to emphasize this *is* the old Wild West incarnate."

Mary said one of the other teachers found a recent copy abandoned in her schoolroom and showed it around. She giggled. "I wanted to see if you wore tights, too."

Griz guffawed and slapped his leg. "That I want to see!"

"You buy 'em and I'll put 'em on," Red challenged him.

"Where would I get them?"

"You find out." She cocked her head in satisfaction.

A barmaid approached them. Red hesitated, then asked Mary, "What will you have?"

Mary shook her head.

"Not even a beer?"

Another shake of the head.

Red turned to the barmaid. "Ask Tim if he can spare a shot of his root beer. I guess you know what Griz and I will have."

Tim was the bartender. Red explained that so many men sought to buy him a drink every day that he had to fake it occasionally by pouring himself a shot of root beer under the bar.

"What's next for you two?" Red asked.

Griz put his hands in his pockets, stretched his legs full out under the table. "I'm staying right here."

Red looked thoughtfully at Mary. "And leaving you to fend for yourself?"

Mary shrugged. "We can't seem to agree."

"Shame on you," Red taxed Griz. "Where's your sense of chivalry?"

Mary sought quickly to take him off the hook. "I wanted him to join me at the Opera House dance. I go there every Saturday night, but . . . " She shrugged again.

Griz waggled his head. "I don't dance."

"Hogwash!" Red fixed him with her cat's eyes. "Did you even try?"

"Never wanted to and I'm not going to start now!"

Red turned to Mary. "When he gets stubborn like this, retreat and try a new tack." Then to Griz: "Mind if I make a suggestion?

Why not take Mary to the Argonaut instead?" Griz started to sputter. "Yes, I know. You never go there anymore because the place is overrun with women. Had your supper, Mary?"

"Sure."

"Then you can have another, honey. I hear their suppers are galumptious. And it won't cost him a penny. They're on the house."

Griz began squirming again in his chair and rubbing his whiskered mouth with a hand no longer stuffed in a pocket.

The Redhead pushed her advantage. "It will do you good to get out of the Nugget for a change. On Saturday night 'specially, which should be your night to howl. And to prowl. Get back with your kind of people again, Griz."

He pulled in his long legs, sat up straight again and opened his mouth to speak, took one sad look at each of them, shook his head and said nothing.

Mary caught a look of deep affection in Red's eyes as she dropped her tone to one that was soft and persuasive. "Give her a break, Griz." She rested her hand on the one with which he was drumming the table nervously. "If I were a man . . ."

"Oh, shut up!" he snapped. "Get off my back!"

But the curious thing, thought Mary, was that he didn't bark back angrily or bitterly. In fact, all through this exchange she was impressed with the rapport between them, like one might expect between a man and his wife.

Her heart flip-flopped at that thought. She wondered if they *were* married and had been keeping it a secret. If so, that would account for the gossip that they slept together every time he came to town. The possibility made her feel better about their pairing off.

Red looked at her watch. "Almost time for my next song."

"Before you leave us," Mary said, "tell me about that minister back there who, Griz says, is in love with you."

"You mean Leckenby?" Red sniffed. "He's harmless. Got a case of being stuck on me, that's all."

"Did he ever make a pass at you?"

"Him? Not on your life. I'm some sort of untouchable to him. I've talked to him a couple of times. He says I inspire him. I don't know why. I can't even inspire Griz to take you to the Argonaut tonight."

The piano player fingered a few notes.

"That's my cue," Red groaned. "This time I'll give them something hot and lively." As good as her word, she gave them "There'll Be a Hot Time in the Old Town Tonight!" Just the thing to remind them this was Cracker Creek's favorite marching song in 1898 bars, which then were called saloons. It stirred men's fighting blood still. It suited their desire to step lively and shout their heads off. And that's what the mountain men in the Nugget started doing the moment Red swung into the first chorus.

First one, then another, and a host of them thereafter were on their feet, snake-dancing behind her, in and out among the tables, until nearly every man in the place had joined the serpentine, singing along with her until the very end when they rent the air with just three ringing words:

FIRE! FIRE! FIRE!

It mattered not that these words had never been in the original song, or that they had no relation to what was written there, but they served to put a punch into a chorus that ended thus:

I just hugged her and I kissed her, and to me then she said:
"Please, oh please, oh do not let me fall,
You're all mine, and I love you best of all,
And you must be my man or I'll have no man at all,
There'll be a hot time in the old town tonight."

As a war song it made no sense whatever, but as a march it was terrific. The second time around Mary Meakin caught the fever.

"Let's join it, too!" she screamed in Griz's ear and pulled him to his feet. Griz put his hands on her hips and steered her around all obstacles. She was too little to be sure where she was going, but she sang at the top of her voice and thrust her little fist toward the rafters every time they shouted:

FIRE! FIRE! FIRE!

Griz pulled her out of the line as the song neared its final chorus. Waving a hand at the Redhead across the room, he pushed Mary toward the swinging half-doors.

"Just a minute." She stopped him as they drew abreast of Leckenby, the evangelist. "I want to speak to him."

Griz gave her a puzzled look.

"You wouldn't understand," she said and stepped up to the parson. He hadn't yet taken his eyes off Red. He was completely oblivious of the little girl standing at his feet—hundreds of miles below his level of concentration. And to her, looking up, it seemed that his head was lost in the rafters, a head that was craggy and bore the fierce eyes and hooked nose of an eagle. He was the tallest man she had ever seen.

"I know just how you feel, Reverend," she said softly.

He stirred slowly, as if he had just been awakened from a prolonged sleep, trying to get his bearings. Instead of bending over to look down on her, he recoiled sharply, leaning back to put her farther away and trying to focus on her through bare slits in his eyelids.

He mumbled, "Eh? . . . Eh? . . . "

"I said I know just how you feel."

Now his eyes came slightly open as he stood fully erect, so he *could* look down on her, but from a great height. But he was still fumbling for words. They came out haltingly. "You say . . .you feel . . . like I . . . do . . . about her? Impossible!"

"No. I understand *how* you feel about her. It's such a hopeless feeling, isn't it?"

He looked away, seeming to weigh what she had said. "What I feel about her is unimportant. All that counts is saving her soul." He drew himself up proudly. "I am the instrument of Jehovah, dedicated to saving her. She's worth saving, you know."

"Why, of course."

"I come here every Saturday night to see what gains we have made." His voice drifted off again. "If I could see her once in white . . . pure white . . . and none of these frills and furbelows like she's wearing now, then I could be sure . . . sure . . . sure."

"Sure of what, Reverend?"

The faraway look had come into his eyes again. "That she is the reincarnation of Mary Magdalen." He said the name with such reverence that she barely heard it.

"All in white," he repeated. "That's when I shall know."

14

Mary said, "You knew her name was Mary, too?"

"It was always Mary." But just the way he said it and tried to locate her, now that the song and excitement were over, told Mary he didn't know her real name was Mary.

He smiled to himself when he found his Magdalen. Mary's audience with him had ended. She shrugged philosophically and looked up at Griz, who had stood by, saying nothing. Now he spoke. "He's nuts. Let's get out of here."

He told her later, "You'd never believe that's the same man who thunders his denunciation of sin in the Creek when he's out from under her spell." He just shook his head.

They got out of the Nugget the same way they sneaked in, using the magic words, "Make way for the little lady!"

Mary pouted when they broke into the clear on the walk. "Where are you taking me now?"

"The Argonaut, of course."

"You mean it?" She screamed the words and threw her arms around him.

"Where else?" he grinned.

"Oh, Griz!" she moaned in wild ecstasy, burying her nose in his corduroy jacket about the third button from the top. He had never seemed taller than he did at this moment.

All around them men stopped and cheered approval of her action, though they had not the slightest idea why she broke free and threw a kiss in the direction of the Nugget. But that was worth another roundhouse cheer.

Only Griz caught and understood the words which she said as she threw the kiss: "Thank you, Mary Too! Thank you for making this possible. I shall never forget."

So saying, she clasped Griz's arm and started to whisk him away toward the Argonaut, only to gasp and stop dead when she spotted Bill Saxon in the shifting throng ahead of them on the boardwalk. She tried to duck out of sight.

Griz yanked her back against him. "What are you up to now?"

She pointed. "Bill Saxon!"

He looked all around them. "I don't see him."

"I did," and her voice was hoarse. "And if he saw me coming out of the Nugget and throwing that kiss back at it, I'm a dead duck. My school principal will know all about it Monday morning."

15

She collapsed, a dead weight on his arm.

"Let's find out," he assured her. "He's certain to show up at the Argonaut. Where women are concerned, he's number one in line."

2

The Argonaut was only a hop, step and a jump off the boardwalk on the side street behind Homer Prentice's bank. Mary perked up with every step toward its hospitality.

"You will never know what you are doing for my morale," she told Griz.

"Just giving you a chance to see how the other half lives," he smiled. "The Nugget and the Argonaut all in one evening."

She recalled once being invited to a Saturday night supper. "Ages ago. I shall never forget how these women tried to impress me with the feeling that they were like the church suppers they used to enjoy 'back home.' Griz, they are never going to get over the feeling that this is only an interlude in their lives, that there is a 'back home' to which they are always going to return. Will they never admit that this is an exciting new world?"

"Not if they came from New England, Pennsylvania, Virginia or any Eastern seaboard place where it is born in their blood to want to come home when they get through with their gallivanting."

"But you come from New England—"

"By way of West Virginia."

"You don't want to go back?"

"At the moment, never!"

"The one time I got to an Argonaut supper Mrs. Prentice asked me. She never did again."

Griz suggested that Amelia Prentice was not the most thoughtful woman in the world. "She likes to give the impression she is always seeking something new to be nice about, forgetting the people she has once been nice to, as if that once should satisfy them. I guess Amelia will never be able to appreciate what it is like to be taken to the mountain top and shown the Promised Land, then never given another chance to enjoy it."

"That's me," sighed Mary. "Why is it that unmarried women like me are never given a chance to join the Argonaut? They welcome bachelors like you with open arms. Why not spinsters?"

"Because it's a man's world still, Mary, even if you would never know it."

The Argonaut was, of course, a re-creation of the original club of that name which died in the fire that wiped out its predecessor in the second decade. It was founded as a haven for men who shunned the common saloon, yet liked to have a drink or two with a leisurely noon meal and perhaps a game of billiards afterwards.

"The mistake we made," said Griz, "in bringing the Argonaut back to life two years ago, was in admitting too many newcomers to membership. When they outnumbered us incorporators, they outvoted us and gave their women and youngsters the run of the club. Not even restricted to certain hours or days of the week. It has never been the same since, except for the *'back bar'*, which the newcomers, almost to a man, voted with us to keep forever barred to women. Now do you understand why I prefer the Nugget? Down there they *know* who runs the place!"

"Oh, come now," she cajoled him. "Don't tell me you aren't as sweet on women as the next man."

She switched tactics quickly. "Maybe you'd think otherwise if you knew that Argonaut women and their children did a really good deed today and needed the club in which to do it."

His only reaction was to lift his eyebrows expectantly.

Mary thought it was one of the few times she had been able to get a good look at his eyes. Normally there was a whiskery overhang. Now there could be no doubt they were the deep brown of cordovan leather.

"Yes," she explained, "the Argonaut *was* overrun this morning with women and youngsters tying off two quilts for the mother of Davey Craig, one of my favorite pupils. His mother is a dressmaker . . . "

"Yes, I know Davey and his mother, too." He laughed. "She never seems to find time to do something for herself."

Suddenly, she babbled: "Did you ever have the fun of tying

off a quilt when you were a boy in Maine?"

"I sure did." He rubbed his whiskered chin, trying to remember. "Seems like I always wanted to work the underside, doing the actual tying off. Yes, it *was* fun, Mary, but you have proved my point. You should know what an Argonaut is."

She smiled. "The Argonauts were a mythical band of ancient Greeks who sailed with Jason in search of the Golden Fleece."

"It seemed like an appropriate name for the original club, and again for us, seeing as how the Creek is now the Mecca for all these human ants crawling all over these mountains again, looking for nuggets. Get my point, Mary?"

"It depends on whether a man would rather pan for gold or raise a family which might be a greater credit to him. It is simply a question of values, isn't it?"

"That's hitting below the belt, Mary."

"Not at all, Griz. You and I and Mary Too are all in the same boat. We have no families, no kids of our own. We are the pariahs, the ones who don't belong. It might be a good thing for us occasionally to see how the other half got that way."

"Only they don't know they are better off," Griz said bitterly. "*That* is what sticks in my craw. They've got to make damn sure they push our heads underwater every time we come up for air."

She looked at him sharply to make sure she had heard him correctly. This was not the hard-bitten Griz who gave no quarter or asked for none. "I could kiss you for those words," she said, hugging his arm.

"Let's not get emotional," he growled, pointing to the Argonaut's door ahead. "Once we go through that door, you're *agin* me. Remember that if you want to have a good time. That pack of females in there will not let you play with them unless you join them, even if you come with me. I am the guy who has been *agin* them from the start, and still am. So they hate my guts." He guffawed. "And I don't blame them. But I want you to know how to play your marbles."

He put his hand on the Argonaut's door. "Ready to run the gauntlet?"

"How do I look?" She ran a hand quickly over her hair and smoothed her dress. "Presentable?"

"You look swell."

For her part, though she asked, she had no misgivings, but woman-like she wanted to be sure he would be proud of her. She always dressed for women anyway. They were the critical sex. Luckily she was wearing her best dress, the sprigged challis, for the Opera House dance. Now she would have a chance to learn whether the conservative tastes of the lady Argonauts agreed with hers. She thought the green of the material set off her brown hair beautifully. And the tiny flowers made her feel so many years younger. Last summer when she was home on vacation, her mother helped her make it. Mother's poor, work-worn hands had put tiny hems in the ruffles adorning the skirt and she herself, with loving patience, had gathered the yards and yards of material. Tucks on the bosom gave her a suggestion of curves she didn't have—she chuckled about this—and the softness of the little lace collar and cuffs made her feel almost regal.

She swelled with pride as she fingered the tiny twinkling buttons that gave her the final touch of elegance with which she wanted to walk into the Argonaut. There was no doubt in her mind that she looked swell, as Griz had put it, but she had wanted to hear him say it.

"I'm ready, Sir Grizzly," she said proudly.

Griz swung the Argonaut door wide open as they stepped inside. All over the lounge, which served as dining room or meeting place as the occasion required, feminine heads popped up to ogle them in response to a nudge here and a hoarse whisper there. It was as if someone had said, "Look who's come to supper!" and everybody had promptly and unashamedly taken a good look.

Then a knife or fork was dropped on the floor by some nervous female. The resultant clatter made every woman jump, suddenly realizing what an ass she was by staring open-mouthed at Mary and Griz. Red-faced, they tried to busy themselves again at the buffet table.

The Grizzly frankly chortled at their discomfiture.

"I see what you mean," Mary muttered under her breath.

"Get ready to join them," Griz hissed at her as Amelia Prentice came forward to welcome Mary. Taking Mary's arm, Amelia ignored Griz completely.

"So nice to see you again," Amelia cooed, turning to gesture toward the other women. "I think you know most of these ladies." She ticked off their names as Mary nodded.

There was Jean Hawkins, the club's most outspoken woman, whose hawk nose beautifully accented her name; little old Mrs. Titcomb, who always spoke barely above a whisper, but prepared the best roast beef of any woman in the club; Mrs. Buxton, an amazon of a woman, who qualified as the club's best piano player; Louise Allen, whose huckleberry pies were out of this world, yet not a woman among them ever suggested she was the most beautiful Argonaut wife.

The culinary star for this night was Constance Nichols, whose husband had bought the smelter, abandoned sixty years earlier, and turned it into a museum on the art of smelting (which it continued to do on a limited basis commercially when sufficient ore was available.)

Unlike Amelia Prentice, who always brought cakes to these suppers, but never gave away a copy of her recipes, Constance had absolutely no skill with the frying pan or the baking oven. She would normally be spotted behind the long service table, somewhere in the vicinity of meats and potato salad. But she had suggested that they make Boston baked beans and brown bread the main dish this Saturday night, the twenty-fifth anniversary of Elihu and Ruth Gerrish. Gerrish ran the government assay office in Cracker Creek.

Mrs. Nichols, however, prepared neither the baked beans (with molasses, of course) nor the brown bread. She persuaded Mary's Mrs. Swenson to do the beans and send them down to the Argonaut, steaming hot, in big brown crocks that gave the proper Bostonian touch to the occasion. Similarly, the brown bread was provided by the home bakery which supplied her table.

Amelia Prentice had turned around from introducing Mary to find Griz still standing where she had ignored him, smirking, she would have said, from the amused look on his face. She frowned her impatience with him and spoke sharply: "Why aren't you back in the bar where you belong?"

"Couldn't take my eyes off that crock pot," Griz replied to Mrs. Prentice. "What's happening around here? I thought you women couldn't put on one of these shindigs without a roast of beef?"

"I'll have you know," she spoke tartly, "that crock pot contains Boston baked beans—"

"You don't have to tell me," he spat back. "I grew up in New England. Had them all my life as a youngster, especially for Sunday morning breakfast. With fishcakes!" he added triumphantly

Amelia made a sour face. "We can do without the fishcakes. The beans and brown bread are in honor of the Gerrishes. It is their anniversary today."

"Nice people," he said. "Guess I'll drink to them. That's if you don't mind?"

She glared at him, yet held her tongue.

"That's for leaving us one room in this club where we can regain our self respect," Griz tossed over his shoulder as he started for the bar. Yet he stopped once more to deliver his final arrow. "I still can't figure out why you didn't try to get your feet inside the bar, too."

"As if we'd want to!" Mary called after him

"That's telling him," seconded Jean Hawkins.

From the way other women echoed this thought, Mary knew she had scored with them. Griz had told her, "To live with them you must join them against me." She had done so with a vengeance.

Amelia called to her. "Give me a hand with these cakes."

It was her way of telling Mary, she decided, that she had qualified to be one of them.

Amelia started counting. "We should have about sixty here tonight and half of them will take cake, mostly women."

Mary guessed that the men would go overboard for Louise Allen's huckleberry pie.

"They always do," Amelia admitted. "Never seem to get enough of it. She knocks herself out every Saturday morning trying to make enough pies to satisfy them. Some men are just pigs. Take two or three pieces. I tell her to make just enough pies to give them each just one piece, but that is not our Louise. She thrives on being a favorite with the men."

"What woman doesn't, except those hipped on women's rights?"

Amelia looked sharply at her. "I hope Quigley isn't one of those who interests you."

"Not a chance," Mary said quickly, lest she give herself away.

"Good! How he ever got to be a member of this club is more than I can understand."

Mary held her tongue and reminded Amelia she hadn't said how to cut the cakes.

"Man-sized pieces out of two of them. Half size the other two. Her eyes twinkled. "That gives the women a choice."

Mary thought, "She is still a very beautiful woman when she smiles. What a pity she is childless."

The front door opened at that moment to admit an attractive couple, Monte Willcox, one of Mary's tablemates at Mrs. Swenson's, and Cara Ames, a piano teacher from Baker, the county seat.

"Cara!" Mary called out with delight. Then she turned to Amelia. "I thought you always said Cara couldn't leave her mother alone more than one night."

"I didn't ask. She simply told me last week she would stay over this Saturday, too. That was good enough for me."

Cara Ames was the daughter Amelia Prentice never had. She smothered her with love every Friday night when she stayed with them overnight. She came up on the morning train every Friday, gave piano lessons that afternoon and Saturday morning to youngsters musically inclined, and took the down train every Saturday afternoon without fail—until school vacations began this very day.

"Are you trying to make a match there?" Mary asked Amelia.

"Why not? They are perfectly suited to each other." With which Mary agreed. She came out from behind the service table to greet them. Cara was tall and lithe, dark and engaging. Monte was an apple-cheeked smiler with the build and easy grace of an athlete.

"Love your dress," Mary said. Cara was a vision all in white, which reminded Mary of the rapture which had consumed Parson Leckenby in the Nugget, barely an hour earlier, when he visualized seeing the Redhead dressed all in white.

What is there about white, she wondered, especially in a woman's dress, that catches a man's fancy?

She never got a chance to satisfy herself as to the answer because, at that moment, there was a terrifying clatter of horses charging past the Argonaut, accompanied by ear-splitting yells and gunshots reminiscent of Indian raids.

At once, men poured into the lounge from the bar, knocking over chairs and scattering tables set up for the supper, striving to reach and comfort their wives, cowering and sniveling against the back wall.

Jean Hawkins, however, was the exception. She had beaten a couple of unattached men to the front door and had her hand on the door knob when there came shouts of "Don't open it," from the back of the lounge.

"Oh, please don't open it," begged little Mrs. Titcomb, the color draining from her wrinkled face.

But Jean had the door open far enough to stick her head out when Griz came through the curtained opening from the bar, his drink still in his hand.

He calmly took a sip from his glass, then looked around at the human frieze of men and women, frozen in attitudes of disbelief, alarm or even fear.

From the door, Mrs. Hawkins turned to keep them posted. "Sure as shooting, they are heading up the hill, past our homes."

There were more shots in the distance.

"Are you sure this isn't just an act," Griz suggested, "another of the stunts the town has in mind to re-create the Old Cracker Creek for the benefit of tourists? There's a lot of them out there on the walk tonight."

"They ought to let us know then, instead of scaring the life out of us," Monte yelled from the back of the room. He was laughing his head off.

His reaction was contagious. Soon people were laughing all over the room and turning to restore the supper setup.

"The last time they shot up the town, a bullet barely missed Amelia," Homer Prentice reminded everybody.

She nodded soberly. "That's right. The hole is still there in our outside wall. If that bullet had gone clear through, it might have killed me because it was aimed right at the seat of my chair."

Joe Buxton guffawed. "And that's a hell of a place to get smacked, isn't it, Amelia? Better luck next time."

On that note the men made a new break for the bar, except for the Grizzly. He broke stride to join them when he caught a glimpse of Cara Ames, looking very radiant and feminine and desirable.

"You know Cara, don't you?" Mary prompted him.

"Yes," he said with obvious enthusiasm, taking Cara's hand, "but only as a busy-bee in a tailored suit, rushing back and forth on the walk between music lessons, never having time for even a brief—"

"Hello, Mr. Grizzly," Cara said with a merry laugh.

"Hello, yourself," he countered, holding her away from him to take a better picture. "You look stunning tonight."

Watching this by-play, Mary's heart did a flip-flop. "Isn't that always the way," she sighed to herself. "He never noticed my dress. But I wasn't all in white!"

There was another flurry of distant shots. Griz canted his head, listening. "Not too near, not too far," he guessed. "They could be doubling back." He went to the door, checked briefly, then turned back to suggest, "It's a great night outside. The moon's out now. Why don't the four of us take a short walk to whet our appetites for beans and brown bread?"

Mary and Monte held up fingers at once. Cara said, "I'm all for it, but wait till I borrow a shawl from someone."

"Perfect," Griz agreed, beaming after her as she checked among the women and soon followed Louise Allen into the ladies parlor. Meanwhile, Mary figuratively groaned to herself, recalling Cara's words: "Wait till I borrow a shawl." The perfect feminine touch. Made Griz think about her as he waits. She wondered why she never thought about playing it that way. "I'm forever pressuring a man, fearful of losing him, once I get a hand on him."

Cara returned, looking absolutely fetching in a fancy shawl that gave her white dress a dash of color, but nothing to match the flush of excitement on her face as she took Monte's arm and held out the other hand to Mary and Griz to join them.

As the four of them stepped out of the club, Mary caught sight of Bill Saxon headed toward the Argonaut. Until that moment she had forgotten about the chance he might have seen her coming out of the Nugget. She panicked, grabbing Griz's arm and groaning, "Oh God, is he going to spoil my evening?"

"What goes?" Griz asked.

"Didn't you see Bill Saxon coming up the sidewalk, headed

for the club? If he saw me coming out of the Nugget and bawls me out before all the Argonauts, I'll die, Griz. I really will."

"He better not," Griz assured her, squeezing the little hand that held his arm.

But in the next breath he showed his mind was more on Cara, calling ahead to Monte, "I think we'd better stick to streets that have sidewalks if we don't want Cara to get dust on that white dress."

There it was again—the white dress that caught a man's eye! Mary smoothed her challis, thinking to herself, "I guess green is not a man's color. Or is it the woman herself who really counts?"

She need not have asked that question because Cara was the most desirable woman she knew. At least five years younger, and she stood up to a man, tall enough to look him in the eye. Mary never felt tinier than she did at this moment.

The four of them walked along the side of the hill that overlooked the town, past the better homes, including the Prentice's. Their homes reflected their prosperity. Two of them had conservatories. Constance Nichols, that night's hostess at the club, had little squares of colored glass framing the big window that looked out over the town and green valley beyond. Roses, poppies and irises gave their yards a bright touch of color.

They stopped to admire one specially pretty flower garden. Resuming their walk, they found they had switched partners.

Cara started to correct the situation, but Mary told her quickly to forget it. One look at Griz said he didn't mind. "It's a good idea to mix people up," he averred.

Within minutes, with their long legs, they were pulling away from Monte and Mary. "Now why did I say that?" she asked Monte. "I'm old shoe to you." She started to call after the other couple.

"Nix," said Monte. "Let it be."

"But Amelia is trying to make a match between you two, isn't she?"

"Don't we both know it," he grimaced. "She's been trying to foist us on each other for more than a year. That's why, until tonight, Cara has refused to stay over for one of these suppers."

"But she always said Cara's mother couldn't be left alone

two nights running."

"Poppycock! That was to put Amelia off the track."

"And all this time I thought Cara was just the type of woman you would go for."

"Oh, I don't say I can't, or won't, but neither of us wants to be pushed."

"Amelia won't like it," Mary warned him, "if she finds out Cara has gone off with Griz." She looked at him sharply. "Did you two switch on us deliberately back there?"

"What do *you* think?"

"I think you did."

"Well, not exactly, but Griz intrigues her and she was asking me so many questions about him before we stopped. She may have played for the switch, unconsciously or otherwise."

"And I'm sure Cara intrigues him, too," she admitted. She looked up at him suddenly with a face drained of color.

"Have you got it that bad, little Mary?"

"Does it show?"

"Probably not enough that he would notice it." He put a brotherly arm around her. "Buck up! The game's young yet."

"Not for me." She tried to match his smile. "But thanks, Monte."

"Don't try so hard."

"That's my trouble, isn't it?"

By now Cara and Griz were well ahead of them, passing out of sight as the street dipped into a natural draw, to rise again up the west side of Schoolhouse Hill. In the distance they heard once more the pounding of horses' hooves coming down that slope at a gallop. Only this time the men's yells sounded more like those of a pack of lovesick coyotes.

They topped the last rise and looked down into the draw to see three horsemen brandishing hand guns, cornering Griz and Cara on the sidewalk, yelling and gesticulating wildly and firing an occasional shot into the ground at Griz's feet.

The moonlight was so bright that Monte and Mary could take in the whole picture, even at that distance.

"They are trying to make Griz dance," exclaimed Mary. "We must do something to help him."

Monte hesitated to get upset. "What bothers me is that those shots don't kick up any dust in the street."

She put her hand to her mouth. "You don't suppose, do you—?"

"Exactly. They're using blanks, not bullets!"

"Are you sure?"

"Look at Griz and then at those two youngsters with the guy who is doing the firing. They're doubled over their saddle horns, cackling hysterically. And Griz is putting on a terrific act, highstepping clumsily in imitation of a drunk and stumbling crazily all over the street."

"And look at Cara," Mary added. "She's standing, as if lashed to that fence, arms outstretched, grasping a picket with each hand, as if the feel of something to hang on to gives her the strength to endure this experience."

"Kitty cat!" Monte admonished her playfully.

"Well, isn't she beautifully posed in that white dress and fetching shawl?"

"Too bad there isn't a camera handy to preserve this whole tableau for the Argonaut's archives!"

She giggled and he doubled over laughing.

"Shall we—?"

"Absolutely," he said. "Get back to the club before they do and have a chance to embellish their story."

3

Supper was in full swing when Monte and Mary returned to the Argonaut. Amelia Prentice rose from the table where she and Homer were saving seats for Monte and Cara. "Where's Cara?" she asked Monte anxiously.

He looked at Mary, as if to say, "Shall we tell her outright or string her out?"

"Has something happened to her?" Obviously, Amelia was on the point of getting excited when neither gave her a quick answer.

"They are just a little delayed," Mary explained.

"What do you mean 'they'?" Amelia demanded.

"Cara and Griz," Monte cut in.

"You mean she's out there somewhere, all alone with that man?" Amelia demanded.

By this time, just about everyone had stopped eating, lest they miss all the details of what promised to be interesting.

"But it's nothing to get excited about," Mary assured Amelia. "They just got way ahead of Monte and me and—"

Amelia cut her short and turned to Monte. "You went out of here with Cara on your arm, didn't you?"

"That's right."

"So how did you get separated from her and that man wind up with her instead?"

Monte turned helplessly to Mary. "We don't really know, do we?"

"That's right, Mrs. Prentice. The four of us were just walking along the hillside where you live, stopping from time to time to admire the way that gorgeous moonlight brought out the color in some gardens, and suddenly Monte and I found they were walking away from us, down the draw leading to the west side of Schoolhouse Hill."

"And you didn't call to them?"

"They had dipped out of sight before we decided what to do."

29

"And just then," Monte broke in, "we heard once more the pounding of ponies' hooves coming down that slope at a gallop, and hesitated."

There was a shudder throughout the room as those listening intently began to push their chairs back, in case they had once more to take refuge against the back wall.

"No . . . No!" Monte begged them. "Don't anticipate what I was going to tell you. The town is *not* going to be shot up again tonight. But we had the same reaction as you just had now, until we looked around for cover and crept forward carefully till we could see Griz doing a crazy, drunken dance while one horseman fired blanks at his feet."

"Blanks!" shouted several men.

"That's right," Monte insisted. "They didn't raise any dust in the street. Griz was doing an act and enjoying it."

Laughter swept the room and they all began talking at once. Mayor Bert Ascher's comment was: "So Griz was right all along."

Amelia Prentice turned back to her table in disgust, then belatedly remembered Monte was to sit with them. She called to him. "Might as well join us now. I suppose you have no idea when they will be back."

He shook his head and took his seat.

Just then the front door opened and everyone turned or looked up, expecting it would be Cara and Griz. Instead, it was Bill Saxon, with a big smile on his face. "Hello, everybody. Sorry to be late."

But the smile was replaced, as he spotted Mary Meakin, by a look as deadly as he might have used while impaling a butterfly on a pin. She knew his technique only too well. He had developed it in the courts, as a practicing attorney, but he had honed it to razor sharpness at Mrs. Swenson's table, relishing a battle of wits and words with the other boarders at every opportunity. He fought with an intensity that one might have admired if it were not so apparent that he got an unholy satisfaction out of completely demoralizing whoever opposed him, even if the dispute were nothing more than the proper pronunciation of a simple word.

Mary literally withered; she guessed he must have seen her coming out of the Nugget. Why couldn't he have waited until next morning at the breakfast table? Why humiliate her before

all these people? It was only this morning at Swenson's he had been so sweet to her, remarking that it was going to be such a lovely day that he had half a mind to play hookey and take her for a ride out Cracker Creek way.

"My favorite ride," she bubbled, naughtily trying to trap him because she knew he would never be caught out in his car alone with *any* woman.

Mayor Ascher, sensing that Saxon was about to reprimand Mary for something totally divorced from this occasion, stepped in to dissuade him. "Now, Bill," he said. "Can't you put it off till some other time?"

Looking extremely pained, Saxon focused his eyes on the ceiling. "What I have to say must be said in the presence of the members of this club."

The mayor was not to be dissuaded from stopping him. "I must remind you that Miss Meakin is a guest of a member of this club and should be accorded every courtesy. If you have something important to say, I suggest to make your statement, or whatever it is, to the board at its next meeting."

Saxon glared at him and fired at Mary, "Who brought you here?"

"Don't answer that," Ascher said.

"I don't mind," she told the mayor. Then to Saxon, "I came with Griz."

"You mean Quigley!" he corrected her sharply.

The door had opened quietly during this exchange as Cara and Griz returned to the Argonaut.

"Did I hear somebody paging me?" Griz inquired, feigning surprise.

"I mean exactly what I said," Mary insisted. She had learned at Swenson's how to stand up to him. "I call him Griz and so do a lot of other folks. Why should I change because you don't like him?"

"Because I don't like to see you associating with a bar bum. I did, didn't I, tonight on the boardwalk?"

There it was right out in the open, the only question being whether or not he had seen her leaving the Nugget. She glanced quickly at the mayor. His wink of encouragement gave her the courage to play it cool.

"Perhaps," she said softly with a little toss of her head.

The mayor turned to Saxon. "You mean you saw her with the Grizzly?"

"Damn right, and his name is Quigley, not some fancy nickname some slut in a bar thought up."

"I like Grizzly. It fits him better. But the point is, he brought Mary to the supper tonight."

"He did?" Saxon hit one hand with his other fist, bouncing up and down in his anger and getting red in his screwed-up face. "That's what I mean. Let the bars down and he starts associating with nice women like Mary and"—he turned his head—"this other woman who just walked in the door with him—"

Amelia was on her feet instantly. "Don't you dare insult her by suggesting she picked him up! She's my guest."

"I did no such thing," Saxon spat back at her, "but we ought to expel him from the club—"

The mayor said, "We can't do that, Bill. You're an attorney. You ought to know that. There's nothing in our by-laws that says he can't go into a boardwalk bar and have an occasional drink."

"But whenever he's in town, I know this for a fact, he sleeps there overnight—"

"That will do!" thundered Homer Prentice, finally getting to his feet. "We will have no more foul language in the presence of ladies."

"And what I want to know, Mr. Saxon," demanded Amelia Prentice—she would have called him Bill normally—"is why you object to that man inviting her here"—she still could not bring herself to call him Griz—"when you sit at the same table with her every day at Swenson's and have never once invited her to be your guest here. I know you don't like to be encumbered, as you would say in lawyers' language, so you always come alone. No heart, that's what I would say!"

"Amen," said the mayor.

Forced to stand his ground, Saxon shook a finger at Mary. "I could stop you from ever being seen again with him! You know that, don't you?"

"You mean by going to my principal?"

With a straight face, he nodded. "I hope I never have to do that."

Cara had been standing by, mouth open, unable to believe that anyone could be so vicious to a guest in the presence of virtually all the Argonauts. Now she boiled over. "You wretch!" she cried. "If I were Mary, I'd slap your face for making that threat!"

Saxon recoiled as if she were going to carry it out herself. He frowned, taking Cara in from tip to toe. She was at least two inches taller than he. Apparently he had not been aware of her until this moment. He turned to the mayor. "Who is this woman?"

"Miss Cara Ames, guest of the Prentices," said the mayor. Pointedly, he did not introduce Saxon to Cara.

"Miss Ames," Saxon repeated the name, accompanied by a slight, stiff bow. "Ames?" He seemed to be combing his memory. "Ames? . . . Ames?" Each time with rising inflection. Then his eyes gave away the fact that he had found the right pigeonhole.

"You wouldn't be the daughter of Clifford Ames?"

Cara nodded cautiously.

"You would have been about eleven or twelve at the time?"

"Ten."

"Pretty child, I seem to remember."

"I was scrawny then."

"You haven't forgotten?"

"I'm not likely to."

Mary now recalled that, in an unguarded moment, Cara had said her father deserted her and her mother when she was only a child. "The last thing he said to me was that I must be a big girl now and look after Mother, no matter what happened to him. He seemed to know that Mother would never make it on her own, so I started giving piano lessons when I was fifteen, while Mother folded up with every ache and pain in the book."

The reason for the desertion came out now. Saxon was putting on an act, shaking his head, pretending to be sympathetic with Cara's bitterness. "I can understand how you feel. Of course, you know I was only doing my duty as an attorney."

Cara was not to be assuaged. "Mother says you were only asked to find him, not to wreck the lives of two women."

Saxon bristled. "But he was a bigamist!"

"You have no proof of that." She turned to the mayor. "All I know is that he handed my father a piece of paper, which Father crumpled up and stuffed in his pocket as soon as he had read it, while this man"—she pointed to Saxon—"kept croaking at him like a bullfrog . . . "

"I beg your pardon!" scowled Saxon angrily. He began backing away and found himself hemmed in by curious and encroaching Argonauts.

Amelia Prentice put her hand on Cara's arm and tried to lead her away. "It's time to sit down to supper."

But Cara had to get in one more thrust. "You might have had some compassion after seeing the three of us, instead of pocketing the fee."

Mayor Ascher raised his hands in a conciliatory gesture. "Everybody sit down to eat, please."

Bill Saxon made his escape during the shuffle.

The mayor put a fatherly arm around Mary's shoulders and beamed at her and Cara. "I don't suppose you two realize," he said, "what a show you two put on for us tonight. We must ask you to come here more often. You're good for our tired blood."

Mary looked up at him. "You don't know how near I came to slapping Bill's face. For Cara's sake."

"For a moment I was afraid you *were* going to do so."

"You and me both," Cara agreed.

"But you haven't yet told us what happened eventually to your father," he reminded her.

Cara hesitated only for a moment. "I'll tell you two since you have been so understainding. But I never want to discuss the subject again. He took the next train east. We never saw him again and he never wrote."

Cara heard Amelia calling to her, excused herself and joined Monte and the Prentices.

The mayor asked Mary with whom she was sitting.

"Presumably with Griz, but he seems to have disappeared."

"No doubt to the bar," he smiled. "Let's get seats where he can join us."

They were among the last to go through the buffet line. Running through her mind was that moment when he put a fatherly arm around her shoulders, after she and Cara had

34

put Bill Saxon to flight, and complimented them on the show they had put on for the Argonauts. It was so exciting to be appreciated by a man who seemed to be the very personification of the father image: kindly, affectionate and tolerant.

She had always wanted to know him better. She judged he was a lonely person like herself. A widower and most likely in his early fifties. He didn't fit her picture of what a mayor should be. He was a veterinarian and proud of his love for horses and dogs.

Someone had once said he had gone to Heidelberg to study medicine and flunked out. If that were true, he was one of those rare individuals who can take the bitter and come up smiling and affable. She suspected that beer helped, too. That would account for his rotund belly.

They had barely started eating when Homer Prentice stood up, knocking his chair over in doing so, and rapped his glass with a spoon for attention.

On his feet like this, among friends, Prentice dispelled the appearance of being gruff and stuffy, as he did during banking hours, and became a warm and hearty man. He chuckled when he reminded the women that they were rarely given a chance to drink anything alcoholic at the Argonaut.

There was a scurrying among the tables as wine glasses were passed around to toast the Gerrishes. Ruth Gerrish fingered the stem of her glass nervously. She tried to smile as Jean Hawkins began to fill it, but her lips were pressed tightly together in a straight line.

"Just a mite," she begged, shaking. "I don't know how I can drink more than a drop." She looked up, pale and colorless. "I never touched anything before."

Elihu Gerrish caressed her shoulder gently. "Come now, Mother. A couple of drops won't hurt you. You will never have another twenty-fifth."

Tentatively, her lips touched the glass.

"That's the girl, Ruth," said Prentice. Then he swung around, holding his glass high. "Ladies and gentlemen of the Argonaut, I give you Elihu and Ruth Gerrish of the good old Commonwealth of Massachusetts. May they have another twenty five years in the love and sight of each other!"

Gerrish, in his turn, rose and toasted his clubmates. Impulsively, Mary turned to toast Bert Ascher silently, to which he responded with a twinkle in his eyes, raising his glass to her and draining it. Only then did she begin to wonder what had happened to Griz. She shifted around to look toward the curtains cloaking the bar door.

"He looked in once," Bert told her, "gave me the high sign to let it be, and ducked back in again."

Rather than reassuring her, Griz's reaction sent her momentarily into a tailspin. Was he annoyed? Would he now expect Bert to take her home? Oh, how could she have been so thoughtless as to leave him without a dinner partner when he had been badgered into taking her here? She was so absorbed in such thoughts that she barely heard Bert offer to go into the bar and ask Griz to come out and change places with him.

"Oh, no, I can't let you do that . . . but he hasn't had anything to eat."

"I'm sure the bartender slipped out and made him up a plate at the buffet table while we were so busy eating, trying to catch up."

"You think I'm silly to think about that, don't you?"

"No," he said slowly, smiling. "I think I understand."

"Does it show that badly?" asked Mary. He looked off over the heads of the other diners, seeming to be trying to come up with a good answer. Eventually he spoke quietly. "I don't blame you. There's a great deal more to that young man than most people realize or are willing to admit."

"*I* know it." She was surprised that her voice was husky.

"My advice is: Never give up, but don't show it. He has a block with women. He was married once, you know." She nodded. "She died suddenly. "Spinal meningitis or something like that. He gives you the impression that he has never gotten over her death. But that's not true. We all do in time." He stopped, shaking his head. "I'm a good one to talk like this. I never realized what I was losing until my wife died. I didn't appreciate what I had until I didn't have it anymore. Does that make sense?"

"Perfectly."

"What I'm trying to say in an old man's way is: Don't be

too hard on him every time he looks at another woman." He nodded toward Cara at the Prentice table.

"You noticed that, too?"

"Perhaps his real hangup is that he is afraid of being hurt again if he gets tied to another woman. He may be playing the field for that reason. So my advice is to hang tough, be handy, but never possessive, and never force the issue."

"But he will never think of me as anything more than his little sister," she sighed.

"Don't downplay that affinity. Give him every chance to become accustomed to you. That's half of what marriage is. Getting to know each other and accepting what you didn't know about the other half."

"What about the woman they call the Redhead? In the Nugget. Is he in love with her?"

His eyes masked what he was thinking when he hesitated.

"Don't pretend you don't know who I mean," Mary said. "I won't say where and when I met her, but she's quite a woman, although I can't figure out what the attraction is between them. She could be the only one who counts. And her name is Mary, too," she added, somewhat bitterly.

"I've heard tell it is."

"I ask it again: Is he in love with her and, if so, why? I want a man's opinion."

"I have only a hunch. nothing to base it on."

"That's good enough. Out with it, Bert."

"Offhand I'd say"—he hesitated, as if searching for just the right words—"she is his refuge when he needs one. They are too much alike to fall in love. She has had a bad time, too, as I suspect you know. So the two of them stick together against anyone who might hurt either of them.

"But mark my word, Mary, she's got to be on your side if you ever hope to catch him. I'll put it delicately. They are like two peas in a pod, sharing the same pod whenever it suits them. But, as for it meaning anything beyond that, forget it!"

At that moment, Homer Prentice rapped again on his tumbler for attention.

"Let's clear the tables and chairs away now, folks," he said. "We're long past the time for dancing."

Bert excused himself to help fold the setups and stow them

37

away, but the women waved Mary away from the kitchen cleanup. She was told, "Mind you are a guest. Just find yourself an easy chair and relax."

She did as she was told, putting her head back and closing her eyes, as she did as a child when she was shooed out of the kitchen at grange and church suppers. She had forgotten how she used to be thrilled, listening to the cacophony of sounds created in the breakup of these suppers. The game was to identify sounds with people.

Dishes were scraped and stacked, silverware dumped. She could always tell who were the busy-bee scrapers and who were the lazy ones. Women with high-pitched voices let their nervous energy escape, scraping with a fork or spoon. Contraltos sort of played harmony to the pizzicato of someone like Mrs. Titcomb. Constance Nichols, who had supplied the beans and brown bread for the night's specialty, was the sleepy sort. She most likely made an art of defoliating each dish.

But, however poorly she may have guessed otherwise, there could be no doubt as to the identity of the woman who dumped silverware all at once into a metal dishpan. When the pan finally stopped ringing after a score or more of shattering drops, Mary named the guilty one with no hesitation—Jean Hawkins. Such a technique could only be attributed to someone born for the cymbals.

All this time she had also been conscious of the bass notes provided by table tops and sawhorses being hauled away by the men and stacked elsewhere like so much lumber. No finesse, no cadence; just business-like, as men were supposed to be.

She was glad that Griz was not a business or professional man who lived by rote. None of this up-by-the-clock routine, a hasty breakfast, a quick kiss, off for the day (unless he came home for lunch), back by six, tired out, edgy perhaps, supper in silence, falling sleep in his chair after supper, until it was time to go to bed early.

Perhaps this was why Griz appealed to her. Here today, gone to his diggings tomorrow. Not that she believed he was dead serious any longer about prospecting. He was basically an outdoorsman. Whatever he did, he wanted to do it on his own, and apparently he came up with enough pay ore to make a living.

He admitted he came to the Creek originally with the hope of landing a job at the reopened smelter, for which his mining engineer background qualified him. But as yet, Monte Willcox had told him, it was a borderline success only, kept alive mostly by tourist tours six months a year. Monte was the manager of the smelter.

Mary jumped as someone touched her shoulder.

"Time to wake up," Bert said. The lounge had been changed into a ballroom.

"But I wasn't asleep," Mary protested. "Just listening with my eyes closed to all the fascinating sounds you folks made in creating this transformation."

"I shall try it sometime," he said, "if it will leave me with such a smile of happiness on my face."

"Prettily said," she fenced with him, and took the hand he offered to help her to her feet. He was such a darling. He made a woman feel so feminine.

At the piano, busty Mrs. Buxton was tickling the keys with the first notes of an opening waltz.

Mary stole a look at the curtained bar. "Do you want me to call him out?" Bert asked her.

"No, I think you told me, 'Don't be possessive.' I was just wondering how long he can stay in there." As an afterthought, she asked: "Is there a back door in there?"

He laughed. "Yes, and guessing what you are now thinking, I'll also say, 'Yes, he could be sitting this dance out at the Nugget.' "

"That's if he doesn't dance, as he said in turning me down when I wanted him to go with me to the Opera House dance." She turned back to Bert. "Now I think I'd like to dance." And despite the bulk of him, she found he was amazingly light on his feet and gave her an exciting waltz. Later they teamed up with Monte and Cara, exchanging partners many times.

Amelia Prentice cornered them to tell Cara, "They want you to play the hymn we always close with. I'm sure you know it. 'Abide With Me.' "

Amelia turned to Mary. "The old Argonaut Club destroyed in the fire always closed with that hymn and we felt we should keep the tradition going."

Cara looked over to Mrs. Buxton at the piano. A vigorous bobbing of that woman's head said she heartily approved.

Cara turned to Mary. "I suppose I can't say no."

"It's their way of saying they want to hear you play," Amelia said. "Most of them never have."

Mary clapped her hands, saying she and Bert would have a chance to dance to Cara's music for the first time.

"That settles it," Cara said. "For you two I'll do it."

Mrs. Buston gave the piano stool a few extra turns to make it high enough for Cara's long legs. Cara acknowledged the applause with a sweet smile and began playing "Message of the Violet," a haunting waltz by Victor Herbert.

Halfway through, Mary said to Bert, "There's nobody can waltz like you do." She was swinging it like a Viennese herself, putting exhilaration into every step, dreaming that it might be like this, too, with Griz.

"You are daydreaming again," Bert said softly.

She put her head back to see his face. "How do you know?" she said saucily.

"Because I see that faraway look in your big hazel eyes. So I'm better than he is?"

Now she blushed and nearly got out of step. "Okay, so I was wondering, but this was going to be the first chance to find out."

"Tough luck. I'll see that he asks you again."

Just then Griz walked in the front door and waved his hand.

Bert Ascher stopped dancing at once and signalled with a come-hither finger for Griz to take his place. Griz used the same sign language to point to his feet, shaking his head that he couldn't dance, and pointed to the bar, where he was headed.

Mary's back was to Griz, so she was completely puzzled by all the gestures Bert was making. "What's going on?" she asked.

Bert turned her so she could just see Griz disappearing behind the bar's protective curtain. "I was trying to coax him into changing places with me so you could have the last dance with him. He pointed to his feet, shaking his head to say that he couldn't dance."

Before Mary could say anything, Cara gave the musical phrase with which each stanza of the closing hymn ended.

Soon everyone was singing with hushed reverence:

Abide with me: Fast falls the eventide;
The darkness deepens; Lord, with me abide:
When other helpers fail, and comforts flee,
Help of the helpless, abide with me.
Swift to its close ebbs out life's little day;
Earth's joys grow dim, its glories pass away,
Change and decay in all around I see . . .

Their voices trailed off into shocked silence as Cara stopped playing. Nobody had heard the door open, but Bill Saxon lay there, half inside, begging Monte to come help him. His head and face were a bloddy mess and one eye was half closed. Monte and the mayor rushed to his side.

"What happened?" they both wanted to know.

"I've been mugged!" he managed to say with lips bruised and swollen.

"Any idea who did it? Did you recognize any of them? Where did it happen?"

The questions were coming fast from Monte and Bert, both of whom signalled to the Argonauts to leave quietly, while they took care of Saxon. First they had to get Saxon inside and away from the door.

"Can you stand up?"

"Not unless you help me." Which they did, and sat him in a chair. "Now tell us where and why?"

He opened his mouth to do so as Griz walked in from the bar, drink in hand.

"Why you—" he began. Monte clapped a hand over his mouth, reminding him, "No swearing in the Argonaut."

"I would also like to know where this all happened," Griz said, pursing his lips and shaking his head.

"Right back of the Nugget!" Saxon shouted at him. "Two big bruisers grabbed me. I had barely gotten inside and they had their hands on me and grabbed me out the back door and beat me up."

Mary Meakin stepped up to him. "Tell me why you, of all men, went into the Nugget at this time of the night. We all thought you went home to Mrs. Swenson's when you left here. Did you want to see whether you fancied the Redhead, too?"

she sneered.

"No!" he thundered, pointing to Griz. "To see if he had walked out on you here and gone back to her."

Mary shot a look at Griz, but he simply shook his head and pursed his lips again. "However," Mary thought to herself, "he left me in the lurch when it came time to have supper, came out of the bar to find Bert and I at supper and retreated to the bar again, until the dancing was almost over, when he came in the *front door* and made for the bar again."

Amelia and Homer Prentice were still waiting for Monte to squire Cara home. "Ready?" Homer said to Monte, breaking in on his and Bert's efforts to get Saxon in shape for a ride home to Swenson's.

"But I can't leave Saxon now," Monte protested. "It will take both Bert and me to get him in a car and out again and up those steps and into bed after we get there." He turned to Cara. "Griz will take you home."

"He will do no such thing!" Amelia exclaimed. "She's coming with us."

"Oh, no, she isn't," Monte insisted. "She came as my guest and I'm responsible for seeing that she gets back to your house, properly escorted."

Amelia snorted, glaring at him. Then to Homer, "Aren't you going to do something about this?"

"Yes, my dear. You know I never make any decisions except at the bank."

Mary almost laughed out loud. She suspected the mosquito had at last stung the queen bee.

Amelia hesitated, then apparently thought better of what she wanted to say. She took Homer's arm and literally yanked him underway. But she called back, "We shall be right ahead of you, Cara."

Bert asked Mary to come along with them in the car taking Saxon home. "When we get there, you might call the doctor while we get him into bed."

"And the marshal, too," Saxon spoke up. "I want him to investigate how come I got mugged."

Seeing Griz set off with Cara on his arm, Mary could not swallow for the lump in her throat. Griz had not so much as said one word of regret for missing the whole evening with her.

Ascher read the thoughts in her eyes. "Hang tough," he said.

"What does that mean?" Monte asked, as he started the car.

"Just a thought for the day," Mary said bravely.

4

Cracker Creek could be quite hot and muggy in June, more so than in August. This was one of those days.

Mary scowled at herself in the mirror. Her room was stifling. Heat and humidity seemed to shrink it to a tiny cell. "Couldn't throw a cat around in here by its tail," she hissed between her teeth.

And this was going to be one of those days of all days! Even more exciting than last Saturday night at the Argonaut had promised to be. She was going to be a bridesmaid at a wedding this afternoon and Griz was coming to supper. Bad cess to him if he spoiled this one, too.

She had not seen Griz in a week. Presumably he was out at his diggings, prospecting or simply keeping out of sight. She wondered which. Conceivably he could be a little sheepish about having given her short shrift at the Argonaut that night, then maneuvering himself into taking Cara home while Monte and Bert ministered to Saxon's cuts and bruises and tucked him in bed.

Momentarily she blew her lungs up to the point where she thought they would burst, reacting to her still smoldering anger for that night's treatment, but she broke off suddenly, letting the air of resentment escape its tiny bellows, determined to believe he was not the kind of man who would do that deliberately. If he were, where was she going from here?

It could be a deadly, if not embarrassing, game between her and Cara if he should start playing one against the other. They were both long-time friends, but each needed a husband—Cara to make a break from a demanding mother; she to become a mother before her heart broke from tending cuddly little tots all day at school and having none to come home to at night.

She wished she might have seen Griz's face that night when

he said goodbye to Cara at the Prentices. She would never have much of a chance with Griz if Cara were becoming interested in him. She was younger by seven or eight years. She had a stunning figure and long, attractive legs. Griz would like that. She remembered how they had stepped out briskly and left her and Monte far behind the night of the hillside walk in the moonlight.

They were a good match physically, too. Cara could look Griz right in the eye and sass him to his face if she had a mind to. Griz would like that, too. She sensed this in his attitude toward the Redhead. He would never expect either one of them to be cute and cuddly.

So, what did she have going for herself? Again she stared at the mirror. The scowl that had been wrinkling her face had given way to a washed-out look of utter desolation. She had so little to offer and Cara had so much. Even Cara's tiff with Bill Saxon had worked out to her advantage. Griz had learned, perhaps for the first time, that Cara had been without a father since she was ten. He must have guessed the rest of the story, that she had been the sole support of her mother for years. Mary had an instinctive feeling that such a hard luck story would have great appeal to Griz. How could Cara be so lucky?

The mirror reminded her that her lower lip was sagging. The mugginess in the room was beginning to get to her, though she had discarded her dress on returning to her room from mid-day dinner. In another moment of exasperation she began to rip off more clothes. She got down to her slip and panties before she felt any relief and this came through her feet. The straw matting on the floor was cool. Unbelievably cool. She paraded around the room, wriggling her toes, until she had a sudden impulse to take the slip and panties off, to prove by the mirror that she had a feminine figure, if only a skinny one!

She stepped to the mirror again, to stare at the travesty of a woman's breasts reflected there. Once, in jest, she had called them her brown-eyed susans! She turned this way and that, trying to achieve some encouragement from a different angle. No luck whatever. They were just as flat as pancakes! She recalled that Griz had never stolen a look in their direction, although she had caught him ogling Cara's ample contour.

45

In her mind, she cried out: "Why must I be so puny and insignificant in all that counts about a woman's figure?"

Just the day before she had heard Mrs. Swenson and one of the neighbors talking about her at the foot of the stairs, unaware that she had come home early. "Poor Mary," the neighbor had said, "if she could only puff up her bust a bit. It would make such a change in her appearance."

"Wearing a bra stuffed with tissue paper might do it," offered Mrs. Swenson.

"I don't know," the other sighed. "The trouble is she is boyish all over. And it's the way she walks, swinging her hips as if she were a boy . . . " Her voice trailed off, then came back strong. "But she is never going to get a man the way she is now."

Mary had shuddered. Thirty-one and still going nowhere.

She remembered how, when she was growing up, someone had suggested that rubbing cocoa butter on her nubbins would make them grow bigger, but it didn't work.

So Mrs. Swenson had suggested using tissue paper to stuff her bra? She dug into a bureau drawer for her supply and rolled two big snowballs, placing them inside her bra. The result was startling! "By golly," she crowed, "I've got a bust!" The side view was even more satisfying. She couldn't remember when she was so pleased with herself. In fact, she was so excited, she kissed herself in the mirror.

That made up her mind. She would leave them in place for the wedding and for supper. If nothing else, Griz must see her in her new facade. He wouldn't be fooled, of course, but that would be half the fun of showing off—if he approved.

She bustled around with renewed vigor, no longer mindful of the mugginess, intent on getting ready for the wedding. She soon learned that she had better pin her puffballs in place, otherwise they tended to get lopsided or droopy every time she laughed or stooped over. That done, she hummed merrily to herself and wriggled into her best dress.

All she remembered later of the wedding was that she caught the bride's bouquet. Harry, the bridegroom, was one of the seven men at the boarding house who had never made a pass at Mary. He was marrying a girl named Jocelyn. Marriage ended any boarder's stay. When love came in, out went the man who dared to break Mrs. Swenson's devotion to celibacy. She wanted no married couples giving the other boarders naughty ideas.

Harry's defection created a vacancy at the table and a room for rent upstairs. Mary had a wild idea she might be able to sell Mrs. Swenson and Griz on making *him* the seventh boarder. She sent word through the Redhead—she knew no other way to reach Griz—that there was a vacancy coming up and Mrs. Swenson would listen to whatever he had to say if he came to supper that night after the wedding. As Mary's guest, of course.

Back came the word quickly that he would be there. In fact, Mary wondered if the Redhead had accepted for him without reaching Griz. She chuckled to herself, relishing this possibility.

She got an answer of sorts when Griz showed up wearing a new suit of store clothes and sporting a Vandyke beard, while the tangle of whiskers that usually hid the rest of his face had been trimmed neatly and close for the first time anyone recalled.

"Griz!" Mary shrieked, throwing her arms around his midriff and hugging him ecstatically. She looked up, eyes sparkling, "You look so distinguished!" Then she stood off to look him over from all angles and clapped her hands, turning to those gathered on the veranda, "Isn't he terrific?"

Monte Willcox, coming up the steps at that moment with Cara Ames, caught the words. With the soberest of faces, he advanced stiffly and bowed from the waist. "King Grizzly," he said breathlessly, turning to take Cara's hand, "may I present the Lady Cara, Your Majesty?" Barely able to suppress her mirth, Cara made a delightful curtsy and skittered for cover when Monte ducked just in time to escape a swipe of Griz's hand aimed at his head.

Cara then made her way to Griz on her own, declaring, "You are ravishing," as she shook his hand.

Mary started to turn away, stung by that greeting. All her machinations to get Griz to come to supper, so she could have him all to herself while everyone else concentrated on the newly married couple, were going awry. She had no idea Cara would be staying overnight for a second Saturday.

Cara caught the trembling lower lip on Mary's face and put

a finger to her own lips, adding: "I'll tell you later."

Monte joined them and fingered Griz's store clothes. "Good goods," he snickered. "Much better than corduroy."

Everyone knew that Griz never wore anything but corduroy jacket and britches, no matter what the occasion, even as he did in taking Mary to the Argonaut.

"What does Red think of the new outfit?" Monte asked.

"She put me up to buying them."

"That figures. The Vandyke and overall trim, too?"

"Yep."

Mary wanted to ask, "Did she pick out the suit, too?" It had been her observation that anytime a man let a woman pick out his clothes for him, they were either married or going to be.

Griz shuffled his feet, remarking, "I still don't feel good in longies," and jostled Mary. Turning quickly to apologize, he exclaimed, "Good gosh! What has happened to our little Mary?"

"You noticed!" she exulted, giving him a quick squeeze. "The first one to do it!"

"Why, it's true!" laughed Cara.

Grizz took Mary's hand and caused her to pirouette as if she were a ballet dancer and he her partner.

"Wonderful!" he assured her. "They do a lot for you." His eyes twinkled as he introduced her to Cara with a wave of his hand. "The new Miss Meakin, Miss Ames." Then down the line of those gathered on the veranda. "Mr. Willcox . . . Mr. King . . . the other Mr. King" and so on, naming all those standing around except Bill Saxon, whom he deliberately snubbed.

Cara put an arm around Mary and squeezed her. "I like it immensely!" Mary blushed deeply and unconsciously crossed her arms over the two pufflets, become all the more embarrassed when she realized that, in doing so, she had drawn all the more attention to them.

What meant the most of all to her was that Griz had noticed the subterfuge, guessed at its secret, hailed her for carrying it off so well, and never embarrassed her by even the slightest hint that he knew they were false. If he could be so considerate in such circumstances, could she not hope that some day he might come to love her for her own sake?

Now it was time to go in for supper, Mrs. Swenson said.

On the way in Cara whispered that the reason she stayed over was that Monte said they were going to give the newlyweds a shivaree later that evening and he thought she might like to take part in it.

Mary was relieved to learn that Mrs. Swenson was treating this as a social occasion and considered it her prerogative to tell everyone where they should sit.

"The bride and groom will sit on either side of me," she said as she took her place solemnly at the head of the table. "Harry on my right and Jocelyn left." She was a stickler for presiding at all meals except breakfast. "Miss Meakin and Mr. Willcox at those two places at the far end, so that Miss Ames is at Mr. Willcox's right and Miss Meakin's guest is at her left." Everybody else fill in where you find a vacant chair."

Mary noted Mrs. Swenson had carefully avoided calling Griz by name. She hoped this did not bode ill for his bid to be given the room Harry was vacating. Mrs. Swenson had said she would give him a fair chance to convince her he was a proper enough person to join her exclusive menage.

Suddenly she realized that Griz's "trial by fire" had begun. Mrs. Swenson had deliberately placed the four of them opposite her at the other end of the table, so she could observe Griz's manners, especially his table manners, and his comportment with people he knew well. There was nothing she could do to warn him, because if she leaned over to whisper to him, Mrs. Swenson would certainly think she was coaching him.

Besides, Griz was enjoying himself. For a man who had no home except a shack in the mountains and who cooked his own grub, this meal was heavenly manna. Even when he got to town, he had to settle for free snacks at the Nugget bar or fried food at some cafe, unless Red cooked for him, too.

The supper was built around heaping platters of cold cuts to offset the enervating effect of the day's heat and humidity. But for those who liked something hot there were red flannel hash and chicken livers. Hot baking-powder biscuits and honey provided the stuffing for anyone who was still unsatisfied, and damson plum preserves and cookies were the dessert.

Griz ate with such relish he had little time to talk, which made Mary wish she could get through to Mrs. Swenson how much this man needed a home again. But she must not try to speak for him at the interview. Mrs. Swenson had always said, "A man speaks best for himself. Nobody else can make impressions for him. All others say only empty words."

It seemed to Mary that Mrs. Swenson's eyes never left Griz during the entire meal. Whenever Mary looked up, the four of them seemed to be under intense scrutiny, but the all-seeing eyes were focussed on Griz. She was relieved when Mrs. Swenson spread her hands to give the signal that supper was over. No one ever dared leave the table until she gave this signal. It might be only a gracious dip of her head. Other times she felt obliged to remind her boarders to observe certain social amenities. This was one of those occasions.

She rapped lightly on the table. "I'm sure I don't need to suggest," she said, "that the least we can do for Harry and Jocelyn is to gather in the parlor and drink to their health."

Mary whispered in Griz's ear. "That is her way of saying, 'Coffee will be served in the parlor.' " They winked at each other since they dared not snicker lest they get caught at it.

Mrs. Swenson finished her cup quickly and turned to Mary. "Might as well get it over with if he wants to talk with me." She led the way to her private sitting room. She was just as curt when they were seated. She eyed Griz critically. "Miss Meakin says you want to talk about that room upstairs."

"That's the general idea."

"Well, make up your mind. Either you want it, or you don't. Which is it?"

There was a flicker of a smile at a corner of her mouth. Griz returned it without otherwise changing his expression. Too bad, Mary thought, that Monte wasn't in the room to enjoy the sparring. Being a former boxer, he would have said they exchanged left jabs, feeling each other out, and liked the response in each case.

Mrs. Swenson led again. "What makes you think you fit in here?"

"I'm a college graduate like the rest of them."

"Argonaut Club, too," she countered with a smirk.

"I wasn't going to mention that."

"I shouldn't think you would."

"It's not that important."

"The Argonauts got no reason to put on airs."

"I agree with you there."

"Some of their women don't like you."

"I know. It's mutual."

"Maybe you like the women at that boardwalk bar better."

"That was a low blow. Mary held her breath, fearing Griz would lose his temper, but he only thrust his hands in his pockets angrily to hide his clenched fists.

"Mrs. Swenson," he said quietly, "if you are going to rent me that room, why don't you say so?"

"Mr. Quigley, I run a good, clean house. That's my answer."

More than anything else, Mary thought, calling him Quigley told Griz exactly where he stood with her. It was the first time this night she had given him a name and she chose to use the one that was certain to infuriate him. From that moment Mary was certain he would make a fight for the room.

"Mrs. Swenson," he said acidly, "what does one have to do to qualify for your 'good, clean house'?"

"You have got to start clean and stay clean all the way."

Despite her resolve to hold her tongue, Mary broke in. "Please, Mrs. Swenson, he has never had a chance to lead a normal life since his wife died."

"I didn't know he had been married, but what has that got to do with what he is now?"

Griz shook his head at Mary, then fired at close range at Mrs. Swenson, his face close to hers. "Now I want to ask *you* a question. How would you go about getting a bank loan from Homer Prentice?"

"I'm never going to ask Mr. Prentice for a loan.

"But suppose you *had to have* a loan?"

"That is never going to happen!"

"You are awfully positive—"

"You bet I am!" Her mouth was a thin, straight line.

"But what if you don't have any credit?"

"I don't ask for credit. I pay cash."

"But what if you are out of cash?"

"Then I'll have to close the boarding house."

"You wouldn't even beg to save it?"

"Never!"

"Then you will understand why *I* shall never beg now, or

at any other time in the future, for you to give me a room and board here." He turned to Mary. "Come, the night is still young."

"And there's the shivaree to come," Mary reminded him. She still did not know if he was diappointed or if he was only making a play for the room because he sensed she was trying to wean him away from the Redhead's available bed.

When Griz and Mary returned to the parlor, they found Cara at the piano, accompanied by the King twins on mandolin and guitar, entertaining the newlyweds and the rest of the household. As they ended that piece, Cara turned on her stool to say, "Just one more piece, then I must beg off. What would you like?"

"Singing in the Rain," Mary cried out.

"The bride and groom must dance to it?" Monte shouted. Sheepishly the young couple complied, to much hand-clapping.

Mary whispered in Griz's ear: "When they swing into the second chorus, that's the signal for the shivaree to begin."

The second time around everyone the parlor started singing with an abandon that was catching, a prelude to the moment when all hell broke loose outside.

Mary was stunned by that initial jolt, though she was waiting for it. She hung onto Griz for a moment, during which her eyes kept getting larger as excitement built up inside her. Then she screamed, "Shiva-ree-eee!" and scampered out the door.

The newlyweds froze, the bride clinging to her husband, terrified, until he forced her to sit on a settee, then joined her. Everyone else stood in place, open-mouthed or chattering, expectant, hands raised as if to ward off goblins. Mrs. Swenson moved to a position commanding the doorway.

From out of the night, accelerating in volume and tempo, came an awful clatter of sticks and stones being pounded on pots and pans, steel tools being played across washboards with a spine-chilling scream; of wailing sirens, cowbells and horns, and anything else that could contribute to this appalling bedlam.

Mary stuck her head inside the door, her eyes flashing. "They are yelling for you two to stick your heads outdoors!"

"Do we have to?" cried Jocelyn, the bride.

"They will come and get you if you don't!" Mary promised, pretending she was a Halloween goblin.

Mrs. Swenson shrugged. "Stay put," she told the bride. "They will come in anyway. All they ever have in mind is, 'What you got to eat? You got to feed us to get rid of us.' " She moved off toward the kitchen. "I guess I can dig up something."

As if she hadn't planned on it and had everything ready, Griz snickered to himself. He remembered only too well how she had looked at her watch when he was being dismissed minutes earlier.

Once Mrs. Swenson had quit guarding the door, Mary waved her hands to the raucous crowd outside and they poured inside, snakedancing and howling around the young couple and separating them so effectively that the bride did not know Harry had been spirited away until she found herself penned inside a prancing circle of women only.

"Harry!" Jocelyn screamed, trying to break out of the symbolic wedding circle. The circle collapsed on her instead.

Cara sat entranced on the piano stool, watching the saturnalia until Mary shouted, "Music, Cara," after which piano, mandolin and guitar contributed to the din, giving it tempo and a heartbeat!

Youngsters and men came snakedancing inside again, but there was no Harry with them.

"I want my husband!" the bride wailed, burying her head on Mary's shoulder as the women released her and cut back into the weaving line of prancers. Music and pure hullabaloo were now blended into one steady beat like that of a tom-tom.

"It's all right," Mary told the bride, soothing her as she would have done a child. "It's all in fun, Jocelyn. See there's Les and Mark, Jim and Andy, and Monte, too." She called off their names as they paraded by. "They won't let anything happen to Harry. You just wait and see. They will bring him back in a little while."

The snakedance was now one tremendous necklace, coiling to the street and back again. "Come with us," Mary said, taking the bride by the hand. "Have fun." She made a place for both of them in the serpentine, then reached out and grabbed Griz out of a comfortable chair where he sat enjoying the spectacle.

"You, too!" she shouted, pulling him to his feet. "Don't think you can sit out this dance just because you can't dance!"

He had never seen her so flushed and excited. She yanked him into line behind her and clamped his hands on her tiny hips. "Shake it!" she cried, bouncing up and down with each step, trying to inspire him to match her exuberance.

But not for long. Mrs. Swenson appeared with coffee, cider, doughnuts and cookies and there was no more shivaree. The revelers jammed the hall, parlor and dining room, eating, drinking, laughing, gobbling and cheering on Jocelyn's behalf when Harry was restored to her. And a rock specialist took Cara's place at the piano, rallying them to new heights of song.

Sometime during this aftermath the newlyweds slipped quietly away to the room Harry was vacating on the morrow, when they were to start their honeymoon by taking the afternoon train to Baker, along with Cara.

But they were not missed by anyone except Mary, whose eyes had not left them since they were reunited. She could not stop thinking what it would be like to change places with them in the night ahead. All evening there had been a restless stirring deep inside her that called for satisfaction. Her cheeks were burning up with desire. She knew now how a Vermont maple tree must feel in the spring when its sap began to flow.

Unable to withstand the tension any longer, she slipped outside unnoticed—or so she thought. She stepped into shadow on the veranda, from which she could look up to the window of Harry's room. Lucky Jocelyn, up there in Harry's arms.

Her hands slipped defensively to her hips, smoothed her dress carefully, and came to rest on her abdomen. Flat and firm to the touch, narrow like a man's. Nothing there to excite a man. It must be true what people said about her—destined to be an old maid schoolmarm. Never to cuddle children of her own or to comb their hair and wash their dirty little faces. . . .

She heard nothing as Griz came up softly behind her. Not until he put his arms gently around her. It seemed this was all a part of her fantastic daydreaming until he spoke.

"We missed you, or at least I did."

She shuddered, coming out of her trance. "It comes harder

every time one of them gets married."

"You poor kid!" he comforted her, crushing her to his chest. Then the dam broke and she sobbed her heart out in the comfort of his embrace.

After a little while he asked if she was feeling better. Her head bobbed up and down. Her big eyes had been washed so clean of what was troubling her that they fairly sparkled like crystal.

"Anybody special?" he asked, releasing her.

Blinking a couple of times and putting on a sober face, she again bobbed her head up and down . . . but very slowly.

"Monte?" he exploded, obviously certain he had guessed the right man.

"She shook her head, smiling coyly.

"Bert Ascher?"

She looked off into the night, seeming to weigh her answer. "Not yet, at least."

"Anyway, I've gotten you out of the dumps."

She looked up at him. "No more guesses?"

"Me?" he inkled with chuckle.

Her reaction instantly sobered him. "I only meant to be facetious," he protested, but there was no longer even the vestige of a smile on his face. Her wide open eyes never wavered as he looked into their infinite depths. She realized that he was shocked by what he read there.

How long they stood there, facing each other, transfixed, Mary had no idea. Moments only, most likely, but from far away she heard Griz eventually suggest that what she needed most of all, right now, was to take a long, vigorous walk with him.

"A moonlight stroll to get the muffins out of our systems," he said, making an effort to sound light-hearted. "Down to the park and back, maybe?"

She jumped at the chance. "I'd love to!" she sang out, taking his arm smartly and setting in invigorating pace down Schoolhouse Hill. The park was down by the river, at the other end of the boardwalk.

But no matter how briskly they walked, she could not stifle her thoughts. If she had only laughed in his face when he said, "Me?" Anything would have been better than standing there tongue-tied, staring at him helplessly, laying her heart bare. She had spoiled every chance he might have had to discover for himself that he was falling in love with her.

They set foot on the boardwalk, where their heels clicked out the first sounds that had passed between them in minutes. "You're very talkative," he suggested humorously. "Unlike you."

She gave him a fleeting smile. "I was thinking of the time when I was a little girl. I come from the wheat country between Pendleton and Hermiston. My father still has a farm there. Growing up on a farm, you never think much about the difference between a boy and a girl until you grow up. We used to go skinny-dipping in our swimming hole without thinking twice about it. It was not the rule, just a matter of choice, depending mostly on the weather or whether it was harvest time.

"That's when we'd get so caked up with dust and chaff, helping around the thresher, that someone would yell, 'Last one in is a nincompoop!' and there would be a stampede for the creek. And nobody would stop to climb out of overalls or shoes, but jump or dive in and take them off underwater because the boy or girl who became the nincompoop got royally ducked and cascaded with water.

"That's all it was, Griz; just a game—until my father put the kibosh on my playing it any longer when I reached the fifth grade. We didn't think much about sex in those days."

A sad smile flickered across her lips. "I guess that's when my luck ran out. The boys discovered it made a difference when they had to think of me as a girl. Girls were a nuisance. They no longer would let me play baseball with them. Soon— it came about so fast—we were all grown up and I was still the runt and the ugly duckling. One by one my girl friends got married in their teens to boys I had once played baseball with, and gone skinny-dipping with when we were just kids, while I kept going on alone, still untagged, haunting the auction picnics, hoping I'd find some kid who remembered I'd never been a nincompoop."

"Auction picnics?" He wrinkled his nose.

"Those picnics where a girl brings a box lunch for a boy and herself, not marked, mind you, so nobody is supposed to know who's the girl behind each box marked 'boy.' But don't believe it. Mine was always one of the last to draw a bid and I usually got a klunk."

"Try *me* sometime," he suggested.

"You mean it?"

"I said, 'Try me.' "

"You like picnics?" In just two words he had said she had not lost him entirely. She wondered if he would flick an eyelash if she then told him outright that she was in love with him. She laughed softly at the thought.

"What's so funny?" he asked.

"You."

"What about me?"

"You never would have made a good nincompoop!"

The soft crunch of pine needles underfoot told them they had entered the clearing down by the river where all outdoor civic affairs, except baseball and rock drilling, were held. Riverside Park was an expression of Bert Ascher's dream of elegance for a Cracker Creek that was otherwise impudent and brash, for a Cracker Creek that could draw tourists.

It had a perfect setting, flush with the Powder River at the point where Cracker Creek tumbled into the mainstream and created a lazy overflow of meandering sloughs for canoeing and young couples in love.

To one side were the huge pits where whole sides of beef were barbecued on Labor Day for the midday picnic. And in the very center of the clearing was a birdcage of a bandstand, painted a bright yellow, with a huge ball on top.

Anyone who knew Bert Ascher could have guessed the source of his taste for the excessive ornamentation under which his bandstand fairly sagged. It was pure baroque and reflected his German birth. Six carved columns held up the peaked roof. Uprights for the railing were carved and pierced in devious and intricate designs. Lights were strung in festoons from under the roof to the six corners of the hexagon. It was a perfect setting for romance. Almost any evening but Wednesdays in summer couples could be seen spooning on the bandstand's steps or in the shadows of the podium.

Wednesday nights were reserved for the hometown band Ascher was organizing. He had played trumpet in his youth

57

and found he still had the lip for it. He had recruited the King twins from Mrs. Swenson's and a couple of real tooters from the mines. Others, after coming to rehearsals to snicker, had joined up if they had any musical talent.

Bert's most satisfying achievement was to get Homer Prentice to admit he had a piccolo kicking around the house somewhere and to persuade him to find it. Mary would never forget the first time she heard Homer piping away with all the intensity and determination of that colonial with the bandaged head in the painting, "Spirit of '76," as he, Homer, put his heart into John Philip Sousa's "Under the Spreading Eagle."

Griz gestured toward the bandstand steps. Though it was Saturday night no spooners had beaten them to this sanctuary. "Guess the shivaree used up the youngsters' energy," he laughed. "Shall we sit down?"

"Such a lovely night," Mary purred, making a place for him to sit beside her.

The heady scent of pine and fir was intoxicating. A slight breeze off the river made certain it would not be long before they came under its spell.

"You sound as if you are relaxed now," he remarked. "The walk did you good?"

She wanted to say, "Just being with you was all I needed to settle down." She smiled at him instead, closing her eyes and nodding a yes with her head.

For awhile they were content to say nothing more. Mary sat hugging her knees, watching the fireflies circling the sweet-smelling, orange-flowered bushes Ascher had planted around the base of the bandstand.

Her thoughts were going round and round, too. She would never be satisfied she knew the key to Griz's heart until she understood why he still carried the torch for his dead wife, Alice. Finally curiosity got the better of her and she blurted out words which tripped her tongue: "Was she very beautiful, Griz?"

"Huh?" He came to with a start. Apparently he had been in a reverie of his own. "You mean Alice?"

Seeing the look on his face, she regretted her question.

"Forget it, Griz. I shouldn't have asked."

He thought about it for what seemed a long time, looking up at the stars for an answer, finally turning to put an arm around her and give her a quick squeeze. "Nobody has a better right to ask," he assured her. "Maybe I should get it out in the open where I can face it. I've kept it bottled up too long already. Too long!" His voice trailed off.

She waited patiently, content to have his arm around her.

At length he turned to look into those big hazel eyes which always seemed to fascinate him. "Yes," he admitted, "she was very, very beautiful, both in mind and in body. Why she married me I shall never know."

"Tall?" She dreaded to ask, but she must know.

"Yes, and with a beautiful carriage."

She thought he had started to say, "Like Cara," but had caught himself in time. Mary was looking up into his face now, anxiously anticipating every detail. "She wore her hair piled high on her head and carried herself like a queen. Her hands were lovely to look at and soft to the touch, even though she did all her own housework."

"You loved her very much?"

"I worshipped her."

Mary caught her breath at his emphasis on "worshipped." How could a little runt like she was—" Yet, something clicked in her head. She had asked if he *had loved* Alice very much. He had said nether yes nor no. Only that he "worshipped" her. There was a distinction here, or was she grasping at straws? Had Alice been so perfect that he stood in awe of her, instead of loving her as the only woman among all women?

Suddenly Griz stood up, sticking his hands in his pockets and walking back and forth in front of her.

Quickly she was on her feet, too, all apologies. "I kick myself for asking you such an impertinent question."

He quit pacing long enough to rumple her hair. "Forget it, kid. I should have talked about this long ago. Never could, except with the Redhead; least of all with you."

Her heart faltered at the warning implied in those words. "Why me least of all?" she whispered.

"Because you remind me of the baby girl I lost, too!" Now that he had said it he seemed to be impelled to talk. "It was bad enough to lose a wife, but to lose a daughter, too, to the same scourge, was more than I could take at the time—and ever since."

"Why didn't you tell me before? You must have known that at least I, with my background, would understand."

He sighed deeply. "I've never been able to talk about it after I told Red and afterward regretted it. This is something I have to live with, Mary. It isn't that I'm still grieving, but I can't face the possibility of it happening again."

If only to make him forget his obsession and perhaps recall some happier moments in his life with his daughter, she asked, "Was she beautiful, too?"

"Beautiful as her mother. If she had lived, she would have been about your size."

It was a very sober face she held up to him. "Is that why I remind you of her?"

"Absolutely!" He put an arm around her and squeezed her to his side. Any other time she would have said to herself: "The touch of a man is a wonderous thing," and twisted around to be cuddled against his chest like a little kitten. But he had crushed her hopes of ever being loved by him for herself alone. She slumped within the curve of his arm and turned away, heartsick that he apparently had never accepted her as a woman to be loved or in love.

He did now, however. The look on his face when she said, "Take me home now, Griz. I'm cured," gave away his realization that he, too, had failed miserably to do anything about relieving the sap in her veins this night when she was the chief goblin at the shivaree.

5

Mary did not see Griz again until the Fourth of July. With school out for the summer, she had gone home for a short visit with her folks. But home was not the same anymore.

Mama was not getting any younger. She expected Mary to help with the housework. Mary was willing, but it wasn't much of a vacation if she had to be on her feet all day long. Mama didn't see it that way. She always said, "I never had a vacation in my life," and was proud of it.

Everything Mary used to love about farm life had curdled since the excitement of Cracker Creek. She remembered the thrill, as a youngster, hovering over the wash-boiler as it bubbled away, begging for a chance to stir it up with the sawed-off broomstick. But Mama always said no because she might scald herself.

Now, hair stringing down her sweating face and looking ten years older than she really was, Mama made her feel guilty if she didn't take all the washing and ironing off her hands.

The barnyard smells which she always accepted as characteristic of farm life now nauseated her. She asked what had happened to the barricade of stately populars which stood off the wind that always seemed to whistle across this rolling landscape. Or the hollyhocks she loved, nestling against the house, and the rows of phlox lining the front walk.

"Too much trouble looking after them," Mama said.

"And the poplars?"

"Ask your Dad. Think he said they drew lightning."

And the front lawn no longer was green, but scruffy and thin, like a man growing bald. And chicken droppings everywhere. Mama always said that to let hens run made them tastier eating.

So Mary was glad she had signed up with Mr. Cole at Cracker Creek's Emporium, to spell his help during summer vacations, rather than stay at home until threshing time, when the crews had to be provided with heaping midday meals. Papa could afford to hire a couple of husky farm girls to do more for Mama than she could.

She had been on the Emporium job only two days before she was smitten with the hustle and excitement of it. She loved the pungent smell of oilcloth, the colorful patterns of calico and the rustle of silks and satins as she unrolled their bolts and slit them crosswise with one swift zip of a scissors to provide customers with the exact yardage they desired.

She wondered why this might not be more satisfying work than teaching, until she remembered nothing could ever replace her schoolchildren in her heart.

Yet the chance to chatter all day with women filled a void in her life. Between living in a house dominated by seven men and devoting all her weekdays to children, she had little chance to socialize with her sex. She needed to brush up against women, weeks on end, to discover what was lacking in her makeup and in her rapport with other women—and through them especially with men.

"Men!" she snorted as she let her mind run on while luxuriating in bed this Fourth of July morning, until she realized with a jolt she intended to get up early to watch the baseball excursion take off for Baker.

At supper the night before all the men except Bill Saxon were saying this game would settle the Eastern Oregon championship. Going into the game, both teams were undefeated.

She bounded out of bed to run to the open window. Sure enough, she could hear a hubbub in the making down by the depot. She slipped quickly into her clothes and clattered downstairs to breakfast.

"Where's everyone?" she exclaimed on finding Bill Saxon alone at the table.

"Gone to the excursion, I guess. Disgusting exhibition!"

"Baseball?"

"No, the riffraff you have to associate with on such an occasion. I'll take my baseball when I can walk to it and sit with whom I wish to converse."

He used his napkin to wipe his lips so carefully Mary thought he was trying to purge them of the aftertaste of his disgust.

"But I'm only going down to see the fun as they load up and pull out," she protested, finishing a quick cup of coffee and a doughnut.

"You would," he retorted with undisguised sarcasm. "You're partial to big muscled men who smell of sweat and murder the king's English."

In response, she gave him a flick of her fingers on his bald spot and scampered down the front steps.

Before she reached the depot she could hear the uproar of an angry crowd, massed around the locomotive and harassing Depotmaster Jillson, who had taken refuge atop a baggage truck from which he was shouting, "There's no more seats, I tell you. Go home!" He was having no more effect than if he had said, "Shoo fly!"

"Get more cars!" the massed crowd fired back at him. The cry was carried back, wave on wave, in a chant to the far reaches of the jam.

The truth was, the narrow gauge railway had been unable to come up with rolling stock adapted for passenger use. Eighty years earlier when it was in its heyday it was devoted mostly to hauling logs down to sawmills in Baker from the vast reaches of the Blue Mountains to the south, as far as John Day country. Then it boasted only one passenger train daily from Baker to Prairie City and back. This was the train Easterners, lured to Cracker Creek during the gold boom, nicknamed "the Five O'Clock" because its 26-mile afternoon run into Baker was far more exciting than their commuter trains on the Eastern seaboard.

"There's no more cars!" the depotmaster kept shouting, hoarsely.

Someone shouted: "The yard is full of flat-cars!"

Mary's heart did a flip-flop! Griz's voice! She looked around widly, torn between seeking him out and ducking out of sight. Not a word had passed between them since he took her home the night of the shivaree. They had parted swiftly at the Swenson porch steps. He had tweaked her shoulder and said, "Good night, kid," sort of father-like, before she ran up the steps to keep him from seeing her start to bawl.

She hesitated now to bring herself back into his focus when he might be dead serious about that outcry. In this timber

63

country flat-cars ordinarily were used for hauling logs. His cry had created an instant hush, during which everyone turned to look up the tracks.

The depotmaster scratched his head. "Flat-cars?"

"Yes, flat-cars," Griz shouted, pushing forward. "If they can haul logs, why not people, too?"

In that moment Mary abandoned all resolutions not to make up with Griz until he made the first move. She had spent many sleepless hours at the farm, trying to think out that last heartbreaking night with him. Now she had melted like a wax candle at the first sound of his voice and only a glimpse of him in a thicket of angry baeball fans.

He might have been a Pied Piper when the crowd took up his cry for flat-cars, and some even took off up the tracks, determined to haul them back to the depot by sheer strength, if necessary. But Mary knew she no longer needed to decide whether he was worth fighting for.

The depotmaster held up his hand. "Wait! I want to talk to Abe." Abe was the railway's only engineer qualified to drive a passenger train. Another hush while they conferred on the baggage truck and gestured repeatedly toward the rail yards. Finally Jillson announced: "Abe doesn't think the railway would approve."

The terrific roar of the crowd's disapproval hushed when Griz struck again. Shaking an angry finger, he yelled: "Then you're not going to move that train out of here today!"

Jillson bristled. "Who says?"

"We do!" came the answer in one swelling voice.

Jillson lost his temper, shook his fist at them. "It's against the law! I'm going to call the marshal."

From the back of the crowd came the familiar voice of Abe Long, Town Marshal. "I'm right here, Matt. What seems to be the trouble?"

"I want you to arrest these people. They won't let this train get underway."

"Be sensible, Matt. I've got no one hundred deputies."

"Well, then, arrest that big fellow there, Quigley. He's the ringleader."

That did it for Mary. Unable to see what was going on, she followed in the marshal's wake when he worked past her.

"Right over there, Abe," Jillson pointed to Griz. "Arrest him and the rest will stop this nonsense."

"Can't do that either, Matt," Long said as he reached the baggage truck. "He's one of my deputies."

"Since when?" the depotmaster bristled.

"Oh, maybe a couple of minutes ago—while I was walking up here."

"I'll have you fired by the city council!" Jillson swore.

The crowd hushed as Griz asked in a cool, clear voice: "There's nothing in the law, is there, Abe, that says a man can't sit down on the rails here, when there are no benches or anything else but the ground to squat on, if he's tired from waiting for a seat on this damned train?"

At once there was a movement among those jammed around the locomotive to sit down in the roadbed ahead of it.

"Stop them!" scramed the depotmaster, jumping up and down.

Long shook his head. "Can't do."

"Why not? They're committing a crime."

"What's the crime?"

"They're blocking the railway. That's illegal."

Long laughed, shaking his head. "That's trespassing. Nothing more."

"On private property?" Jillson reminded him. "Read that sign over there. It says, 'Trespassing on this property will be prosecuted to the full extent of the law!' "

"In a civil suit," the marshal reminded him. "It's like as if Griz here might hold out his arms to keep you from passing him on the boardwalk, and moving whichever way you did. That wouldn't be a crime. But if he put his hands on you, for whatever reason in the circumstances, that would be assault and you could swear out a warrant against him. I don't see anyone trying to stop that locomotive with his hands."

"Hear that, men?" Griz called to those sitting down ahead of the locomotive. "Don't touch Old Pluto! Not even the *cowcatcher*! That's assault!"

Old Pluto was the name Abe Hiller had given his favorite steed. Why "Old Pluto"? Because its enormous, funnel-shaped smokestack, belching clouds of black smoke, reminded Abe of the mythical Greek god of that name—always belching fire from his nostrils.

The depotmaster turned on Griz, firing a new vocal barrel. "You got a ticket?"

"Right here." Griz held it high.

"All right. You get aboard."

"Where?"

"Anybody else got tickets?" the marshal called out.

Hands went up throughout the crowd, even among those sitting on the ties in front of Old Pluto.

Long scowled at the depotmaster. "What happened?"

"Guess they bought them yesterday, or even a day or two before. How do I know?"

"Don't you know how many tickets you sold?"

"Never counted them. Never sold too many before."

"That's a fat excuse. All those folks on the train now—they got tickets?"

"Not all. Some came early and just climbed aboard. How was I going to stop them?"

"Nobody's saying you should, Matt. But since you can't make good on all the tickets you sold, seems to me there's only one decent thing to do. Call the whole shebang off and refund money to those who present tickets."

All the stuffing collapsed in Jillson with this advice. "Abe," he protested, "you can't do this to me."

"I ain't doing anything to you, Matt. Just trying to be fair and keep the peace. I'm leaving Griz in charge here, just to help you get out of this jam."

The marshal put a hand on Griz's shoulder and gave it a shake of confidence. "I hereby appoint you Deputy Marshal. Take it from there and"—he emphasized with a wink—"get *all these folks* to the ball game in time."

Nobody but a wife could have been any more choked up with delight than Mary over the on-the-spot mandate. She clapped her hands ecstatically. Griz, however, gave no hint of his reaction, except to mumble. "An old Confucius saying says, 'He who speaks up to *tell how* is usually asked *to do it*.' "

He turned abruptly, intending to speak, only to find Mary looking up at him with adoring eyes. Twice as big as usual. His mind hung up with a solution to the problem suddenly tossed at him, he reacted angrily. "What are *you* doing here?"

"Taking in the show," she giggled. "It's terrific! And to think you got chosen to play the lead!"

Obviously nettled, he waved her off, grumbling: "Me and my big mouth!"

Big eyed, she asked, "What are you going to do?"

"I haven't the slightest idea. You come up with one and you are dubbed Deputy-Deputy Marshal."

That told her he had lost his sense of humor momentarily. This was half the battle.

Jillson brought them both back to their senses. Hands cocked on his hips and poking his jaw at Griz, he growled: "Wel-l-l! Time's a-wasting. What do we do?"

Mary inkled, in an undertone, "If they ride on flat-cars, what do they sit on?"

"On their bottoms, of course. What else?" Jillson said out of the corner of his mouth facetiously.

The depotmaster unconsciously provided the answer. "Abe Hiller says it's hellishly dangerous, riding on flat-cars with nothing to hang on to."

"That's it!" Griz shouted, vaulting atop the baggage truck beside Jillson. "Nothing to hang onto! Get it? That's the solution!"

A ripple of excitement led to a chorus of "How's?"

"If Matt here provides the flat-cars," Griz shouted, "we'll come up with the means of *hanging* on and there'll be room for every-y-y-body aboard this train."

This time the response was a roar of approval.

Griz held up his hand again. "Listen to me carefully. I want every man here to go home, back downtown or wherever you can find anything to sit on, or nail down, and bring it back here. Beg, borrow or buy if you have to. Benches, old chairs, boxes, beer kegs and especially wood stumps you use as firewood. And everyone of you must have a chopping block at home. Bring it! You can make yourself a new one next week. And planks to make benches out of boxes and stumps. And don't forget hammers and eight or nine-penny nails."

Mary expected them to fly off at once in every direction, but they stood dumbfounded for the most part.

Griz doubled over with laughing at the reaction, then wiped the grin off his face and explained: "You are going to *nail them on the flat-cars!* Get it?" He spread his arms as if they were the wings of an eagle. "Vamoose!" he thundered.

With those words the ant hill came alive. Griz turned to the depotmaster. "Now, Mr. Jillson," he said with a deferential sweep of his stetson, "if you will now bring up your flat-cars."

Until this moment Mary had given no thought to taking the excursion herself. Certainly not to see the ball game. But she was suddenly intrigued by the possibility it might be a wild escapade to her liking. She knew what Engineer Abe Hiller meant about cracking the whip around every sharp curve on the downhill run to Baker, with a string of flat-cars for a tail.

She gave Griz a quick look, noting that he was standing braced against the onslaught of scurrying ants he had loosed on Cracker Creek, shouting orders like a harried foreman, obviously no longer aware of her presence, and skipped home.

"I want a big stick of firewood," she said to Mrs. Swenson.

The woman gave her a puzzled look. "For what?"

"To sit on, of course," she giggled, collapsing against the ample Swenson breast and laughing herself out of breath. But she got her chunk of firewood, and no more questions were asked.

On her way back to the depot, she was further intrigued with a more cogent reason for joining the excursion. She could look up Cara Ames. She hadn't seen her since the night of the shivaree. Piano lessons were taboo to youngsters during summer vacation.

On second thought it occurred to her that Griz might have the same cute idea—to heck with the ball game, why not look up Cara instead? That possibility gave her goose pimples. Ever since that dreadful night at Riverside Park she had been linking these two together like a couple made for each other. If for no other reason, she must take the excursion to make sure he found her at Cara's if he came a-courting!

With steel in her backbone, she marched up to Griz, her huge chunk of firewood numbing her arms. Out of breath, she puffed: "See, I'm bringing my own seat, like you said."

He made a pass at taking it from her, but she twisted away, clutching it tightly.

"Hang it, Mary," he protested, "you can't ride out there. It's too dangerous."

"If that's so, you should not have suggested it in the first place." She pointed to the monstrosities men were creating on the flat-cars, out of chopping blocks and apple boxes, beer kegs and kerosene cans, old railroad ties and milking stools, a couple of park benches and crosscut slices of legs galore, and planks where connecting links were needed.

Three youngsters had even come up with an old bedspring, which they nailed to the floor of one flat-car and lashed a mattress to. Now they were running and jumping on it.

She shook her head in smiling admiration for the genius of his bizarre idea. "Look at them, Griz. Did you ever see anything that reminded you more of a garden full of toadstools?"

He smiled indulgently, but reminded her that flattery would not get her aboard the excursion.

"Not even if I buy a ticket?"

"Look at you," he scolded her. "No hat or gloves and that dress wouldn't keep a gnat warm!"

"Then you keep me warm!" she challenged him. "I'm a gnat!"

She caught herself starting to throw her arms around him, as she usually did before the shivaree. But it would never do to be demonstrative now. Instead she smoothed the light gingham dress she was wearing. "What's wrong with it? It's one of my prettiest."

Griz bent down to look her right in those big eyes. "You think," he said, stressing every word, "that because it is hot here in the sun, it is going to be delightful sitting out on one of those flat-cars, enjoying the breeze that the train kicks up, fanning your face and riffling your hair. But you have another guess coming, Mary.

"It's going to be damn cold once you get into the canyon. Like when you're out buggy riding and give your nag a flick of the whip and he takes off, galloping like fury, and the wind goes right through you. This ride down the canyon is going to be four times as bad as that."

She searched his face fearfully. "You want me to go home?"

"No! No! Of course not," he said forcefully, but thoughtfully tender.

She was pathetically humble. "I didn't mean to do this, Griz. Honest, I didn't. I just came down to watch the fun and got caught up in the exictement when you took over. All of a sudden I wanted to go if it was the last thing I did. Before I changed my mind, I ran home and Mrs. Swenson gave me this stick of firewood."

"Did you tell her what you wanted it for?"

"Yes. To sit on."

"But not on a flat-car?"

She shook her head.

"Or that you wouldn't be home for dinner or supper?"

"No."

"You might at least have picked up a jacket or sweater."

She smiled sweetly, holding up her purse. "I have this. I never feel well dressed without it. Nothing else matters."

Griz gave her a wry smile. "That's what Alice used to say, too. It beats me what emphasis you women put on certain symbols."

"Alice was right," Mary assured him. "I'm beginning to enjoy every time you speak of her."

But in her mind she was thinking, "Now he can talk about her without feeling disloyal because he no longer puts her on a pedestal."

He sighed deeply, "Women are frustrating."

"Including little runts like me?"

But she was buoyed up by the relaxed way he said it. She was encouraged to make a bold play. "Okay, Griz, I'll go back to Mrs. Swenson's and hold her hand the rest of the day."

"You will do nothing of the sort! Take your stick of firewood over there and stand by till we start boarding."

She inkled, "You'll let me sit beside you?"

"Yep, and keep you warm, too." He gave her a quick hug, just like he used to do. But she told herself she must not let it mean anything more than that.

As he predicted, she was a thoroughly chilled young woman by the time the excursion stopped at McEwan, six miles down the track and twenty more to go.

Griz bounded off the train there to talk with engineer Hiller. He came back shortly to tell Mary Abe said she could ride down the canyon in the cab with him.

"What about you?" she asked anxiously.

"Oh, yes. Me, too," he said, steering her forward quickly. "I'm still a kid when it comes to railroading. I'll just stand back out of the way, watching how you take it."

That ride down the canyon of Powder River in the cab was an experience neither of them would soon forget. Mary sat for a time in the fireman's seat, watching Mr. Gadsby chuck four-foot slaps of cordwood into an open firebox, which consumed them with the fury of a forest fire. It seemed Gadsby would not stop stoking this inferno until there was a noticeable difference in the click of Old Pluto's wheels on the rails. Hiller was throttling down for the canyon.

When Gadsby finally slammed the fire-door shut, Hiller beckoned for Mary to cross to his side of the cab. The Powder River was tumbling joyfully down the rapids at his right. "I don't want you to miss this next mile," he shouted in her ear. "Stand behind me so you can see the slot as we hit it."

Mary stole an excited look at Griz. He was the picture of an indulgent father enjoying his child's reaction to this experience. She had never seen him more relaxed as he leaned against the cordwood piled in the coal car, resting his elbows on the top layer. Even his beard twitched.

She rubbed her backsides to convey to him her gratitude for the heat from the firebox that had proved he was right about her meager attire. The gesture drew from him an even broader grin that was nothing short of affectionate. But she bemoaned inwardly that his heart could go out to her as a child, though not as a woman.

Abe Hiller touched her arm, drawing attention to Pluto's funnel-shaped smokestack, now giving off a trailing veil of black lace. Its top was capped with a bent-inward rim to keep sparks from escaping to set fire to the neighboring grasses and hillsides.

No question now but Old Pluto was sneaking up on the canyon and its strangled torrent of white water. He slithered around a score or more of tight curves, purring silently on each change of direction; ducked behind an outcrop now and then, circled the Pillar and suddenly burst in full view of the notch that lay dead ahead. Then he entered the chute on even terms with the river and rattled over the bridge that put him on the left bank. Then it was a race through the gorge to see which came out first.

Pluto was on solid ground here. The granite roadbed had been blasted out of the canyon's wall to provide a wide shelf well above flood stage. The rails were new and of a heavier steel, well ballasted.

"Hang tight now," Hiller shouted in Mary's ear. "Here's the rapids."

In this final, twisting, headlong quarter mile, she was whipped about on her feet, like sheets on a clothesline in a squall, hanging on for dear life.

Suddenly she cried out, pointing to the surging river, "We're going backward," never having experienced this phenomenon before.

Abe Hiller gave her a big grin. "That's because you are letting your eyes run ahead with the river. That's because the river is going faster than we are. Now look back."

That way, Mary discovered, Old Pluto was walking away from the river. It was very disconcerting that the eyes could be fooled so easily.

But she caught sight of something far more fascinating. The last two flat-cars were whipping around the curves on hundreds of male legs because the men on them, for the most part, had quit their makeshift seats and were sitting along the sides of the cars, dangling their legs overboard and kicking at the tall grass growing close to the narrow roadbed. Touching the engineer and pointing back, she giggled: "A thousand-legged centipede is chasing us!"

Then they were in open country once more. All around them lay green meadowland. The Powder River had gone off by itself. Old Pluto was being given his head again, loudly exhaling clouds of black smoke to the rhythm of his wheels on the breaks in the ribbon of steel.

Gadsby tapped Mary, pointing to the whistle cord and holding up three fingers. "Three long ones," he shouted.

She grasped the knot with both hands and yanked. The resultant blast was so startling she let go and staggered back into Griz's arms. "Two more," Griz laughed as the fireman held up two fingers.

This time she pulled the cord with one hand and put the other over one ear to deafen the blast. Griz explained that she had just signaled the train would make a flag stop at

Salisbury. He handed her down there and steered her to one of the coaches. She balked furiously when he tried to help her board.

"But I want to get back out there with you," she begged.

"You are going inside this time," he said, just as firmly as the father image with which she had been endowing him. "I'm not going to let you get chilled again. Do you want me to go inside with you and help you find a seat?"

She bristled. This was carrying the idea of proxy fatherhood too far! "No, I'll find my own seat!" she fired back and scampered up the steps. All at once she felt like skipping down the aisle, humming to herself like his make-believe child.

She was certain now, however, that, ball game or no, he would turn up at Cara's, as she had speculated. All she need do to guarantee this was to corner Monte, who was somewhere in this excursion crowd, and ask him to pick her up at Cara's for the return run to Cracker Creek. Preferably doing so in Griz's presence.

6

When the excursion reached Baker, its horde of baseball fans marched en masse down Depot Street until it came to the turnoff for the ball park. Mary and Griz were in the thick of this rooting, tooting mob, stretching from curb to curb.

Mary had not yet told Griz she had no intention of going to the game. Already she was sensing a change in his attitude toward her. He was no longer the pseudo doting father, warmed by an emotional experience, shared with her in the cab of Old Pluto.

Now his eyes were darting in every direction, seeking out men in the moving throng he could salute with a wave of his hand and a few hearty words. He was a hail-fellow-well-met, thriving on the infectious camaraderie of the rollicking crowd. He was not even aware she was no longer keeping step with him.

Fearful that she might wait too long to tell him of her decision, she looked around desperately for Monte. She was three or four yards behind Griz, being swallowed up in the crowd before he realized she was lagging and stopped to let her catch up.

"What's up?" he asked solicitously.

Before she answered, she thought to herself, "How nice that he *did* miss me!" Wrinkling her forehead, she complained: "I can't find Monte."

He craned his neck in circles until he spotted him. "Right over there," he pointed and took her hand. "come with me."

When they joined Monte, she slipped between them and locked arms. As one, they got in step with the marching horde.

"The Three Musketeers are we!" Monte boasted, setting the cadence and stepping out briskly, an infectious lilt to his enthusiasm.

Mary gulped, then blurted out what she was determined to say. "I'm not going to the ball game with you guys." Then to

Monte quickly, "Will you pick me up at Cara's after the game? I don't want to miss my ride back to the Creek."

Done with considerable finesse despite her nervousness, she said to herself. Short, sweet and to the point. Now each knew she was going to spend the day with Cara.

She caught a quick exchange of glances between the two men, which might explain the step which Griz missed when she asked Monte, rather than Griz, to pick her up at Cara's. He had to execute some fancy footwork to get back in stride.

Griz put on a long face which didn't fool her one bit, "so you're going to dump me now."

"How come?"

"Dumping me for Monte!" He arched his eyebrows, grinning at Monte through his whiskers. "Suit yourself."

She pretended to be surprised. "You can come, too, if you like. I only asked Monte because he knows where she lives and I thought I had been enough of a nuisance for one day without asking you to squire me back to the Creek, too."

"Suit yourself," he said again, but with a suggestion of displeausre this time. He deliberately avoided looking at her.

She would always be grateful to Monte for saving her neck at this point. He asked, "What do you say, Griz? You or me?"

Mary held her breath. They had reached the turnoff for the baseball park. Her little game hung in the balance.

Griz pursed his lips, stroking his beard thoughtfully, then cackled in their faces. "You didn't think I was giving it real hard thought, did you? No, sirree! I don't think it matters which one of us picks her up. We might even flip for it."

Monte frowned. "Shame on you, Griz! You just deflated the little gal."

He was so right, but she put on a brave smile and tossed her head as if it didn't matter which. "The one who wins the toss gets his *choice*."

"Not on your tintype!" said Griz emphatically. "The one who wins gets to pick you up and chaperone you all the way back to Mrs. Swenson's."

Monte chuckled. "You got out of that one neatly."

"On the other hand," Griz suggested, "maybe we both can come pick her up—"

"And get a chance to see Cara, too!" Monte cut in.

Griz cocked his head, thinking. "That's an idea, isn't it?" he said eventually. Too innocently, in fact.

"Oh, come off it," Monte protested. "You were working around to that alternative all the time."

"Oh, shut up!" Then Griz turned to Mary. "Let's leave it this way. One of us will positively show up. That I can promise you. Maybe both," he smiled slyly. "Who knows?"

Whereupon they both fell upon each other, back-slapping and laughing gleefully until they realized they were leaving Mary out of their act, reached out and enveloped her, too, and gave her a good, roundhouse two-man hug which took all the wind out of her. When she got her breath again, flushed and too overcome to say anything, Griz tipped his hat to her, said, "Let's get going!" to Monte and away they loped to overtake the tail-end of the march to the ball park.

"So I was right about the bait!" Mary said to herself, with that satisfaction about her lips that reminded her of a cat who has just caught a mouse. She laughed out loud, causing a cat on a nearby fence to stir and open its eyes. Impulsively, she walked over and titillated its white neck, then stroked its silken fur from the neck to the tip of its tail, which came straight up, bringing the cat to its feet, purring furiously.

"You know just how I feel, don't you, Tabitha?"

But even the cat knew when it had had enough of the ultimate in ecstasy. When its claws began to shred the pine wood under its paws, Mary guessed it was time to get on her way to Cara's. She took a big, deep breath and sounded off again, but not for Tabitha's benefit. "Cara," she sang gaily to herself, "Here I come!"

It was a great deal farther to Cara's house than she had anticipated. She was hot and tired when she caught sight of a wide veranda ahead, sheltered by luxuriant honeysuckle vines.

"Come in, child," said a voice from the recesses of the porch as she climbed steep steps. Rocking quietly in a huge rattan chair was a tiny, sharp-faced woman, spectacles pushed back on her forehead. She was snapping green beans and cutting them up into a granite kettle.

"You look all tuckered out," said the woman, whom Mary

took for Cara's mother, Louella Ames. "Take a chair and I'll call my daughter." She pitched her voice an octave higher to call: "Ca-a-a-ara! We've got company."

Mary held out her hand. "Mrs. Ames, I'm Mary Meakin from Cracker Creek."

"Land sakes," the old woman said. "I ought to know you. Heard enough about you. Schoolteacher, aren't you? Why, you aren't much bigger than the kids you teach."

Mary thought, "What about yourself?" but Cara appeared and exclaimed, "What on earth are you doing here at this time of the day, Mary?"

"I came down on the baseball excursion."

Cara laughed. "Not really?"

"Down and back in the same day."

"How wonderful! But you don't want to go to the game, do you?"

Mary shook her head.

"Then stay here and just visit with us."

"I was hoping you would say that."

"Stay to dinner and maybe we'll have time for a bite of supper, too, before traintime."

Mrs Ames broke in. "Not much for dinner except beans. Cara doesn't seem to have time to get good vittles together any more."

"Now, Mother," Cara said, patting her shoulder lightly. "There's plenty in the refrigerator, if you'd only eat it, and I think there are just enough strawberries left on the vines for a shortcake."

"Oh, let me help you pick them," Mary begged.

"Well, dear, you girls can have the berries," Mrs. Ames said with resignation. "Those last ones I had gave me an awful spell of heartburn. Just give me a dish of applesauce." She turned to Mary. "You see, I really don't eat enough to keep a bird alive, but somehow or other the good Lord keeps me going, and why I don't know, because I'm no good to Cara or anyone else."

"Now, Mother, stop talking that way. I'll make us a cool drink and while I'm stirring up the shortcake, you just sit and chat with Mary."

The beans disposed of, Mrs. Ames hitched her chair around

77

until she sat almost toe to toe with Mary. She fixed Mary with sad, watery eyes. "Humph!" she sniffed. "I thought you were a big grownup woman the way Cara talked about you."

Mary kept her cool, though she was getting mighty tired of such remarks.

Louella Ames looked furtively toward the screen door, then dropped her voice. "How well do you know my daughter?"

Mary recognized this as the opening gambit of a fishing expedition. This could only mean that she had become suspicious when Cara stayed over a second night with the Prentices.

"Now give me some straight answers," the woman said, "because I'm going to give you some straight questions."

Mary decided to stall for time. "If you mean intimately, Mrs. Ames, I don't know Cara that well, but already I love her dearly and everybody I know feels the same way about her. She is such a lovely person."

"She is lovely, all right," Mrs. Ames agreed, "but what I want to know is"—she dropped her voice almost to a whisper—"is there a man up there at Cracker Creek who has taken a liking to her, or she to him?"

Mary would have liked to answer, "That's what I'd like to know, too." Then it was all she could do to keep from bursting out laughing. She wondered what the woman would think when not one, but possibly two men from the Creek showed up at the door to take her home.

Mentally crossing her fingers, Mary said, "Not that I am aware of." She wished she could be certain too.

"Now, girlie, don't try to fool me." The woman's eyes snapped. "I've got to know, but when I ask Cara she just laughs and puts me off. I'm an old woman and I feel it in my bones I won't be around much longer, but while I'm here I need my girl. What's going to happen to me if she gets married?"

Mary would have liked to reply sharply to that challenge, but Cara's return stilled her tongue.

"Time for a little rest before dinner," Cara told her mother, helping her out of her chair and into the house. When she returned, Cara settled in a chair, fanning herself with the end of her apron. "Bet Mother's been pumping you on my love life," she laughed.

Mary blushed, but held her tongue.

"It's getting to be an obsession with her," Cara admitted. "I'll never hear the end of that second night I stayed over for the shivaree." Still, she smiled and laughed it off. "Something to be lived with."

Mary kept thinking how pretty she looked, relaxed in an apron and strawberry stains showing on her fingers. It took no stretch of the imagination to picture her sitting comfortably at the breakfast table, pouring and serving up eggs for a doting husband. "Yes," Mary admitted to herself, "she will make a perfect housewife."

"Maybe if you got married she would *have* to care for herself," Mary suggested. (A tentative feeler on Mary's part as to Cara's attitude toward marriage.)

Cara smiled. "He would have to be an exceptionally understanding young man to marry me and my mother, too, because it would have to be that, much as I regret it."

Mary now dared to make an even more reckless gambit.

"There are a couple of young men in Cracker Creek who might be willing to take that gamble."

"That's possible," Cara laughed, "but I shall never spend the rest of my life in Cracker Creek."

"I thought you loved it."

"Sure, for a couple of days at a time it's exciting. But as for living there permanently, no! Really, Mary, it is nothing more than the mining camp it recreated from the past. But every other building on the boardwalk is a saloon, even if they now call it a bar, and upstairs over every one of them is a massage parlor, where before there was a brothel—" She stopped short and put a hand on Mary's arm. "I'm sorry. I have offended you."

"Oh, no. It's just that—"

"I want you to believe that I love you and the Prentices, and people like Griz and Monte, but here we have a Carnegie Library and a Little Theater, glee clubs and a women's club, and lovely specialty stores to shop in, not like the Emporium, which is little more than an old fashioned dry goods store." She put her hand to her mouth. "Oh, dear! There I go offending you again! How's the new job?"

"Fine. I've only been at it two days so far."

"You must forgive me for being so critical of Cracker Creek, but I just could not take it as a steady diet."

Cara looked at her watch. "Time to think about dinner. The noon whistle at the lumber mill should blow any minute now. Mary, will you set the table for me? Afterwards, let's go down and look around the shops. You might find some things you can't buy at the Emporium."

Which is exactly what they did and Mary came back to the Ames home with her arms full of packages. "Lucky I have a man to help me carry them to the train," she told Mrs. Ames.

Louella Ames was at once alert. "What man?"

"Maybe two," Mary said saucily.

"You know these men?" the mother asked Cara sharply.

"I can guess," laughed Cara.

"Griz and Monte," Mary admitted. "Griz for sure, maybe Monte." Then to Mrs. Ames: "They promised to come for me in time to catch the excursion's trip back home."

Later, when she got over being flabbergasted by the size of these two men, Louella Ames looked them over as carefully as if she were buying horseflesh, then asked impertinently, "Which one of you is stuck on Cara?"

"I think they both are!" Mary squeaked with impish delight.

Griz swallowed so abruptly from the shock effect that he choked and had to be pounded on the back. Monte turned a fiery red and developed instant laryngitis.

Quickly Cara headed for the kitchen, telling Griz: "I'll get you a glass of cold water."

"Make that two," Monte called after her, mopping his forehead. "I seem to have become uncommonly hot. Wouldn't be a bit surprised if I didn't get a touch of sunstroke at the game."

"That's no sunstroke," Mary kidded him, testing his brow with her hand for signs of a temperature.

All this time Mrs. Ames was sitting rigid in her rocking chair, tight-fisted hands clutching the chair's arms, her jaw sagging half open, head turning back and forth, eyes focusing sharply on whoever was speaking at the moment.

"Young lady," Mrs. Ames cut in. "Seems like you are playing with this one." She pointed to Monte. "Is he in or out? A straight answer now!"

Mary giggled. "Mrs. Ames, I eat breakfast with him every morning."

Louella gasped. "You're married?"

"No."

"Related?"

"No. We just live in the same boarding house."

Louella snorted and turned toward Griz. Cara had just handed him the promised drink of water, which he had just started to drink when Louella pounced. "So this is the man who is stuck on Cara!" she gloated.

Griz choked a second time and staggered across the room, coughing his head off, till he managed to steady himself on an old pump organ.

"Mother!" Cara said firmly, but patiently. "Nobody is stuck on anybody here. We are just four old friends, happy to be all together again."

Louella Ames looked from one to another, anxiously trying to satisfy herself this was true.

For his part, Griz sought to get this woman's mind off the subject. The nasal twang in her voice suggested a way. Leaning back on the organ's beautifully carved walnut case and smoothing its finish with one hand, he said: "Mrs. Ames, you remind me of my grandmother."

"I don't know whether to take that as a dig or a compliment," she hedged.

"A compliment, of course. You just proved my point by your question. My grandmother believed in speaking her mind when, as she would have said, the situation called for it."

"Always have," she said proudly, with a toss of her head.

"You come from New England?" Griz asked.

"No, sir! Born and raised right here in Eastern Oregon."

"Any of your folks come from New England?"

"My grandmother did. From Maine."

"There!" crowed Griz. "I thought so! My grandmother was from Maine, too."

"Mine was from Bangor," Mrs. Ames said proudly.

"Mine too!"

"What a small world," commented Mary. "However did you spot her background?"

He chuckled. "First, she came right out with what was on

her mind. *'Maine-iacs,'* as I like to call them. They pride themselves on being forthright."

"That's Mother," Cara laughed.

"You see," Griz continued, "you must have been around your grandmother a lot when you were a child, Mrs. Ames."

"Spent half my summers with her."

"That accounts for the trace of Down East twang."

"And proud of it!" Her eyes snapped. Then she was out of her chair quickly and across the room till she stood beside Griz.

(And this was the woman, thought Mary, who said she was half dead already!)

"See this organ you're leaning on, young man."

Griz stood off to get it in better focus while the others crowded in to caress its finish and trace its carvings with the fingers.

"The keys haven't yet even begun to get yellow," Mary said.

"I want you to know," Louella cut in, "my grandmother brought this all the way to Oregon when she was nineteen. They hauled it overland across the Isthmus of Panama, while she and her two sisters rode pack horses, and a packet ship brought it to Portland."

Cara opened the Gothic-carved doors below the keyboard, on either side of the recess where one's legs pump the pedals, revealing shelves where sheet music presumably would be stored. "These cubbyholes," Cara explained, "are our secret hiding places for family papers." Giving Mary a significant wink, she added, "God only knows what you might find there."

In the little time left before the Cracker Creek trio had to make a run for the excursion train, Cara fed them a quick supper of iced tea, sandwiches and homemade cake.

"Did you make this?" Monte asked, trying to get his mouth around one bite from a huge hunk of cake.

Cara smiled. "Sure."

"M-m-m-ummm!" he hummed, getting frosting all over his fingers, trying to keep crumbs from falling on the floor.

Out of respect for his first mouthful of cake, Griz let his beard do the twitching and his eyes do the talking. But there was little doubt Cara had made an impression on both men with her kitchen potential.

So, Mary said to herself, perhaps it was a mistake to encourage Griz to see Cara in her home. She was a great catch on every score—not beautiful, but a fine looking woman; quite talented, thoughtful, even tempered, good sense of humor, and, best of all from a man's viewpoint, a good wife in the making. What more could Griz ask if he were in the mood for asking?

On the way to the train Mary asked Griz if he loved New England.

"Sure did," he said.

"Ever want to go back?"

He answered with an emphatic no.

That closes one exit, Mary said to herself.

She had borrowed a warm jacket from Cara so that Griz could not refuse to let her ride out back again. But he had outfoxed her. "See," she waved the jacket on her arm, "I can take the cold wind this time."

He brought her up short when she sought to head for the flat-cars. "I have it all fixed up for you to ride home with the Redhead."

She whipped around. "Why didn't you tell me?"

"Because I knew you would be pig-headed again."

She stamped her foot. "How dare you do my thinking for me!" And just as quickly regretted it. After the smooth sweetness of Cara, how could she *dare* to snap at him? She guessed she would never learn to be politic where a man was concerned. She came back very slowly, putting one foot at a time carefully in front of the other, quite penitent.

"Whatever you say, Griz."

Which is one reason she rode all the way to the Canyon with Mary Too in a passenger coach. At that point, as the train crept painfully upgrade after clearing the chute, there was a hullaballoo alongside that brought Red and Mary to their feet, scurrying to the car's rear platform, to see men leaping from the flat-cars behind them and fanning out on the hillside above and below the roadbed whooping it up and picking wild daisies as they kept pace with the train.

Someone spotted the Redhead on the platform and called out, "Hey, Red! See what we're picking for you." He held up his tribute, taking his eyes off his footing, stepped in a gopher hole and promptly tumbled to the edge of the river. But he came up, dripping, grinning and holding up his handful of daisies, much as a Nez Perce Indian of these parts might have done three generations earlier with a fresh scalp, and chased after the train, trying to hand it to Mary Too before he fell on his face again.

The very fascination of what these men were doing was too much for Mary. "I'm going to join them," she giggled, and slipped down the coach's steps, from which it was only a short drop to the roadbed. Griz and Monte, she quickly discovered, were on foot too, back alongside the flat-cars—just for the exercise, they later told her. Not a moment too soon, Griz up with her, lifting her bodily off footing too treacherous for a woman's heels and hoisting her, kicking legs and all, onto the nearest flat-car, despite the furious tattoo she was beating on his shoulders and neck with her little fists.

"Now stay there!" he admonished her, "and behave yourself! If you want to do something worthwhile, tell these men to bring their bouquets to you, so you can make them into one big armful for Red."

The suggestion appealed to her. She dropped to her knees on the flat-car and held out her arms. "Bring your daisies to me," she called to the men. "I'll keep them for you—to give to the Redhead if you wish." She repeated the appeal as she came abreast of new groups. The childish look of her touched their hearts and they responded handsomely.

A big, grinning lumberjack was the first to step up and hand her what he had picked. Bashfully bobbing his head, he said: "For the Redhead!"

She held them high for all to see. "For the Redhead!" she shouted.

"For the Redhead!" a dozen others cried out, until the words became a chant up and down the hillside. Soon Mary could hold no more in her hands. She gathered her skirt up like an apron and held it out as a target for all to shoot at, usually on the dead run. She guessed her slip was showing, but that made the game more entertaining.

When her skirt began to sag with the harvest, Griz called a halt and ordered everyone back aboard the train. At the last stop, McEwan, before the run into the Creek, he called the Redhead to the platform of her coach for the presentation of the daisies.

A quartet from the Bonanza mine sang a very impromptu version of "I Love You Truly," as Griz pointed to a miner, "You get the first kiss!" The crowd hooted as the embarrassed hunk of a man collected, with little more than a peck. Griz next singled out a veritable Paul Bunyan for the second and last kiss. This man made no mistake about his approach and execution. He gave Red such a thorough bussing that he knocked her flowered hat askew.

"Break!" cried Griz as the crowd rocked with cheers and guffaws, and anew when Griz held the man's hand high, hailing him as the new champion of the Blue Mountains.

Then Griz turned to Mary. "The daisies, please." He had to help her up the steps. There were so many she could hold them all only by wrapping both arms around them.

"From all those men out there who love you," Mary said to Red in making the presentation.

They cheered the Redhead lustily. But her smile cracked a little bit as she tried to take them from Mary. Deciding they were making a mess of it, she held up her hand to halt their wild applause. "There are two Marys here," she told them. "This is Mary Meakin, who collected all those daisies you picked for me and my real name is Mary, too, in case you didn't know it. I think we should give half the daisies to this other Mary. What do you say?"

A roaring yes was the answer.

She returned half the daisies to little Mary, who hid her face momentarily in them, then kissed Red impulsively.

"Go on, get out of here," said Mary the Redhead. "Do you want me to bawl, too?"

Thus ended the daylong excursion, which saw Cracker Creek lose the baseball championship to Baker. Townspeople scattered to their homes for a belated supper. With nothing in their bellies but sandwiches and beer at the ball park since breakfast, men from the mines and logging camps had no choice but the boardwalk. More often than not, they chose the handouts at bars to satisfy their ravenous hunger, against sitting down in a cafe with no hard liquor for a chaser.

85

Inevitably, this led to jam-packed bars and mounting truculence. Then swinging fists and a show of guns.

A couple of hours after midnight, a man picked himself up from the boardwalk, drew a pistol and fired pointblank at the swinging doors of a bar from which he had just been ejected.

Inside, an innocent man fell dead.

7

Mary did not see Griz again until the week of "Sunday closing."

The moment Mayor Ascher heard about the shooting from Marshal Abe Long the next morning, he said at once: "There's going to be hell to pay," and he was so right.

The local newspaper screamed, "SENSELESS KILLING" in headline type two inches high, with a subhead decrying the smear on the town's successful efforts to recreate the Cracker Creek of the Old West, without any of the blood and thunder of those days.

True to the pattern which the town had set, it had fostered a revival of the Women's Christian Temperance Union and of the Salvation Army's street corner fight against "John Barleycorn," with drum and brass. Now these two organizations seized the opportunity to call for a big demonstration on the boardwalk to demand the town council enact an ordinance permanently closing all public bars or taverns from midnight Saturdays to midnight Sundays.

Parson Leckenby rallied the churches to endorse this move to keep the Sabbath holy, and Bill Saxon led the fight in the council that, within ten days, passed such an ordinance and set the first Saturday midnight in August for it to take effect.

It mattered not that the fatal shooting on July 5th did not occur on a Saturday or Sunday. It was simply the spark that set a smoldering, long-time fight on fire.

Hardest hit by Sunday closing, the mayor and marshal agreed, would be the men from the mines and lumber camps who worked five and a half days a week and now would have only Saturday nights, till midnight, and what there was left of Sunday night "to go on the town," as they put it.

Mary ran into Griz on the boardwalk in midweek before the fateful Saturday night of the first Sunday closing. He made a sour face. "Yes, I was going to sit this one out at my digs and come in Sunday, but Abe Long says he's going to hold me to the badge he pinned on me that day at the depot. He's expecting a bad time and needs help. Not from the bars and taverns. They are apparently willing to shut down promptly at midnight, but asked how they're going to get the men out at midnight if they simply refuse to move?"

Mary laughed. "That's easy. Just outfox them!"

She could see he wasn't impressed with her flip remark, so before he could say, "How?" she said, "Give me time. I might think up something, or ask Bill Saxon."

Griz made a face. "If he had kept his mouth shut, the council might have fooled around long enough so everybody would have forgotten about the shooting."

"He wants to be mayor," she suggested.

"If he ever gets the job, that's when I move out."

Nothing could have chilled her more than those last three words. If he were to leave the Creek, she would bet he'd head straight down the tracks for Baker and Cara's front doorsteps. And at a time when he never looked more attractive to Mary. Not once since the Redhead persuaded him to trim his beard in anticipation of impressing Mrs. Swenson had he failed to keep it just as neat. But she realized the real reason why he looked so brown and healthy was that he had gone into intensive training for the Labor Day rock-drilling championship.

She had read somewhere that behind every great man there was a woman who had made him think great. All he needed now, she believed, was a woman who loved him beyond everything else in the world and who would spoil him rotten, telling him how great he was and that nothing could stop him from beating Jim McLeod, the perennial champion, this coming Labor Day. She knew she could, and should be that woman.

"How's training coming?" she asked, trying to be as concerned as a wife might be.

He mopped his brow and the back of his neck, where sweat induced by the humidity stood out like droplets of condensation on a cold water pipe.

"It's tough on a day like this," he said, "swinging a sledge-hammer with everything you've got for even five minutes at a time, let alone the fifteen we have to go when it's for real.

Guess I'll stop on my way back to my digs to take a dip."

Her face lighted up. "In the creek, you mean?"

"Sure thing. Found a wonderful spot, off the road and out of sight in a grove of trees where you'd never suspect there was a swimming hole. Over my head in spots, too. The creek got dammed up apparently by a rock slide."

"How far out?"

"About two miles. Always heard there was one in those parts but never thought much about it until I needed to dunk myself after one of these sessions. Guess it is a favorite spot for necking."

She could not resist teasing him. "You wouldn't know about that, of course."

The hair framing his brow gave way as he popped his eyes at her. "You want to give it a whirl? Get your bathing suit and I'll drive us out and back."

"You forget, Mr. Grizzly," she said importantly, "that *I* am a business woman now. Mr. Cole would have a fit if he knew that I had even tarried to chat with you on my way back from the bank."

"Some other time?"

"I'd love to. I have Saturday afternoon off this week if you are interested. That's in case it is as hot as it is today."

He hesitated. "The afternoon before Sunday closing?"

She started to say forget it, to show her annoyance, but he raised a finger to hold her tongue. "I suppose I might as well show up early instead of late for that damnable night. You remember I said I have to wear the star again?"

"Yes, I remember. You might wear it in swimming."

"It's a deal. I'll pick you up at Mrs. Swenson's around two o-clock. And wearing the star!" he snickered. "Okay?"

"I might even meet you somewhere along the road. I like to walk a lot and haven't been getting much chance recently to do so, since I started at the Emporium. The Bourne road?"

He nodded.

She made sure she was well out of town before two o'clock that Saturday afternoon. She had no desire for Mrs. Swenson to see her going out of the house, bathing suit in hand, to join Griz in his ancient jalopy. So she wore it under her wraparound.

It was a lovely day for a dip. Hot, but not humid. More than anything else this summer she had missed swimming. Working her summer vacation this year had deprived her of that enjoyment.

Cracker Creek had swimming of a sort in the brackish water of a slough of the Powder River, below the point where Cracker Creek flowed into it, but it was too shallow for grownups, besides being dirty.

She broke a switch off a willow bush beside the road and used it like a whip on the long grass and golden rod growing alongside. It helped her to think out what she had let herself in for, by agreeing to join Griz in this escapade. She looked around desperately for a place to hide, in case she wanted to call it off. She could sneak back to town after Griz had driven by and tell him later she had to work unexpectedly that afternoon and had no way to let him know.

But sober thought told her she was acting like a ninny. She was a grown woman, even if there was some doubt about that. If she were afraid he might try to rape her, given the secluded setting, it would be wise to call it off. But she shook her head and smiled. Not the Griz who thought of her only as the little daughter he lost, now grown up.

Griz and his jalopy came upon Mary shortly, lustily switching to the right as if to rout every grasshopper on the seven miles between the Creek and Bourne. This was his stamping ground, the road to his diggings. It was one of the three cornucopias which fed gold-laden ore seventy years ago to the smelter at the Creek. Within a radius of two miles of Bourne there had been five great mines—the Argonaut, Golconda, Eureka-and-Excelsior, Columbia and North Pole—all deserted now except for the inevitable prospectors, like Griz, who for perhaps no other reason but that they loved the outdoors, liked to poke around on the chance they might come up lucky.

Mary burst into superlatives when Griz drew up beside her. "I never felt so great in my life!" she bubbled. "The most beautiful day! A terrific walk!" She turned her head into the soft breeze. "I can hardly wait until I dunk myself!"

Griz chuckled to himself. Two words could only describe her: "Intensity personified!" Then to Mary: "Hop in, you walked right by the turnoff. We've got to double back."

Instead of going over to the passenger's seat in the jalopy, she whacked him in the leg instead. "Move over," she giggled. "I'm taking over."

"You're what?"

"You heard me! I'm driving. Always wanted to drive one of these contraptions. If you think I'm not capable of riding as good a brake as you do, I was driving a tractor on the farm when you were still in knee pants. Git over!"

He grinned a big gap in his whiskers and slid across the seat.

She climbed into the driver's seat, put her tiny foot on the accelerator, released the brake, and backed around to head in the opposite direction. "You say when we reach the turnoff."

Griz made a pretense of hanging on to the dash with both hands. She slapped the nearest one sharply. "Just like in school," she said, "I don't let my pupils get fresh with me."

Griz let it pass, then pointed. "Behind that stand of trees."

There was nothing but a faint dirt path now to follow.

The jalopy rocked sharply going over an upthrust stone. "Gosh that was nice," she purred. "Made me think I was back on the farm again."

He pointed to a gap in the trees. She drove through it, to emerge in a little dream world where the only sound was of Cracker Creek tumbling over upstream rocks and a warm sun poured its blessing on them through a rent in the blue sky above.

Mary caught her breath. "I can't believe it!" she cried.

Loose rock had created a huge pothole, big enough for a dozen people to swim and dive into without crowding, when a rock slide had dammed the creek downstream.

Each picked his own clump of bushes to undress behind, so Mary was thrilled when Griz came out skinny. "You remembered!" she exulted, tearing off her one-piece bathing suit and shouting, "Last one in is a nincompoop," as she dived in ahead of him.

They came up, shaking the water out of their hair in a spray of diamond drops reflecting the sun, and gamboled like a couple of dolphins, climbing out frequently to sit on the carpet of pine needles skirting the pool. Once or twice Mary held her breath when their antics caused them to collide in a way that might easily have led to intimacies.

At these times she wished she was as sure of herself as she was of Griz, no matter how much she wanted to be loved by him. That night of the shivaree he had made it clear that he thought of her only as the incarnation of the baby daughter he had lost. The supposition that he slept with the Redhead did not lessen her love for him. Bert Ascher had told her that they were too much alike ever to get married.

That night in the park she would have let him make love to her, no matter what the consequences. She was ready and aching for it. But her sap was not running this day, in solitude broken only by rippling mountain water and the invigorating lift it had given to every part of her body, so why take a chance of another turndown?

They were sitting on their cushion of pine needles when Griz suggested they had better get going if she did not want to be late for her supper.

Her eyes sought his hopefully. "One last time?"

He nodded yes and hit the water before she did, shouting, "Who's the nincompoop this time?"

They thrashed around for the sheer exhilaration of it. A dragon fly landed on the surface near Griz. He took a mighty swipe at it and doused her when he missed. She took the dousing for a challenge and replied in kind.

At once they were a couple of kids again, engaged in a water fight in which no quarter was asked and none given. They tumbled over and under, flipped backward and sidewise, and did everything possible to gain an advantage from which to drown each other out with torrents of water delivered by the heel of the hand.

In the last of these maneuvers Griz came up from a dive so close behind Mary he had no choice but to catch her in his arms as she backed into him. On another woman his hands would have been clasped around the woman's waist, but on Mary they came to rest on her breasts. Unfortunately, she assumed this was deliberate. She flared with a fury neither he nor anyone else had ever heard her express before.

"Take your hands off me *there!*" she screamed, breaking his hold and twisting out of his grasp. She splashed ashore, red-faced and trembling all over and climbed out, making at once for the bush behind which she had undressed.

Utterly flabbergasted by her outburst, Griz treaded water for several minutes, obviously trying to make up his mind what to do. The more he seemed to be trying to think it out, he shook his head, eventually swimming ashore and striding up the bank until he was within earshot of her protective bush.

He called out: "Do you hear me, Mary?"

"Yes, I hear you. I want you to take me home at once!"

"Won't you tell me what this is all about?"

No answer to this or several other questions.

She was dressed before he was and in the passenger seat of his jalopy before he joined her.

Softly, very thoughtfully now, he asked: "Now will you tell me what this is all about?"

She covered her face with her hands, leaning forward on her elbows. "I'll try . . . but it is so hard to talk about it. It was so wonderful, going skinny again in swimming, not the least bit self-conscious of our anatomy. So it came to me instantly, as a ghastly shock, that you should grab me here"—she touched her breasts—"as if you had waited until the last time we were in the pool to make a pass at me. I never got so far as to wonder if you meant to make love to me on the pine cones after we got ashore and dried off. I just panicked and made a run for it."

Now she raised her head and gave him, unconsciously, the full impact of her big hazel eyes—and as usual he blinked twice—hopeful he would understand and forgive the mess she had made of everything.

Griz did not respond at once. He seemed to be searching for the right words to square things.

"You must understand," she continued, "it was not so much that you touched me here, which would only be natural in a man, but as you saw for the first time today, I have nothing there, absolutely nothing, to excite and delight a man. That is my cross and why I was so distraught. It meant that never again would you think of me as a normal woman, with all that implies, including my own babies eventually at my breast."

There were tears in her eyes now. He gathered her in his arms. "Never mind, little Mary, it is no longer important that they be breast-fed. It was my fault, too, that I was daydreaming in that pool today, thinking again of you as the personification of the daughter I lost, instead of a grown woman with all the appetites and reactions of a woman in love."

He socked himself in the jaw with his fist. "Next time use your fists on me, instead of words."

For which encouragement, she snuggled up to him, lulled by the hum of swarms of insects and refreshed by the breath of a breeze which had set the pines and firs to rustling. Before she knew it, she was fighting to keep awake. She tried to focus on a swarm of bees keeping pace with them and swooping from time to time to chase butterflies, but she got cross-eyed instead.

She never knew for certain if she had gone to sleep and dreamed up an idea for Griz to get the men out of the bars and taverns that night by midnight, when Sunday closing first took effect, but it was clear to her now how to carry out her glib remark, "Just outfox 'em," which he had treated with scant interest.

Now the problem was how to phrase the idea, so that he would not dismiss this one quickly. She decided to hold off till they reached the boardwalk. Seeing Schoolhouse Hill ahead crystallized it. She made him start with the suddenness of her attack.

"Tonight at midnight," she reminded him. "You wondered how you could get everybody out of the bars and taverns in time. The key to it must be something that makes them come running outdoors to see what all the hullabaloo is about. A fire on the boardwalk would do it. Ringing all the church bells might, but only as a part of some other stunt. I have a feeling that music is the answer. I keep thinking that this hill"—his jalopy had already started to climb it—"has to come into the act somehow."

"Why the hill?" he asked.

"I don't know," she admitted, "but I had a dream, or maybe it was only a figment of my imagination, that something was coming down this hill tonight, and everybody was on the boardwalk, waiting and watching for it to happen."

He shook his head. "That's a wild one, Mary, but I'll give it a whirl."

Thrilled that he did not dismiss it, she jumped out of the car as he drew up at the boarding house steps and turned at the top to remind him, "See you tonight."

"You'd better not!" he called after her and drove away.

At supper that night there was a good deal of discussion about the wisdom of venturing on the boardwalk that night, in view of the Sunday closing at midnight. Monte said to Mary, "I wouldn't go down there tonight, if I were you."

"Of course, I shall," she said with a typical toss of her head. "It's dance night at the Opera House."

"That's a pretty poor excuse," he chided her. "You haven't been very faithful lately."

"I know. But I have a very special reason for wanting to be there tonight." She leaned over to whisper in his ear. "Griz is going to wear the star tonight."

"Humph! More reason that I should go with you."

Firecrackers set the tempo for that night on the boardwalk. They crackled early and often.

The fire bell was another harbinger of things to come. Someone gave it a terrific workout before he was chased away.

Mountain men raced swift ponies through the side streets off the boardwalk, pretending to shoot up the town (with blanks), then hooted at people who looked at them from behind drawn window shades.

When the boardwalk itself came to life, with a milling throng blanking out the planks from the foot of Schoolhouse hill to the Opera House, Marshal Long and Griz as his deputy made a quick round of possible trouble spots. They moved in fast when glass was broken at a smoke shop, only to find that a happily inebriated miner had put his arm accidentally through a window. Sitting propped up on the sidewalk, eyes closed while his arm was being bandaged, he was trying to sing about Dixie.

"You're a long way from home, partner," Long kidded him. Then to Griz: "Let's go. When it isn't a police matter, learn not to stick around. People might get a notion you're looking for trouble and see that you get it."

Somebody started tinkering with the fire bell again.

"There's an idea, Abe," Griz said. "Why not get all the

ministers to ring their church bells at midnight?"

"That sounds like a whale of a good idea," the Marshal said.

"Will you see they get the message?"

At this moment Griz spotted Monte in the crowd, some distance away. He waved a hand, which Monte acknowledged.

"There's Griz over there," Monte told Mary, dwarfed out of Griz's sight, beside him. "Shall we join him?"

"Do you think he saw me?" she asked, crouching down, hopefully out of sight.

He shook his head.

"I don't want to see him because he told me to keep away from the boardwalk tonight. You go see him and tell him I've made it to the Opera house okay."

He turned to spot Griz again. When he had done so, Mary had disappeared. Since the Opera House was at hand, he assumed she had escaped inside.

Griz's first words were to ask if he had seen Mary

"Yes," he admitted. "Brought her down here, but she just gave me the slip, presumably to go in the Opera House for the dance."

"Find her!" Griz charged him. "And don't let her out of your sight till you get her safely home. Will you do that for me?"

Mentally they shook hands on it.

But Mary never caught up with Monte again until Sunday closing was in force and she wanted him to take her home.

A shot started everyone running toward the Opera House, Griz and Monte among them.

They were a half block away, in tough going, trying to make headway in that mob. They got within fifty feet before they were stopped, locked in tightly, to see an angry crowd had a vigilante pinned against the side of the building, unable to use his gun. More vigilantes inside the door were holding people at bay with rifles and shotguns at the ready. It was a standoff.

At that point Griz remembered the advice Long had given him. (When it isn't a police matter, learn not to stick around.)

"Situation well in hand," he called out in a loud voice for all to hear. He turned to retrace his steps up the boardwalk, speaking to several men left and right, touching his hat to the occasional woman he knew. The crowd gave way cheerfully and followed in his wake. Another situation solved without having to act like a cop. He was impressed.

An hour later, however, there was no doubt the night was coming to a climax. Smashing store windows had become commonplace, although there was no looting. The noise along the walk was deafening.

Getting the first of the big plate glass windows at Homer Prentice's bank put a stop to this sport. It shattered in giant pieces, some of which fell to the street with the horrible swish of a guillotine's knife. The nearest man escaped with only a badly gashed leg.

Meantime, Griz had cornered the marshal to ask if he could draft twenty vigilantes from the Opera House defenders.

"Twenty?" Long was visibly astounded. "I don't think they've got half that many with guns. What for?

"No guns. Just to turn the key in twenty bars and taverns."

"How are you going to accomplish that?"

"Will you trust me? If it doesn't work, you didn't know anything about it. If it does, you take the credit."

"That's fair enough. You think you can empty them to the last man on time?"

"That's the idea—if it works!"

"Well, I got no idea how to do it, so let's try yours. You say twenty men?"

"Twenty men I can count on, one in each bar or tavern, with ironclad instructions to lock every door at midnight sharp. Men who will pay no attention to what's going on outside, even if all hell breaks loose."

"Where will I hook up with you again?" Long asked.

Griz chuckled. "You won't have any trouble finding me if my idea works. Otherwise. . . ."

"You lose the star? Not as far as I'm concerned. You're coming up with these ideas, which is more than I'm doing. Get going!"

Even as Long said, "You're coming up with ideas," Griz had a pang of conscience that he could not give credit where credit was due for what was about to come off. Yet he knew Abe would have never gone along with what he planned if he knew it was Mary's brainchild.

Quite frankly he would have felt better about it if he only knew that Mary was following every move he made. Runt that she called herself, she was having no difficulty keeping him from spotting her, by using big men, of whom there was an abundance, to screen her from his roving eye.

Knowing that the time to midnight was less than an hour away, she saw Griz and Long confer, and seem to come to some agreement. The marshal then went off toward the Opera House as Griz went in the opposite direction, stopped to talk with someone in the crowd, pointed to the fire bell, left the walk and started up the Schoolhouse Hill. It was all very confusing. If she only knew what to expect!

She did not see Griz again until the witching hour, but his moves began to make sense when the fire bell started tolling at a quarter to twelve. When nobody put a stop to it and its cadence became distinctly funereal, the significance of its dirge became apparent. At first, men inside and on the walk shrugged their shoulders and said, in effect, "To heck with it!"

Five minutes later, word spread, like a forest fire, that there was a fire on the boardwalk. Who started it, and why, was never officially revealed, but men scattered frantically with the first twisting bursts of flame, fearful of being blamed for setting it, but flight quickly turned to feeding it with a hitching rail ripped from its posts. Dogs barked madly and men began parading around the bonfire as flames leaped higher, chanting the Redhead's favorite song, "There'll Be a Hot Time in the Old Town Tonight," winding up with the usual three shouted cries of "Fire! Fire! Fire!"

Now the fun began, and that is what they meant it to be, as men poured from the bars and taverns, intent on forming bucket brigades and pretending to put out the fire—with empty buckets! At the height of this hysteria, a church bell rang. Another joined in, then a third—till there were twelve in all, making the godawfulest tintinabulation ever heard in the Creek's memory.

Mary, watching and listening to every step of this ruse to empty the bars and taverns, was experiencing near hysteria herself, clapping her hands and jumping up and down like a high school cheerleader. She did not mind if Griz spotted her now. He had used her idea!

The effect of the bells on everybody, inside and outdoors, was electrifying. If they had not emptied the bars and taverns, what came next did.

A great fanfare of brass from the head of Schoolhouse Hill was followed by the ta-ta . . . ta-ta-taaaah-ta of a base drum, pounding out the tempo for a motley lot of musicians from the Opera House and the Salvation Army, flanked by youngsters carrying flaming torches who began parading downhill to the jaunty cadence of "Onward, Christian Soldiers."

Tears streamed down Mary's face when she recognized that, leading them, with a broomstick for a baton, his torso arched 'way over back, and kicking his heels high like a real drum major, was the man of her heart, the Grizzly! He had exploited every suggestion she had made, even to using the hill, as she had dreamed, as the stage and sounding board for the final impact of sound and music.

She was thrilled by the way his motley band stomped out the cadence, right up to the spot on the boardwalk where there was a charred hole in the planking. Yes, there were jeers and boos aplenty, as well as applause and chuckles, too. But the huge crowd had been so mesmerized by the bells, music and overall noise that even those close up had failed to realize that a real bucket brigade had put out the bonfire.

Griz raised his broomstick baton to halt the stomp, stomp, stomping. Promptly the church bells began dying out, the fire bell stopped tolling and the Salvation Army made a semicircle around the late bonfire hole. Only then did Griz blow his whistle for the last time.

The silence which ensued was deafening.

Raising his voice so that he could be heard by those far back up the walk, the Salvation Army lieutenant shouted: "Men, this is Sunday morning. Let us pray!"

Then came a mad dash in every direction for the nearest bar or tavern, only to find them all locked up tight and blacked out. Abe Long and his vigilantes, the Grizzly and his musical brass, had done their work well. The howl that went up drowned out the lieutenant's prayer, but Sunday closing was now the law of Cracker Creek.

In the breakup of the crowd that followed, Mary found Monte. Together they went looking for Griz and found him, where else, in front of the Nugget. He was the center of an admiring crowd, which included Abe Long, proudly slapping him on the back, and a grinning pack of vigilantes, justifiably excited because they had carried out their part of the ruse so slickly.

When Griz caught sight of Mary, she gave him a tiny wave of her hand, held close to her face in case he might be embarrassed if anyone happened to see it.

He came over at once, a big grin on his face, and lifted her off her feet. "Did you see how it worked, Mary? Everything you suggested!"

"Sh-h-h!" she cautioned him. "Not so loud. They might hear you and spoil it all."

"But I want to tell them . . ."

"And you know you must not. Don't spoil a perfect ending."

A confused Monte broke in. "Do you mind telling me what all this is about?"

She broke out of Griz's arms. "I'll tell you on the way home."

"Yes," Griz spoke up. "Don't let her give you the slip again, Monte. I want to make sure she gets home in one piece. There's a lot of men around here now who may be just looking for trouble to satisfy their anger. Now shove off, I don't want anyone to think you're associated with me and decide to mug you two to get back at me."

"What about you?" Monte asked.

"I'm going in the back door here at the Nugget as soon as Abe and the vigilantes scatter. That's one way to play it safe on my part."

She did not need to be told that he would spend it with the Redhead.

When Griz slipped in the Nugget's back door, he found Tim, the bartender, holding a lamp on a strange tableau. The Redhead was standing over a man who knelt, head bowed low, at her feet.

Griz stopped short when he recognized the Reverend Jeremiah Leckenby. "What the—?" he exploded.

Red chuckled. "The parson, no less. We found him in the corner after the lights were turned off. He says he's my guardian angel. He's praying for me, Griz. That's more than you ever did."

Leckenby looked up at her without rising. "Praying for you

and all other sinners on the boardwalk tonight," he said. "Hoping that by your act of ending the desecration of the Sabbath, you will set your feet hereafter on the path of righteousness."

"Now that's a pretty speech, Lecky."

"Leckenby, Ma'am. And it's a prayer, not a speech. I've been praying for you every night for a long time."

Red asked, "Are you getting sweet on me, Parson?"

Suddenly he was tongue-tied. "I . . . I . . ."

She bent over to help him to his feet. "Why don't you go now. You got your wish in closing us down."

Leckenby reached out to touch the hem of her dress. "I think of you as Mary Magdalen. I must save you, Mary, if it is the last thing I do." His voice trailed off. "I must . . ."

Tim the bartender pulled a dollar bill from his pocket. "This is for your collection plate today. You don't want to be found here, Parson."

Griz put a five-dollar bill in Leckenby's hand. The parson looked at each of them in turn and dipped his head, allowing them to let him out the back door.

Red grinned at Griz. "So you're pretty cocky after the show you put on tonight. But all pooped out now, of course."

"No, raring to go more than ever."

"That's what I thought." The way she took his arm and steered him toward the stairs said, better than words, that she sensed what he needed most of all now.

8

Mary first heard from Mary Too that Griz was taking the first steps toward a drastic change in his lifestyle. The Redhead came into the Emporium to shop on his behalf. "He has taken a house in town!" she exclaimed. "Imagine that!"

"I don't believe it!" Mary gasped, stunned to a whisper.

"It all happened so fast. . . ."

Mary never heard the rest of the sentence, she was so intent on wondering why. Her best guess was that he had asked Red to marry him. Her heart did a violent flip-flop at the very thought.

But she managed to gush her reaction, with appropriate fluttering of her eyes. "I hope you and Griz are going to be very happy."

Red snorted before Mary could be more expansive. "Heaven forbid! All I'm doing is helping him fix it up. I've got to get bedding, dishes and pots and pans."

"No furniture?"

Red shook her head. "I guess he's got enough of the essentials at his digs."

"Then he's not getting married—at least not right away." Mary had been holding her breath. Now she let it all out visibly.

Red patted her arm lightly. "Don't worry, sweet, He has never given me the slightest hint that he would take that step some day. I tell him he ought to get himself a wife to do what I'm doing for him today, and he laughs at me."

They agreed, to save time, Red would call off a list of what Griz needed for the house and Mary would pick the items out and box them for Griz to pick up later.

Mary ventured to suggest that Red hadn't told her why Griz was moving into town.

"So I haven't," Red laughed. "Shows how my mind works. I get so annoyed with him sometimes. When he wants something done, he expects me to do it without being asked."

'*Why* is he moving into town?" Mary repeated firmly.

"Oh, yes!" said Red, putting her mind to it. "He says he's going to take a job with the dredge."

"What's a dredge?" The word meant nothing to Mary.

"It's something that will float on the Powder, Griz says, and has a snout ahead of it that will burrow into the riverbed like an earthworm, sucking and scooping up soil, sand and gravel that's been washed down from the mountains millions of years ago."

Still confused, Mary asked, "What for?"

Red said she asked the same question. "To wash out the gold and other minerals in that *fluvial* residue, he calls it. He says it's just like panning for gold with a steam shovel and that it would take a thousand miners, panning by hand, to do what a dredge can do in a day. It's a Utah outfit that wants him to be a mining engineer for the whole shebang."

"How wonderful for him," Mary exclaimed, "finally to be offered something for which he is best qualified. Is he going to take the job?"

"Seems like it. Otherwise why would he want me to buy all this junk for him? He's been down to Baker twice already to talk to the dredge people. In fact he's there today. To sign up, I guess. These men! Takes them forever to make up their minds. Now me. . . ."

The Redhead kept on talking, but Mary's love for Griz had been given another jolt. She was sunk, thinking the worst—that the real reason Griz was spending so much time in Baker was Cara Ames. Why was he so anxious to set himself up in a home before she did say yes? Unless, she thought, he was using the house as bait in making a play for Cara's hand!

"I'll get this order put up right away," Mary said.

"No hurry," Red told her. "Griz says he'll go straight back to his digs when he gets back tomorrow and won't be using the house until after Labor Day. He says he and his partner need every aching moment—that's right, he emphasized *every aching moment*—to perfect their rhythm in changing drills without a hitch if they ever expect to win the rock drilling title."

It was with a heart still heavy with thoughts of where Cara

figured in Griz's moving into town and taking a dredge job that Mary sat down to supper that night. When she could no longer hold back her news, she broke it obliquely to her tablemates. "Is there anything to the rumor," she asked quietly, "that a dredge is going to root up the Powder River?" She could not have expressed it more sensationally. Bill Saxon choked violently on a mouthful of mashed potato and glowered at her after he had swallowed half a glass of water.

"Who says?" snapped Monte, manager at the smelter, boring into her with angry eyes.

She was a bit floored by their responses. She had meant only to elicit more information than the Rehead had given her. Apparently there were overtones to this news of which Red was unaware.

"Give, Mary!" Monte persisted. "I want to know *who* said *what*. It's very important, if true."

"I want to know, too!" Bill Saxon challenged her.

Monte turned to Saxon in surprise. "What's it to you?"

Saxon ignored him.

Now Mary was thoroughly frightened. She did not want to name the Redhead. She tried another tack. Wide-eyed, as if she could not understand why they were getting so worked up about it, she said simply, "Griz has taken a house in town."

A perfectly innocuous response, she thought, but she had not reckoned with Monte, who hit the table with his fist. "I knew it!" he cried, as the silverware ceased jangling.

"Mr. Willcox!" Mrs. Swenson admonished him from the head of the table. "May I remind you that I require strict decorum at meals."

"Begging your pardon, Mrs. Swenson," he responded, "but may I explain that Miss Meakin has just let the cat out of the bag about something that is going to shake this town to its roots." He rose to his feet. "May I have your permission, Mrs. Swenson, to leave the table to make a telephone call? I must do so immediately."

"Granted," she replied.

A hush fell over the table. Mary guessed that everyone, like herself, would be straining ears now to learn whom Monte felt obliged to call in such a hurry. Since the only telephone in the house was in the hall just outside the dining room, conversations on it were not very private. They heard Monte ring Central on the wall telephone replica of an early twentieth century wall phone, by several vigorous turns of its crank, and say, "Howard Nichols's home, please, Effie."

Whatever Monte said thereafter when he made a connection was lost to the ears of those at the table when Saxon blasted Mary suddenly, "Why didn't you keep your mouth shut? Quigley asked me to keep it a secret until after Labor Day."

She shook her head, helpless. "I don't know what I said that was so awful." Tears welled in her eyes.

"And I'll be damned," Saxon swore, getting to his feet, "if I know who tipped you off, unless it was the red-headed. . . ."

Mrs. Swenson stopped him cold with a stentorian command: "*MIS-TER* Saxon! I'll thank you to remember that I permit no profanity or vulgarities here! One more outburst out of you *and* Mr. Willcox and I shall ask you both to remove your belongings from this house."

Saxon sat down abruptly, apologizing in his best courtroom manner.

When Monte returned to the table, he wanted to know why Saxon was so interested in Griz's job with the dredge.

"Because I recommended him for it," Saxon said with a fiendish grin.

"That figures, because you hate his guts."

"Why would he do it out of spite?" Mary broke in, anxious to avoid another flareup that might anger Mrs. Swenson.

"Because," said Monte, "if he takes the job, he can become the most hated man in Cracker Creek." He turned to the others. "You all know to whom I talked on the phone?" Several nodded yes. "I thought so. All right, that was Howard Nichols. He owns the smelter. My boss, of course. He was offered the dredge job six months ago. Turned it down flat, too. Because that dredge will wipe out that beautiful, lush green meadowland approach to Cracker Creek and leave nothing in its wake but mounds of gravel, caked with dried mud. A gruesome monument to greed."

"Oh, no!" Mary protested in a whisper.

"That's what one man will do if he helps the dredge come in here," Monte continued. "What was your reason, Bill, for recommending Griz?"

"You mean Quigley, of course," said Saxon with his usual ingratiating grin. "I thought he did a terrific job the night of Sunday closing, getting all those men out on the boardwalk with that crazy stunt of his. Any man who can come up with new ideas like that on the spur of the moment deserves a chance to take a challenging job like the dredge."

"Poppycock! You know what they want is a good metals man. Someone on whom they can count to make sure they don't lose a flake of gold in the final residue of their operation. For my money, I think *you* are counting on Griz to fall flat on his face, because he hasn't been working as a mining engineer for seven years."

Saxon turned angry red and asked to be excused from the table. And Mary was suddenly sick to her stomach, realizing that the ideas she had fed Griz to help him carry out his end of Sunday closing had apparently motivated Saxon to recommend him for the dredge job. She, too, asked to be excused to go to her room to lie down. When she regained her composure, she joined the others for coffee in the parlor.

Monte signaled to her to sit beside him. "I want to apologize to you," he said, "for seeming to give you such a bad time, but when you said Griz was moving into town, I knew why. I had to tell my boss immediately because that meant we had lost our fight to keep the dredge out."

"Should we try to stop him?" she asked anxiously.

"Are you game to go out to his diggings to do that? I haven't seen him since that night."

"Neither have I and Red said he was coming back tomorrow from Baker and going straight out there at once."

He looked at her sharply. "That's a sure sign he's ducking us and I think you know why."

She avoided his eyes, saying hopelessly, "Oh, Monte, you are the only one I can say this to, but I'm a hard loser. I think he's getting ready to bring a wife into that house and I think I knew whom to fight."

"Who do you think?"

Her lips silently formed the word "Cara."

He shook his head. "I don't think so. I could be wrong but I think Cara is too much like his Alice was. He told me once he made a mistake in idolizing her too much and I sense he's now doing the same with Cara. When he gets wise to himself, he will back off fast. Besides, she's *my* girl, if we ever get around to doing something about it."

She put a hand over his. "She told me on our visit to her the Fourth of July that she would never spend the rest of her life in Cracker Creek."

"I've gotten the same message from her several times. But never is a long time," Monte reflected. "The dredge will have sucked up all it is going to get out of that meadowland in four or five years. So get in there and fight for him," he urged, squeezing her arm.

"I'll try," she promised, but with none of her usual spunk.

"But look out for the dark horse," he warned.

She frowned, obviously puzzled.

"Your friend, the Redhead."

"But she protested she wanted no part of marriage when I offered my congratulations."

"Remember your Shakespeare, Mary. Especially that passage in the play *Hamlet*, where his mother, the Queen, says, 'The lady doth protest too much, methinks.' If I were you, I'd wonder *why* Red is taking so much interest in outfitting Griz's house for *another* woman!"

Mary sagged again, this time for good. She laid her cheek against his arm and held tightly to his sleeve. She was shaking her head from side to side. "Just when I was ready to accept your guess that Cara was not the target, you remind me that the one who has the least to gain by marrying him may be the one who has always had the inside track."

The Tuttle cottage, which Red had said Griz had chosen for his abode, now became the focus of all that threatened to cut him forever out of her life. She must know at once whether it had the makings of a home for a man who, for three years, had had nothing but the shabbiest of shacks in the mountains as a place he might call home.

On Saturday morning, enroute to work, she went out of her way to size up the cottage. She knew the house, but it had left little impression on her in the past. This time the first quick look gave her a sinking feeling. It was neat and tidy, surrounded by a carefully clipped hedge. The right woman could make it impress a man every time he came home from work.

She peered in a front window. "What a doll of a house!" she thought. If she were arranging the furniture in the tiny parlor, she would put a love seat in one corner, either braided rugs on the bare floor or a flowered carpet. She could make out a boxlike stairway, presumably to a second story bedroom..

Coming around the back, she looked in the kitchen window. An electric range and breakfast table were basics. In her mind's eye she could see frilly curtains in the windows and pots of geraniums on the sills.

Mignonette and bachelor buttons still flowered in a tiny garden. Dorothy Perkins roses trailed over a trellis on one side of the cottage. If only she had a home like this, how she would love and cherish it!

Later that day, when business slacked off, she began work on Red's order for the cottage, having a devil of a time putting her heart into it. To buy for Griz would have been a delight, but for another woman—ugh!

The first item was bedding. Could she honestly be objective if the cottage were to put the Redhead permanently in his bed? Now if this were to be his and her bed, she knew exactly what color blankets to choose, provided Griz would let her do the wallpaper over to match. And she would have no "boughten" quilts, but make her own, in patchwork, brilliant in every color and pattern imaginable.

So much for dreaming! She tapped her pencil on her front teeth and began to select sheets to match the color scheme a man would approve for quilts and blankets. By dint of forcing herself to concentrate and to leave emotion out of her thinking, she was doing quite well when Mayor Ascher suddenly startled her. She had not heard him coming up the aisle.

"What are you up to?" he wanted to know, indicating the spread of the articles in both directions on the counter. Told that she was putting up an order for the Grizzly's new house, he laid his packages down and offered her his hand. "Am I to congratulate the bride-to-be?" he beamed.

The look that swept over her face made him realize what a mistake he had made.

Thoughtfully, she covered for him. "The Redhead asked me

to do this. You know, of course, he's going to take a job with the dredge?"

"First I've heard of it."

"Oh, Mr. Mayor, should he? Monte says it will make him one of the most hated men in town. We can't let that happen to Griz, can we?"

He shrugged. "A man must work at what he knows best. God knows he has waited long enough for something he can put his heart into."

"I wonder whether he has simply given up, convinced that nothing better will come along, or whether he has other fish to fry."

Bert Ascher's eyes narrowed with understanding, but he laughed, "Having a ready-made home hasn't made me any more attractive to uncommitted females hereabouts!"

She laid an affectionate hand on his arm. "You're a dear. Even I might surprise you some day."

Momentarily he lifted his eyebrows at that last remark. "Now if you are looking for ideas on how to fix up a house for a 'bach,' you should come see my setup. Since Emma died three years ago, I've become pretty good at housekeeping."

"But it was a woman's home first," she objected.

"Even so, I've made changes to fit my needs and habits. Come see me sometime. Better still, come to supper tonight and we can compare what you are laying out for Griz with my layout."

She begged off. "People would talk, my coming into your house at night. Enough people think me a flibbertigibbet as it is without calling me a tramp, too."

The Mayor chuckled quietly. "Then let's make it tomorrow morning instead. We can go to church afterward."

"Perfect!" she agreed. "I'll be there."

She caught her breath when she walked into his kitchen next morning. Sunlight streaming through yellow ruffled curtains, a canary poking its head about and eyeing her with suspicion, the kitchen range purring away with contentment, and an oilcloth-covered table against the opposite wall, set with salt and pepper shakers, silverware in a holder and his napkin in a ring—everything said this was the room in which he lived except for sleeping.

Clapping her hands with delight, she cried out: "I simply

can't believe it! At home on my family's farm, our kitchen is the family room, just like this. You make me homesick, Mr. Mayor."

"Bert," he corrected her.

"Bert," she repeated after him, clasping both his hands. "It's going to be hard to call you anything but Mr. Mayor because I've always looked up to you as someone pretty important."

"Right now," he smiled, "the only matter of importance is to cook you a rib-sticking breakfast." He pulled a checkered apron off a peg and started to tie it around his generous middle.

She yanked it out of his hands and tied it around her tiny waist instead. "Pardon me, Bert, but this is where I come in. I don't know when I last had a chance to cook breakfast for a man."

She took his arm and sat him down at the table. "Now you sit there and drink a cup of coffee while I give you a lesson in cooking flapjacks. Mama used to say I was the best little flapjacker in seven counties."

She walked over to the range. "Mmmmm. Mmmmmm! I never saw such service! You've got everything ready."

Deftly testing the big iron griddle and giving the batter an extra twirl, she poured out the first pair, each at least six inches across, on the sizzling surface.

Reaching for the skillet next, she asked, "How will you have your eggs? Sunny side up or over and easy?"

"To tell the truth," he admitted, "I never break an egg without getting some of the shell into it, so I have given up doing anything but boiling them."

"Then it shall be scrambled today so you can have a special treat."

"Marvelous!" he exclaimed.

She was spooning them on his plate before he half realized she had broken the eggs.

"Somewhere along the line I lost track of when you began scrambling them," he complained.

"I use both hands," she laughed. "That's my secret."

When she sat down to eat with him—the tea kettle purring, the sun pouring its blessing through yellow ruffled curtains, the canary eyeing her with less suspicion, and another round of flapjacks rising half an inch thick on the black griddle— everything combining to create a homeyness that had been missing from her life in the boarding house, she wanted to cry for the pure joy of it all.

She thought to herself: "He is a good man, but a lonely soul— like me." She studied the look of infinite enjoyment on his face. He was savoring the aftertaste of a breakfast he had not had to cook for himself. "There ought to be a middle ground for folks like us," she said to herself, "where we can get together without having to risk social disapproval."

She was startled out of her reverie by a loud squawk above and behind her. "That's the canary, Mr. Pavarotti. He was Emma's pride and joy. As she grew sicker, he became almost her whole life," Bert said. "She would have me place his cage beside her bed so she could talk to him and sing with him. It was hard playing second fiddle to a canary as she slowly faded away, but at least it helped her die happy."

"How did it happen she called him Pavarotti? He's only come into great demand in the last few years."

"She didn't. She called him Tweeter. I never could. When she died, he stopped singing. At first I thought of getting rid of him, but I wondered what Emma would have said if I did. Now he's glad to have me feed him and clean his cage, but he never shows any interest in me, except to salute me occasionally with that awful squawk."

"But why 'Pavarotti' now?"

"Just for the heck of it, if nothing else. Unless it was to shame him into imitating Pavarotti by playing some of his records."

Mary crossed to the cage and poked an exploratory finger through the spokes and whistled softly. Mr. Pavarotti cocked his head on one side, and then on the other. "Hello, Mister Pavarotti . . . tweet, tweet, tweet," she crooned, still coaxing him with a playful finger. He stalked sidewise on his perch, turning his head again and again to look at her before he threw back his head and began to trill!

"Well now, isn't that something!" Bert crowed. "Right you are, Mr. Pavarotti. It's great to have a woman around the house again, isn't it?"

"I suspect," Mary surmised, "that when I unconsciously said

'tweet, tweet, tweet' to him it reminded him of what your Emma may have called him, using the short form of Tweeter."

Nothing else they said or did that morning really mattered. Mary trilled, too, deep inside her, because she and the canary had brought happiness to a man who needed it more than Griz did.

Mary and Bert did not have another breakfast together until they hosted Cara and Monte in Bert's home.

"Our guests are here," Mary called to Bert when she met them at the door. "*Our* guests?" She laughed on realizing what she had said. "Doesn't that sound funny?"

"Perfectly nauseating," jeered Monte.

Cara objected. "It sounds sort of nice to me. Just like they were a comfortably married couple."

Mary liked the way Cara had put it. It was an exciting feeling to be entertaining socially, even if it was not her home and Bert was not her husband. She had proposed they include Monte and Cara when Bert suggested they get together again for breakfast. She was being admittedly selfish when she said, "Let's make it a foursome."

She had checked first with Amelia Prentice to make sure Cara was going to stay over for Labor Day, now that she had resumed music lessons at the Creek.

"Oh, yes!" said Amelia, obviously pleased for having found a new excuse to throw Monte and Cara together. "Monte has accepted our invitation to join us in Homer's bank window to see the rock drilling and to take Cara to supper at the club."

This was all the assurance Mary needed. She was eager to join forces with Amelia to get these two matched, provided her hand in doing so went undetected.

In all her thinking, however, Mary had neglected to think out what was going to happen the rest of the day. This came out when Monte and Cara were taking their leave after breakfast.

"See you at the bank," Monte called back as they left.

"We'll stay here and clean up," she said. "Then maybe. . . ." She hesitated, suddenly aware that she was about to say, "We'll look for you at the barbecue lunch." She realized Bert had said nothing about their coupling up the rest of the day.

Bert was overcome with embarrassment. He was pathetically abject in his apologies. "Mary, I never thought for one moment but that Griz was taking you at least to the barbecue and the Argonaut tonight."

"I haven't seen him or even heard from him in a month," she admitted.

The look on her face was so woebegone, Bert put an arm around her and gave her a little squeeze. "For what you did in putting this breakfast together today, the mayor wants to reward you with a special accolade. You shall be the Mayor's Lady for the day. It is only appropriate that the mayor's hostess should be at his side for all of today's activities!"

The affectionate look in Mary's eyes at that moment should have chased away the humility he had expressed in his apologies. He confirmed her appointment as his hostess with the seal of his lips.

They never caught up with Monte and Cara until they were shown to vantage seats behind one of the three great plate-glass windows in Homer Prentice's bank which commanded an unobstructed view of the rock drilling, less than twenty feet away. Cara and Monte already were in front row seats with the Prentices.

From her seat beside the mayor, Mary was entranced for two reasons. First, the excitement of being introduced by him as his social hostess to all who came up to shake his hand. Second, she had never dreamed she would be able to see Griz make his bid for the championship, let alone from a comfortable seat. Only a select few chosen friends of the promoters had seats on the platform built around the drilling rock, with their backs to the bank's brick wall. The Redhead, Mary noted, was one of these chosen few.

All other spectators had to stand in the street around the three open sides of the platform. Very few women opted to do that. Even for men, wearing for the most part heavy leather boots, three hours standing in the hot sun when there was refreshment galore on the boardwalk nearby, caused a steady ebb and flow among the standees, except for those who could rest their elbows, shoulder high, on the three open sides of the platform.

The drilling stone was a huge block of granite with only its drilling face exposed, in the center of the platform. The rock was five feet high because the winning drill would be close to forty inches. This meant the crowd on foot could see the drilling at eye level, close enough to touch the contestants or their drills if they dared.

Oldtimers in these mountains knew there was more to drilling than just hitting a steel bit with a sledge hammer. The bit had to chisel out a round hole to fit the drill's shaft and had to be turned repeatedly to keep it from becoming stuck. The secret of winning, however, lay in changing drills without a hitch as the hole got deeper and deeper. Griz had been holed up at his digs with his partner, perfecting their rhythm and timing in doing this.

Jim McLeod, defending champion and odds-on favorite, had been unbeaten for years. He had a new partner nearly every year. He demanded tremendous strength in the arms and back. He dumped them as fast as they got to thinking they were as good as he was.

The luck of the draw this year forced McLeod to be among those who drilled early. Determined to set a mark that would stand up, he and his partner poured it on. One couldn't help admiring the way they operated. McLeod was a perfectionist. He never let his partner swing the sledge when they were changing drills.

Bert told Mary this was one of the secrets of McLeod's success—that he was afraid the younger man might flinch momentarily, fearing he might smash the champion's hands. With the sledge in his own hands, McLeod never hesitated.

"You've got to admire him," Bert told her. "His attitude is that his partner better have the new drill well seated in the bore or get his hands smashed." Bert looked at his watch and the size of the new drill, before commenting. "At this rate nobody is going to catch him."

It was spectacular performance. On a predetermined count, the partner yanked the bit on which they had been working out of the bore, swept it back over his shoulder into the standee crowd, as they scurried out of danger, and rammed the next drill home. All the time neither man ever broke rhythm.

McLeod had reached the thirty-six inch drill when those

inside the bank, looking on, caught the sound of frenzied cries among the crowd noises. One look at the remaining drills, spread on the platform floor, told the story. The next drill had been knocked or kicked out of place. In fact it was so far askew that it seemed likely the partner's hand, groping behind him, would never find it.

McLeod backers, waving their arms and shouting wildly, were trying to warn him. One man dared to dart a hand toward the errant drill. The referee wheeled in time to see the helping hand and stomp on it. The man let out a howl that McLeod heard, and for the first time in competition, McLeod flinched. His partner came through with a new drill in time, but not the right one. This was too long and heavier. The partner made only a glancing contact with the bore. McLeod's stroke sent it spinning off the platform, twanging like a gong and scattering those in its line of flight. Luckily nobody was hit by it, but two strokes of the sledge were missed before the correct bit could be rammed into place. How serious this was became clear when their official measurement was announced.

Bert Ascher grinned. "Now McLeod can be beaten."

Mary reacted by tightening both hands and getting excited. "Do you suppose Griz has a chance to win now?"

"As much as any of the others who have not yet competed."

She was tense when Griz mounted the platform. She had to resist shouting encouragement to him, which in any case would have been disgraceful conduct for the mayor's official hostess, as well as useless, since it couldn't be heard through those big plate-glass windows.

Nobody yet had beaten McLeod's mark. But Pescovic, Griz's new, young partner, seemed to thrive on competition, whereas Bert said he had heard he was not particularly impressive in their hideaway training. When this big, blond youngster rammed the ultimate drill into the bore with one minute to go, they had a chance to overtake McLeod.

All that lay ahead was smashing that steel drill, forty-five inches long, into that sixty-inch granite rock as far as sheer brute strength could do it, with an assist from the man who manipulated the bit. This was the payoff!

Halfway through that final minute, Griz dropped to his knees and took over the delicate job of twisting the drill, nine inches longer than a yardstick and weighing at least one hundred pounds. At least his aching back said that's what it felt like when he lifted and turned it after every shattering blow by Pescovic with the sledge hammer.

He was conscious now for the first time that people were cheering him and Pesky. He could hear the Redhead singing that old favorite, "There'll Be a Hot Time in the Old Town Tonight" from her ringside seat not ten feet away, encouraging the crowd to sing with her to spur them on to victory. And he sensed that those ensconsed in the plush seats behind the bank's plate-glass windows were standing and waving them on, though he had eyes only for the silvery bit and the bore from which it worked up and down, intent on keeping it loose as the drive shaft on Old Pluto.

"Smash it, man!" he yelled to Pesky in their final seconds. "Smash it! . . . And again! . . . And again!" He was literally counting the cadence of the strokes and the crowd was counting them with him. Though his hands stung with the vengeance of the youngster's powerful smashes, he was completely oblivious to the passage of time and the stream of water which was siphoned by a tube from a barrel and sloshed over his sweating head and shoulders to keep him cool.

Then three men in derby hats and long yellow dusters, watches in hand, yelled, "Time!" and he sagged in place, out of breath, aching in every part of his body, vowing that, whatever the result, he would never submit himself to this torture again, yet wishing that someone would give him a hand to help him to his feet, only to wave it away when a helping hand was offered.

The official measurement said they had beaten McLeod by one-quarter of an inch. "Fair enough," Griz said, "but never again. McLeod can have it back next year."

The Redhead had her arm around him as he left the platform, to be pushed, back-slapped and bear-hugged by those who had bet on him—"and the few who really cared," said Red.

"And that's you," he told her, giving a big hug.

"And Mary especially," she added.

He stopped a minute to weigh that thought. "That's fair enough," he agreed.

But when Mary skipped down the bank's front steps to intercept him, she found him beset by a moving swarm of wellwishers who gave way reluctantly to let her get close enough to tell him, "You were wonderful, Griz. I'm so happy for you and that young man. . . ."

At which point she was elbowed out of the way by another one of the mountain men eager to get his arms around Griz and tell him, "You're the greatest!"

The Redhead, who had not yet let go of Griz's arm, pushed the drunk back into the swarm with her free hand and yanked Mary back beside him. In fact, Red threw that free arm then around Mary, thus effectively isolating Griz for the moment and kissing Mary in her exuberance.

Red told Griz, "Mary is fixing up the order for all the things you asked me to get for the cottage."

"How do you like it?" he asked Mary eagerly.

"Love it! It's a doll. When are you going to move in?"

"Pretty quick," he guessed.

Red remembered to tell him Mary had been the mayor's official social hostess all that day.

"Will I see you at the Argonaut then tonight?" Mary asked.

Griz shuffled his feet, mumbled a quick, "'Fraid not," drew attention to the fact that he was still naked from the waist up. "Guess what I need most of all this minute is to fall into a tub full of water and just soak for an hour."

Those last few words were said with raised eyebrows as he looked at the Redhead. To her credit she did not blush, but Mary got the message. Red's tub and/or bed were still first base.

9

Two weeks later the invasion of the Powder River by Utah Mining and Dredge began. A corps of men and heavy equipment set to work putting together what everyone eventually would call the Monster.

At first, it was exciting to walk down the banks of the Powder to see this contraption taking place. Mary and Bert were among the first to do this. Back teaching once more, she had little time for the mayor until weekends, when they had taken to breakfasting together on Sundays and doing something special the rest of the day.

That first Sunday they walked downriver from the park and came upon a huge barge floating on a stagnant slough. "Doesn't look like anything much," she observed, but a week later the framework of a three-story building had been built on the barge. This time she likened it to the grain elevators which abounded in Eastern Oregon.

On their third visit to the slough, Mary's floating grain elevator had sprouted the long nose of a Halloween witch, pointed at the North Star, from which hung two wicked-looking fangs encircling a boom on which rode a chain of caterpillar scoops.

"All the better to gobble us up with," fantasized Mary, the bitter truth of which she did not suspect at that moment. Too late to do anything about it, Cracker Creek was to learn that those scoops, endlessly for four years, were to root the guts out of the Powder's inviting threshold to the town, terminus of the first rail link to these gold-bearing mountains in the 1880s.

Once afloat, the dredge could move in any direction by simply devouring the gravel and soil around it, and spitting it out behind. It created its own floating pond as it meandered at will, changing the course of the Powder with every move. In its wake it left livid welts of glacial rubble, everlasting scars when the rains came, revealing the bleached and indigestible gravel of the Monster's craw.

Mary and Bert haunted the scene into October, drawn irresistibly, Mary admitted to herself, by her desire to see Griz at work. They finally caught him on a Saturday. He responded impeccably, giving them a tour of the dredge and explaining all the details of the operation.

But he was cooly impersonal.

"You might have thought he had never known us," Mary complained when they stopped at Bert's house.

"You noticed that, too?"

"All business!" Mary sighed.

"The warmth we always loved in him is gone."

She agreed and they lapsed into an awkward silence until Bert dared to ask: "How do you feel about him now?"

She gave him a quick, half-frightened look. "I don't want to face up to the obvious answer."

"Don't ever tell me what happened," he assured her, "but I wish I could do something to ease what I sometimes read in your eyes."

She lowered them, trying to smile. "It will pass."

"Perhaps it might help if you were to stay for supper. We could talk about everything else but . . . "

She eyed him thoughtfully.

"That's if you will let me do the cooking instead. It's my turn to surprise you."

On which note she cheered up visibly. "You'd like that, wouldn't you?"

"Very much." The soft way he said it was very pleasant.

"Go ahead. And afterward I'll wash and you wipe."

Long after the last dish had been wiped they found themselves still sitting in the kitchen, listening to Mr. Pavarotti, who seemed to sense the mood of the moment and what he could do about it.

Mary smiled when Bert gave a sigh of complete satisfaction. "That is certainly the sound of a contented man," she quipped.

"I know of no better compliment a man can give a woman."

The thought set her to thinking. This is how it should be between a man and a woman. No need to talk except when there is something to say. All that really counts is that they are happiest when they are together, no matter what they are doing, even if it is falling asleep in their chairs.

"You are smiling to youself," Bert noted with amusement.

"Yes," she admitted after a pause. "I was just thinking how cozy this is, sitting here with you, not trying to keep up a conversation, just indulging in what I can only call a feeling of being completely at peace with the world."

"Cara Ames had the words for it," he reminded her, "Labor Day morning when she and Monte came to breakfast: 'Just like an old married couple,' she said."

"I guess you're right," she admitted without looking up.

"If you like it this way," he persisted, "it need not end tonight—or ever, for that matter."

Now she sat up straight and turned her face toward him. "Are you serious?"

"Quite serious." He thought it best not to complicate his simple proposal with more words. What she needed most was some maneuvering room in which to weigh all the pros and cons.

She took a long time to think out her first answer. She was amused, of course, by the clever way in which he had proposed. He didn't ask for a yes or no. This was the essence of what he was saying: If she enjoyed the comfortable company they had kept recently, she could make it permanent by moving in with him—legally, of course.

Oddly enough, this moment had come with somewhat of a shock, even if she had thought about the possibility, but only in an amused sort of way, such as: "Wouldn't it be funny if he asked me to marry him?" She hadn't thought what her answer might be if he did. Now, she suspected, she had been afraid to think that far ahead. She was superstitious about coming up with another rude awakening, as she did that night with Griz in the park.

Now that he had spoken, she could admit to herself how wonderful it would be "to live like this always." The prospect fascinated yet frightened her. No more working for a living, a completely new daily routine, and a man more or less under foot day and night.

She had wanted this sort of life with Griz—yes, ached for it for a long time. Yet she wondered now whether he would ever again be equal to it. Despite the impression he gave everyone, he had been frustrated in his marriage. She doubted he would marry again, unless it was for love, with the Redhead available to provide the fruits of marriage without his having to assume any of its responsibilities. She was certain there was no love now in his heart for her.

"I don't know what to say," she finally told Bert.

He waited, content to let her think out loud.

She said, "I'm not going to say any of the usual words that women use—that I'm honored, you leave me speechless, or I'm not good enough for you —and then say no. On the contrary, I am quite touched, Bert, especially in the way you phrased it and built up to the mood of this evening over several weeks. Was that deliberate?"

He smiled affectionately. "In a way, yes."

"You are a very sly old dear, Bert. I congratulate you."

"Thank you, Mary."

"Which does not obscure the fact that you do not love me, does it, Bert?"

He hesitated.

"And the same goes for me," she added. "Let's be honest about it."

"I'm not going to pretend that, in time, we may come to love each other."

"We just don't know, do we?"

"That's right. We don't."

Mary rose, holding out her hand. He took it between both of his and held it tightly. It was a warm and heartening expression of something more than good friendship.

"I want to think about it for a few days," she said, smiling affectionately at him for the first time. On this note they parted, although she knew exactly what she would say eventually. It just didn't seem respectable to say it so soon after he asked her.

A few days later she caught up with Griz on the boardwalk. How to tell him her news? If she were to start with small talk she had two choices —to ask about his job or the cottage. She chose the cottage. This proved to be the direct route.

She made the opening gambit. "By the way, I never did hear how the cottage turned out."

"Fair enough. At least it suits *me*."

"And you don't mind 'baching' it?"

"No more than I did at my digs."

"I thought you were fixing it up for a wife."

"Not me!" he snapped. "I've got no time for a wife. This job is a back-breaker. At home I work halfway through the night, figuring . . . figuring . . . figuring. I could stay at the office and do it faster, but I've just got to get away from that infernal noise a few hours every day."

He said much more, but all she heard were the words, "I've got no time for a wife." Apparently he had become so absorbed in working at his profession once more that he had forgotten how to be the happy-go-lucky man she had always known.

Now, she sensed, was the moment to tell him her news. "There's an opening coming up again at Mrs. Swenson's," she said. "I don't suppose that would interest you now?"

"Nope." Said with marked finality. "Who's moving out?"

"I am."

For the first time he turned to look squarely at her. On his face was an expression of complete disbelief. "You're kidding!"

"No. I'm getting married to Bert Ascher. I haven't told him yet," she grinned, "but I shall tonight. I wanted you to be the first to know."

She got no response. They started to climb Schoolhouse Hill in silence. Now that she had said it, she had a sinking feeling, especially since he made no comment. Telling it first to him made it all seem so final. Deep down, of course, there was still that gnawing at her heart for him. She prayed that this feeling would go away before she married Bert.

Griz finally cleared his throat. "Our little girl is flying high, isn't she?" He chuckled. "Does she realize this will make her the First Lady of Cracker Creek?"

"Oh, Griz, don't make fun of me." She was quickly on the verge of tears. "Bert is a fine man and I just know we are going to be happy."

For once, Griz showed concern. "Of course you will be, and I wish you all the best in the world. And I'm touched you should want me to hear it first from you."

At Mrs. Swenson's steps they stood for a moment as she looked up into his face. The eyes he knew so well were filling now with tears. Suddenly he gave her the old familiar bear hug. "I could wish I still didn't have the same old hangup," he mumbled, shaking his head and hurrying off.

"Thanks, Griz," she called after him and quickly ran up the steps, blinded by her tears and hoping nobody would see her before she reached her room.

Mary and Bert were married two weeks later, with Cara and Monte standing up with them when the Episcopal minister came up from Baker on his monthly visit. The Prentices gave them a wedding breakfast, in the course of which Mary suddenly realized that she no longer had to be invited to the Argonaut Club.

She clapped her hands in delight, with the same lack of restraint she had always shown before she had become the mayor's wife, exclaiming: "Now I can go the Argonaut supper every Saturday night!" She was shocked to see the look of dismay which followed, on the faces of everyone around the table, except for Cara, an outsider like herself.

Bert shook his head. "Wouldn't you know," he sighed ruefully, "that her first thought would be to enjoy something we have killed." Mary had laid a hand lightly on his arm and was looking up at him affectionately. Bert gulped. "I never thought for a moment but that you had heard. Saturday night suppers have been cancelled!"

"Oh, my gosh!" She caught her breath. "So that is why you didn't invite me to the buffet? I wondered. Why, Bert?"

He put his hand over hers. "I'll tell you about it when we get home."

She seized upon the one word he had uttered that eased the dismay she had created.

"Home!" She wrapped the word in ecstasy. "It has been so long since I could call any place home, except where my parents live, that it hits me here"—she touched a spot over her heart—"when you say 'when we get home.' Thank you, Bert, for reminding me I really have a home now."

He told her later that cancellation of the buffets had followed a proposal to vote Goren Trench, taciturn general manager of the dredge, into Argonaut membership. The move split the club wide open, with the Prentices on one side and their best friends, the Nicholses on the other.

"You know what that means?" he asked.

She nodded. "Like four peas in the same pod."

"Exactly. You can't blame Homer Prentice. Trench is giving him all his banking business and renting space on the top floor of the bank. What's more, this has made an impression on suppliers doing business with the dredge, most of them Argonauts. I guess Homer assumed he had only to snap his fingers and Trench would be voted in, hands down. Instead he got blackballed by two votes."

"Who blackballed him?"

"Howard Nichols, for sure, although nobody is saying. If for no other reason than because he has said the dredge will put him and his smelter out of business. He led the fight against Trench. Homer was furious. Never before had he been slapped down so cruelly. Especially by his best friend."

'You have no idea who cast the other blackball?"

Bert's face crinkled up with sly amusement. "I wouldn't be surprised if it were our good friend, Monte Willcox. After all, Monte is the smelter's manager."

"You could be right. I remember that night when I spilled the news at the Swenson supper table that the dredge was hiring Griz. Monte rushed to the phone to call Howard immediately." Then she frowned, asking, "What's this got to do with the buffet suppers?"

"Very simple. Homer reacted by refusing to take Amelia to the next buffet. The next week Howard and Constance retaliated by staying away. In a couple more weeks so many took sides and followed suit, not showing up, there wasn't enough food brought along to make the buffet feasible. Last week they voted to cancel out indefinitely."

Mary thought about his explanation for a long time before venturing to voice her reactions. "I have a feeling," she said slowly, thinking out how she wanted to put it, "that the Argonaut has come to be the very essence of their social life here. If it is not put back on its feet quickly, it will die out for good."

There was a suggestion of a smile on his face when he asked: "So what?"

"Why don't we, the neutrals in this scrap, create in our home a substitute for what they have destroyed so blindly?"

Bert ducked his head as if he had just avoided being clipped on the chin. "When I was a child," he said, "the word I most admired was *elucidate.* After that haymaker you just threw in my direction, I think I should ask you to elucidate."

She had to laugh. "If I may be pardoned for being less profound, what I have in mind is that we should put on a buffet in *our home* every Saturday night until the Argonaut resumes. You're the top man in town, at least for the time being, and I'm the raring-to-go newcomer in the Argonaut, just the right combination to make them come to their senses. I think it is cowardly of them to cancel out their buffets over something that has nothing to do with the club and I'm going to tell them what I think, now that I have a right to do so!"

"Softly, my dear. Your idea of carrying out the tradition right here is brilliant—in keeping with what one might expect from the mayor's lady. But the mayor got where he is, and stays up there, by keeping his opinions to himself."

She was very penitent for her outburst. "I judge I'm being spanked," she began, before he cut her off.

"Not spanked, but complimented for your perspicacity. This is another of my favorite words, calculated to confound the voters. For your penance, look it up in the dictionary. Meantime, how do you propose to go about this?"

"How many people will this house hold comfortably? In the dining and living rooms, of course."

"Ten couples, at the most."

"That would be just about right."

But he objected. She couldn't prepare food for that many people every Saturday night. "Not that I mind paying for it."

She laughed. "I shall have no compunction asking women to bring food, especially pastry, salads and rolls, just as they did to the Argonaut. But we must make it invitational. We shall have the Capulets one week and the Montagues the next."

Bert frowned. "Capulets and Montagues?"

"You know," she giggled. "The warring families in *Romeo and Juliet.*"

He enjoyed a good laugh at her witty choice of malcontents and put an arm around her. "What a prize you turned out to be. And to think you haven't been married ten hours yet."

He kissed her impulsively, a kiss that lifted her spirits more than anything else that had happened that day, including the wedding itself. And the perfunctory kiss that followed.

Within the week the Aschers had begun their buffet suppers. They were a tremendous success. Mary quickly became the social surprise of the season. People said they never would have guessed she had a flair for this sort of thing.

"Where did she get her savvy?" Bert was asked.

"From teaching school, I suspect," he replied expansively. "We forget that a woman teaching the primary grades has to cope with twenty or thirty different personalities, *and* temperaments, five days a week, nine months a year, year after year. The average woman doesn't make that many adjustments to people and situations in five or ten years. After all," he chuckled, "aren't we just little kids grown up?"

He always refrained from making pointed references to the split within the Argonaut when he cited this analogy, but most people got the point.

Despite the enthusiasm of those who came early to their suppers and paid her and Bert the ultimate compliment of calling their home the "Little Argonaut," Mary waited until she was far more sure of herself as a hostess to invite Amelia and Homer Prentice and Constance and Howard Nichols, to the *same* buffet.

The delay proved shrewd on Mary's part. Amelia was so impressed with the rebirth of the Old Argonaut spirit in the Prentice's visit to the Ascher's "Little Argonaut" that she asked Mary to join her in calling on Constance Nichols the following week.

"I needn't tell you," Amelia confided, "that the fun has gone out of this town with the Argonaut all but closed, except for the bar. Since we started the breakaway, I tell Homer we should be the ones to patch it up. But you know how men are!"

Mary clucked, but gave no sign of agreement.

Amelia continued: "I say we women have got to put it together again, and it must start with Constance and me. If you will come along with me . . . who knows?"

Mary started to say, "Why me? I'm nobody." But she gave

herself away with a humble gesture which Amelia cut short.

"Because you are the mayor's wife!" Amelia said. "That's why! It makes quite a difference."

Even so, Mary deferred to Amelia when they set foot on the steps leading up to the broad veranda of the home Howard Nichols had built for Constance "in this God-forsaken place," as she first called it.

Most houses in Cracker Creek were sturdy story-and-a-half affairs, with steeply sloping roofs, meant to shed all but the heaviest winter snow, and walls at least eight inches thick to insulate against the prevailing north wind.

But the house Nichols built towered over the town like a Queen above pawns on a chess board. And its most striking bit was a spectacular bay window, with an interior rim of colored glass squares, framing the valley of the Powder and the mountains beyond.

In Pennsylvania—where the Nicholses lived before they came west to buy and renovate the old smelter to fit into the re-creation of an Old West gold boom town—this house would have fitted best into a setting of stately elms. Here it only served to set them apart from their neighbors.

Mary recalled that its opulence had taken a great deal of living down, particularly when Constance brought along, with her furniture, a grand piano! This was a bit too "tony" for those who had to rough it when they first came to the Creek.

Amelia gave two assertive twirls of the fancy brass doorbell when they reached the stoop. "Any other time," she told Mary, "I would have rung up to ask whether it would be convenient for us to call. But this, I know, is one of her at-home days."

Mary recalled how Constance had amused Cracker Creek women when she introduced the early 1900s custom of "at homes," insisting that, if they were intent on creating the mood of life in the first decade, they should go all the way.

The door opened on a Constance Nichols every bit as precisely dressed as Amelia had expected her to be. And, as always, the living room looked as if she had just finished giving it the last touches before she shoved broom, dustcloth and carpet sweeper in the hall closet as the doorbell rang.

Amelia was radiant as she gently nudged Mary in first. "You see, I brought along the new bride."

"Mrs. Ascher," Constance said, dipping her head ever so slightly as she offered her hand. "How nice of you to come. We had such a lovely time at your buffet. You are both just in time for tea."

"Of course," smiled Amelia.

It had been more than a month since these two old friends had spoken to each other.

Mary's eyes betrayed at once her admiration for the lovely carved furniture. She ran a hand over the back of a settee, near which she was standing. "Ooh!" she murmured, "What an exquisite piece of grape carving."

Constance indicated a chair across from the tea table for Amelia and said to Mary, "Why don't you sit beside me so we can all be more intimate? I'll only be a minute filling the pot."

Mary was sure Amelia did not realize until she sat down that she was facing the bay window with the colored glass squares which now framed the huge, gluttonous Monster that had begun rooting up Powder River. Noting the focus of their attention on her return, Constance remarked, "Not a pretty picture, is it?"

Amelia ignored the obvious dig at Homer's position on the dredge, but became alert again when Constance held out a cup to her, whose wisps of vapor betrayed the fragrance of jasmine. Their eyes met. In that fleeting moment, Mary knew Constance was not being fooled by their visit. Forewarned, Amelia lost no time coming quickly to the point.

"You know why we came, don't you, Constance?"

"Yes." Said very evenly. No inflection whatever. But she never dropped her eyes to the teacup she was holding to her lips.

Mary's lips hovered only a whiff away from the jasmine vapor tantalizing her—unable to take a sip while these two women dueled with their eyes.

"Yet you gave me jasmine . . . " Amelia let her voice trail away.

"Because you like it. Besides, it becomes you."

"Oh, Constance, I wish we could settle this awful mess as easily as this."

"Let's be honest, Amelia, you wouldn't have come here if you thought we could do anything about settling it. So why try?"

Amelia sighed. "I never knew Homer to be so stubborn. It isn't his fault, Constance. He doesn't know what else he can do. The man is a good customer."

"I know. Howard would most likely take the same attitude if he were in Homer's shoes. But the point is: he isn't."

Suddenly Constance became aware that they both were ignoring Mary completely. She apologized abjectly. "But this is the first chance we have had to talk it out."

"And we are not doing very well with it," bemoaned Amelia. "Oh, Constance, we *mustn't* let this come between us."

"You mean you and me?"

"All four of us, but you and me especially. We must try to work on our husbands."

Constance smiled. "That's a laugh. They will expect us to go right down the line with them to the bitter end."

Amelia shook her head sadly. "I'm afraid you are right. I just sort of hoped it might turn out differently if we tried."

She held her teacup up to admire it before she put it down tenderly. "Chelsea Sprig," she told Mary. "I love it!"

Constance offered to freshen her tea but Amelia stayed her hand. "No sense prolonging the agony," she said. "But at least we tried." She rose to leave.

"Homer and Howard tried, too," Constance pointed out ruefully, "but they kept it bottled up here." She touched her breast. "Don't forget it hurts more when it won't come out."

"Yes, I think I shall have another cup," said Mary, passing her cup to Constance. "It isn't every day I have jasmine—especially in Chelsea Sprig."

A rather embarrassed Amelia Prentice sat down quickly and guessed she might have a second cup, too.

"Besides," said Mary, no longer cowed by them, "You two, though you may not know it, have gone a long way toward a reconciliation between your husbands and you must not quit now. Will you do this for me?" she pleaded. "Will you both bring your husbands to our house for the buffet next Saturday night?"

"Both on the same night?"

Mary never knew which said it first.

"Absolutely!"

"What will we tell our husbands?" Constance asked.

"Just us two couples?" Amelia was shaking her head.

"Tell them nothing," Mary said, "except that you are invited back for a second round. From the way they both enjoyed themselves the first time, I can't think they will ever suspect I have crossed the wires this time." She turned to Amelia. "No, I shall have the usual ten couples, half and half. I'll ring you both on the phone and talk over with you which other couples you might suggest."

The two women looked at each other.

"Do you think we dare?" asked Constance.

"We will never forgive ourselves if we don't," replied Amelia.

"Thanks for the jasmine," Amelia told Constance at the door. "It said nothing has changed between us."

"Amen to that," Constance concurred.

Mary's plan for a reconciliation between the Prentices and the Nicholses—her Capulets and Montagues—worked perfectly. The two men stopped cold on catching sight of each other at the Ascher's next buffet. Homer turned at once to demand of Amelia if they had come the wrong night, only to find the two women falling into each other's arms. The starch went out of Howard when he made the same discovery.

Mary stepped quickly between them, abjectly aplogetic. "I must have gotten my wires crossed," she said humbly.

Homer saw the humor of the situation and offered his hand to Howard. In another moment they were whacking each other on the back until Mary cried out: "Break! Let's not overdo it!"

They retaliated by kissing her instead.

"That's really overdoing it," she protested, pushing her displaced topknot back into place. But her heart did a little toe dance, grateful that her ruse had worked!

10

When the Bishop of Eastern Oregon sent word he planned to make Cracker Creek the setting for his service of Thanksgiving that year, the Protestant community at once proposed he conduct the town's usual Union service on that occasion.

Mayor Ascher called a meeting of the town's clergy to decide where it would be held.

The Rev. Mr. Leckenby suggested, "Since he has no church of his own here, I shall offer mine."

"Why not the Opera House?" asked the mayor.

"A dance hall?" snorted one of the ministers.

"A church does not a temple make," Ascher reminded the dissenter.

"The Opera House has merit," said the Baptist minister.

"The whole community could attend," another spoke up.

"Amen," said the rest in turn. It was their way of making the vote unanimous.

The clergy and the mayor guessed well. Thanksgiving Day dawned white and bright after an overnight snowfall that left eight inches on the ground. The air was filled with the sound of bells. Cutters and sleighs blossomed out all over town, jingling the joy of their release from months of storage in barns and stables, bringing hundreds of people to the service, even from as far away as the mines. And all the church bells in town were ringing out the summons to thanksgiving with an outburst surpassed only on that first night of Sunday closing.

Bert Ascher stood in the snow with Mary outside the Opera House, his Mackinaw coat open wide because of the warm sun, his thumbs tucked inside his ample beltline, exulting in the size of the turnout. He was kept busy speaking to all the people he knew.

"You seem to know everybody!" Mary murmured with such great pride in him that it was all she could do to keep from crying out, "This is my husband, folks. See what I have to be thankful for this year. He knows everybody. He loves everybody and everybody loves him. Including me! There, I have said it and I don't care if everybody knows it!"

She looked up at him with such loving eyes that he would have been mesmerized by them had he chanced to turn her way. But at the moment he was spellbound by everybody's response to the Union service.

"I've never seen anything like this since the last time the chautauqua came to town!" he gloated.

"All because of you!" she said, taking his arm. "You talked them into using the Opera House instead of a church."

He smiled, patting her hand. "Don't talk that way." But she could tell by the look in his eyes that he was flattered. "I think we'd better go in now," he suggested.

Mary spotted Griz and the Redhead as soon as they had stepped inside. She wondered how she could have missed them on the way in. Probably because she had been so fascinated watching Bert glad-handing people.

Red was in an aisle seat, with Griz at her side, near the back. Mary touched her lightly, and affectionately, on the shoulder as she passed by. She reminded herself she must be sure to see them after the service.

Mary did not hear much of the service after the first lesson. The bishop had invited gaunt, eagle-eyed Parson Leckenby to read his choice of passages from the Bible. The parson took a deep breath and drew himself up to his full height as he announced chapter and verse: "Matthew, Chapter six: verses 25 through 33."

He swept the throng with his fierce eyes as he waited for them to find the place in their Bibles, then began reading:

"Therefore I say unto you, Be not anxious for your life,
What ye shall eat, or what ye shall drink;
Nor yet for your body, what ye shall put on.
Is not the life more than the food, and the body than
the raiment?
Behold the birds of the heaven, that they sow not neither
do they reap, nor gather into barns;
And your heavenly Father feedeth them.
Are not ye of much more value than they?

And why are ye anxious concerning raiment?
Consider the lilies of the field, how they grow;
They toil not, neither do they spin:
Yet I say unto you, that even Solomon in all his glory
was not arrayed like one of these . . .
Be not therefore anxious, saying, What shall we eat? or
what shall we drink? or, Wherewithal shall we be clothed?
But seek ye first His kingdom, and His righteousness;
And all these things shall be added unto you."

"And this," he said, "from Philippians, Chapter 4, verses 4-7:
"Rejoice in the Lord always; again I say, Rejoice.
Let your forbearance be known unto all men.
The Lord is at hand. In nothing be anxious;
But in everything by prayer and supplication with
thanksgiving let your requests be made known unto
God,
And the peace of God, which passeth all understanding,
shall guard your hearts and your thoughts forever.
Amen."

Mary was a little amused. The parson no longer was the thundering Jeremiah, spitting hellfire and damnation, she had been led to believe he was in the past. Apparently Sunday closing of the saloons had mellowed him.

But she was not prepared for him to come straight down the aisle when he finished the lesson, instead of taking his seat beside the bishop, to present his Bible to Mary the Redhead. Inevitably all those sitting in front of Red turned heads to follow his precipitate steps. He had a look of stark dedication on his face as he made the presentation. Not even the suggestion of a smile. Nor did he say anything. Just handed her the Bible and raised his hand when she half rose in her seat to accept it. She thought he meant for her to sit down, so she did. Afterwards, she wondered if he had been giving her his blessing.

In all her life she had never been so embarrassed. Her cheeks burned with unaccustomed blushing. Except for mumbling, "Thank you, Parson," she had been speechless. She could think of nothing to say except, "Why me?" And she hadn't even said that.

It took Griz to bring the parson's actions into focus. Caught by indulging in a sleepy sort of reverie, no doubt brought on by coming into a warm Opera House, packed with people, Griz had missed the presentation and would have known nothing about it until later, if he had not become conscious of a disquieting pervasive silence around him. It reminded him of those many times in the middle of the night at his digs, when he would come awake suddenly and feel that the silence around him was so oppressive he could actually hear it.

Once again, now in the packed Opera House, he could feel and hear the same frightening silence! A quick look around told him that every eye in the place was turned on him and the Redhead. He leaned over to whisper in her ear, "What happened?"

She showed him the Bible and used a thumb to point toward Mr. Leckenby going back up the aisle to the stage. "He gave it to me," she whispered. "Why, do you suppose?"

There was a knowing smile on his face as he whispered back: "I guess the guy really means it. He's in love with you."

She frowned, shaking her head, but he countered: "Remember the night of Sunday closing? When you found him on his knees in the Nugget, after the doors were locked and all the lights turned off, and there he was praying for you?"

She bobbed her head up and down, a look of sadness beginning to suffuse her eyes. "Poor Lecky," she sighed, turning the Bible over and over in her hands. "I'll bet this was his most treasured possession."

Mary Ascher's first reaction to this unexpected byplay was to exult in her heart that the parson had picked Mary Too and Griz on whom to bestow his public blessing. Of all those whom she held dearest, these two had the least for which to be thankful on this day for giving thanks. Especially Griz. It rankled in her breast that Amelia Prentice had refused to invite him to the dinner following this service, despite Cara's wish that Griz be included, when Monte and Cara were to announce their engagement. Amelia would never accept him as a guest in her house because of his association with the Redhead, whom she called "a woman of ill-repute."

What mattered now, as Mary saw it, was that Griz once more was the respectable professional man for which his education and experience had fitted him. He had a good job, which had not made him the most hated man in Cracker Creek, as Monte had once predicted. He was on Homer Prentice's side in the Argonaut dispute over membership for Goren Trench. How could Amelia forget that, even if Trench was his boss?

Besides all this, Mary felt that Griz was going to need something more than the comfort of the Redhead before the day was out. In telling Mary that she and Monte were announcing their engagement at the dinner, Cara had said Monte was leaving the smelter to go into the banking business in Baker.

Facetiously, Mary had asked: "*What* does Monte know about banking?"

Cara had laughed. "Nothing much. I guess they want him to look after accounts and loans involving mining interests. At least he knows all about that. He is going to be assistant cashier!" Cara added proudly.

So, thought Mary, Cara had won out after all. She had said she would never spend the rest of her life in the Creek. So Monte was doing the moving instead.

But, from Griz's standpoint—and she did not think he had been told yet—the Grizzly was losing his best friend when Monte left town. She had a big lump in her throat as she recalled that night in June, little more than five months before, when the four of them sallied out of the Argonaut on a moonlit walk that ended when they met the trio shooting up the town. They were four young people very much in love with life, but without ties as yet.

Now Griz was the odd man out. Cara and Monte were finally giving in to Amelia's machinations to mate them (although Amelia was satisfied they always intended to marry) but resented her not letting them work it out themselves. And she, Mary, had married Bert Ascher, with whom she now had every reason to believe she was really in love, if affection was the real test of love. Griz was the only loser of that original four, but thank God for Red, Mary said to herself as this service of thanksgiving came to a close, for at least she will give the affection he needs.

Mary quickly cornered Monte and Cara after the service ended and persuaded them to tell Griz their news before he heard it secondhand. "Especially since he won't be at the dinner today," she explained.

"I know," said Cara impatiently. "I tried to change Amelia's mind, but she is adamant."

"When Bert and I decided to get married," Mary said, "I told Griz before I told anyone else. He would have been hurt if he had heard it from Jean Hawkins or one of the other town gossips."

"That does it," announced Monte. "We tell him now."

The four of them caught up with Griz and Red on the boardwalk. Mary introduced Cara to the Redhead.

"Cara," she said, "this is Mary Armittage."

Cara hesitated, looking from one to the other, perplexed. "I thought . . ." she started to say.

Griz guffawed. "In other words," he explained, "this is the Redhead. Mary is just being formal and correct today. You will have to excuse her," he said haughtily to Red. "She is the Mayor's Lady now, you know."

"I was only giving her her proper due," Mary protested. "It isn't everyone who gets singled out like she was at the service. Congratulations, Mary Too."

"Wasn't that something!" Griz exclaimed, doing a little fancy soft shoe in the snow.

"Looks like you're full of it today," Monte grinned.

Griz stopped, looking up at the sky. "I was thinking," he said. "Tonight ought to be a great night for bobsledding. Moonlight, too!" He made a grimace. "Like that night in June, remember?"

Mary said to herself, "He hasn't forgotten!" But she began to fear how Griz would take the news which Cara and Monte were waiting to tell him.

"How about it?" Griz asked, rubbing his hands with eager anticipation. "I know where I can get a bobsled that will just take the six of us."

Monte shook his head regretfully, whereupon the smile faded from Griz's face. "Amelia got you tied up tonight, too?" he said sarcastically.

"It isn't that," Mary assured him, stepping in to put a sympathetic hand on his arm. She thought it best that she break the ice first. "They have something to tell you, Griz."

Griz seemed to sense instantly what it was. "You're going to get married!" He said it before they could.

136

Monte and Cara both burst out laughing and blushing. "You said the punch line before I could say it!" Cara scolded him. "And this is your punishment," with which she gave him a quick kiss on his cheek and drew back, blushing more attractively than she had before.

"I guessed it!" Griz said gleefully, shaking hands with Monte, offering his congratulations. "You two won't believe this, but it shows in your faces today. Good!" Then his chuckle betrayed the twinkle in his eye. "So Amelia won out after all!"

"Not entirely," Cara smiled. "Monte is quitting the smelter and moving to Baker," she said.

Biting her tongue to keep from crying out, Mary watched this news slowly drain the color out of Griz's face. Not even his whiskers could hide the shock. Just as she had suspected, he was taking Monte's defection harder than the end of whatever interest he may have had in Cara. He summed it up in one short sentence. "That's a horse of a different color."

What is more, she thought, there was now a look in his eyes which reminded her of what she had seen so many times in the eyes of a cocker spaniel she knew. To look at him, one might think he had lost his best friend—which, in fact, he had, hadn't he? Until the dredge's coming they had been the closest friends.

Griz apparently was having similar thoughts. "I don't blame you," he told Monte. "I always thought it had to come sometime, but I sort of hoped we could patch it up before you pulled out."

The Prentice sleigh, with sleigh-bells jingling merrily drew alongside and stopped, to end the agonizing. Amelia called out to Cara: "Are you coming with us?"

The bishop and the Nicholses already were in the sleigh.

"Guess we'd better," Monte said ruefully, taking Cara's arm. Pain showed in Monte's eyes as he dipped a farewell to Griz with his head.

As they drove away, Griz said bitterly, "Amelia is still cracking the whip."

"That's why she doesn't like you," ventured Red. "You won't knuckle under."

"No. She's hitting at you."

"Don't I know it." There was a distinct curl to Red's lip as she said it. "The so-called good woman, from her ivory tower, hitting out at me through you!" She hugged to her breast the Bible Parson Leckenby had given her. "This I shall always cherish because of all those women there—all those *good* women especially—he picked me out to say, with the gift of *his* Bible, 'You shall be saved.' "

Griz looked at her with amazement. "You got me half believing it!"

"I do and I don't, Griz," she said. "I do believe that he meant to tell me I'm just as good as Mrs. Prentice and that makes me feel pretty good right here." She patted herself over the heart. "Beyond that,"—she spread her hands in a shrug—"I don't know what good it did either you or me. The Mrs. Prentices of this world will still detest me, the parson notwithstanding."

"What beats me," Griz said, shaking his head, "is that she would invite Trench to her damned old dinner and leave me out."

Mary could take it no longer. She asked what Griz and Red were doing that night.

Griz said: "I was thinking we might take the four o'clock train to Baker and get us a Thanksgiving dinner at the Antlers Hotel."

"That would be nice-e-e-e-e!" said the Redhead. "Why don't you suggest it?"

"You will do nothing of the sort," said Mary firmly. "All that train riding, down today and back tomorrow, and staying over at the Antlers? Just to get back at Amelia and have a Thanksgiving dinner all of your own? That is what it comes to, doesn't it?"

Griz admitted it did.

"And you don't have to work tonight, do you Red?"

"Not tonight."

"Then," said Mary, "you are both coming to our place tonight for a late supper. I can't promise you turkey—"

Red laughed. "Turkey doesn't matter."

"—but I've got all sorts of other good things that you might like better, including love and affection . . ."

"That would be the best part of coming to have supper with you," said Red, breaking in.

"You bet it would," Griz grinned.

So it came about that they all sat down to late supper that evening in the Aschers' warm and cozy kitchen.

"I hope you don't mind?" asked Mary solicitously.

Bert was expansive. "This is where our romance began. Perhaps," he added with a chuckle, "it will do the same for you."

The Redhead smiled. "I guess it's too late for that."

"Oh, I don't know about that," Griz contradicted her. "If I had taken you to the Antlers, who knows?"

"I like it better here," Red said with finality.

And, as if he had deliberately chosen that moment to sound off, Mr. Pavarotti began to trill vigorously.

Red pointed to the canary. "See, even he agrees with me."

But Mary had noted there was something more than mere banter in Griz's words. "Who knows?" he had said. "Who knows?" she said to herself. "Perhaps all he or Red needs is a little urging and we can be happy all around."

The moment for giving this thought a nudge came when they were all sitting around after supper, their chairs pushed back from the kitchen table, feeling mellow and satisfied, toasting themselves in the warmth of the kitchen range, toying with their coffee cups.

"There's no doubt about it," admitted Griz. "This is the life."

"Why don't you and Red get together?" Mary said simply.

Bert Ascher started to bluster, but Red silenced him with a wave of her hand.

"Shush! Why shouldn't she say it out loud if she wants to? It's what everybody thinks."

Mary caught Griz eyeing the Redhead through eyes that were little more than slits, but the cracks in his beard said he was grinning broadly.

On an impulse Mary decided to be even more forthright. "He's got a house—a delightful little cottage and everything that goes with it—except a woman. What's it like, Griz, living alone like that?"

"Stark!" he replied. "Absolutely stark."

Then came an awkward pause when nobody said anything further and Mary thought her nudge had gone for naught.

But Griz's fingers had been drumming nervously on the table.

He looked first at Mary, then at Bert, and finally back to Red. Their eyes met and locked on, for what could have been half a minute, neither blinking.

Eventually, he spoke, "Why don't you move in?"

"I don't like to have to walk to work."

"Who said anything about you working? I mean you move in permanently."

"Are you kidding?"

The way she said it made him back off visibly. He rubbed his eyes while he seemed to be thinking out his next move. Then he made one more try: "It was just a thought," which he said sort of offhand-like.

"Keep it there."

Now he *was* worried. She sounded like she was spanking him for bringing it up. He suddenly wondered if she had misunderstood his motives. "You got me right, didn't you? I was asking you to marry me."

"I knew you were." She patted his hand. "But in front of all these people!"

He held up two fingers. "All these people, huh? Why not? These two are our kind of people. I think they feel the same way about it I do."

"You're sweet, Griz, but we're too much alike. It just wouldn't work."

"We could get married tomorrow and go to Portland on our honeymoon and be back here by Monday forenoon, if the boss would let you take those two days off."

"We don't need a honeymoon, Griz."

"I guess you're right." His enthusiasm collapsed again.

"So why spoil what we have?" she asked, with a wry twist of her lips.

Bert Ascher sighed audibly, shaking his head.

Mary could have cried. Red had said, "Why spoil what we have?" She knew exactly what Red meant. They were happy together as long as neither had any hold on the other. This was the hurdle a married couple had to negotiate. She guessed that Red knew as well as she did that Griz had a mental block to marriage which he might not be able to overcome. Why spoil the good things they already had? But her heart sorrowed for them just the same.

140

Meanwhile, Griz had been thinking, too. If Red would not marry him, he ought to do something special for her, something as dramatic as the parson bestowing his Bible on her. Something that everybody would remember and nobody could forget. The Redhead was the one woman who had stuck with him, come rain or shine.

He asked her: "You've got a birthday coming up?"

"Seventeenth of December."

"Your—?"

"Fortieth." She made a face. "Isn't that disgusting?"

"I don't know," Bert Ascher pursed his lips. "I didn't mind."

Mary punched him. "You can't remember back that far."

"Tell you what I'm going to do," said Griz. "I'm going to give Red a birthday party. A great, big, sensational birthday party such as the Creek has never seen. In the Nugget. Everybody welcome. Especially men whose wives would never think of letting her in their homes."

Mary clapped her hands. "Wonderful! May I come?"

Griz laughed and looked at Bert. "I don't think the mayor would dare approve."

Mary pouted.

"You know how it is," Griz persisted. "In a bar?" He shook his head. "No! Absolutely no!"

"I was in the Nugget that night in June."

"I know. But that was an accident."

Red laid her hand on Mary's. "Thanks for wanting to come. That means a lot to me, but you know he's right."

Mary shook her head. "You won't marry him, but you'll let him give you a big, public birthday party?"

"This one wouldn't be permanent," Red smiled. "That makes the great difference."

Griz asked Red if she would mind his promoting the party openly as being given for Mary Armittage, instead of the Redhead.

"Not if it means that much to you," she said proudly.

"It means everything to me to do this one properly," he said with an equally proud toss of his hand.

The next morning Bert Ascher phoned Mary from his office to say that he had to go down to Baker on the four o'clock train that afternoon on city business.

"I'll miss you tonight," she said wistfully. "It will be the first night we have been separated since our marriage."

"Can't be helped," he assured her tenderly. "Sleep tight."

"I'll try. But in any case I'll meet you at the depot when you come back tomorrow."

She wondered why he chuckled when she said that.

She never guessed she was looking at the answer when he struggled off the train next day, loaded with a huge box that he lugged up the hill to their home, explaining nothing until he got it in the kitchen and laid it on the table.

"This is what I went to Baker for," he laughed as she watched, wide-eyed, while he cut the string and invited her to open the box.

Gingerly, she lifted the cover, peeked in and let off a squeal as she began to burrow in the tissue paper, nearly sending Mr. Pavarotti into hysterics. For there, in all its elegance, lay the most beautiful fur jacket she had ever seen.

"It's seal and Treadwell dye," Bert said proudly as he helped her into it and gently fastened the frog at the throat.

Mary ran to the hall mirror and pirouetted this way and that, pushing the tight sleeves up a little bit to make them puff more, flipping the little back gathers out and adjusting the high collar.

"Oh, my dear, my dear!" she kept saying over and over. "I never dreamed I would own anything so lovely. But why, Bert?" She pulled his head down until his nose was buried in the soft fur, against her breast. "How did you ever come to think of doing this for me?"

He stood up again and enfolded her in his arms, looking off into the sunlight streaming into the kitchen, thinking how she had brought sunlight into his heart and the hearts of so many others.

"Why?" he echoed her question.

She looked up at that moment, her eyes glowing with adoration for him.

"Mostly," he smiled, "because you are so good to me and everybody. I got to thinking the other night, after Griz and Mary left, 'Now why did she do that for them?' And the answer came right back to me: 'Because it's her nature to want to do nice things for people.' And I said to myself, 'Now why don't

I do something nice for her, especially since . . .' "

She had hidden her face against his chest when his words began to be embarrassing, but she looked up when he hesitated. She finished the sentence for him: "Especially now that I am pregnant?"

He said yes with a smile that lighted up his whole face, and crushed her to him.

"Mary, Mary, can you realize what this means to me? If I tried for a thousand years, I could not repay you for this gift."

"Think what it means to me, too," she murmured, every nerve in her body tingling with love for him.

11

December 17 dawned bright and cold in Eastern Oregon. There was an overnight fall of six inches of snow on the boardwalk which, when plowed and shoveled, would bury the hitching posts along both sides. A north wind was being sucked down the mountainside behind Cracker Creek to make one vast ice box of the Powder's valley.

A far cry, Mary Ascher thought, from the night in June when she first met the Redhead and heard her sing "There'll Be a Hot Time in the Old Town Tonight." That night the boardwalk was teeming with human ants, scurrying in and out of the bars. This night the same men would be content to stay indoors, having their own hot time at the birthday party Griz was giving the Redhead in the Nugget.

Griz had huddled repeatedly with Mary during the three weeks they spent working out the details. Once more he was ebullient, bursting with ideas and enthusiasm. The intimate supper party the Aschers had given him and Red on Thanksgiving had been a shot in the arm of his morale. He had come out of his shell.

But Mary found that working with him on such a project had drawbacks. He leaned heavily on her as to how to carry out his ideas. "I'm no good at this sort of thing," he would say. "I'm a mining engineer. Give me a problem in engineering and a slide rule and I can solve it. But I'm no good when it comes to people and what to do about them or with them."

They were thrown together repeatedly because he insisted on checking everything out with her. Inevitably this led to quite a few twinges, reminding her of the old intimacy. She did not regret this, so much as she was bothered that he still could make her tingle when he gave off with bursts of warmth and enthusiasm like the Griz of old.

She had suggested he give the Nugget a festive touch. "Like we did for high school dances in the gymnasium or town hall.

Crepe streamers and rosettes and maybe some bunting."

"I know where I can get some bunting left over from the Fourth of July celebration," he chirped.

"Get it. Anything that will make it look like the setting for a birthday party and not a barroom."

She insisted on checking the final setup on the morning of the party. "Let's make sure," she told him, "that we have not left something undone." Griz took her to the back door, from which they could see the whole interior without being seen. She gasped with delight at the results. The Nugget was festooned from rafter to rafter with twisted paper streamers— great looping garlands of every hue that hung low and criss-crossed each other to create a tangled web overhead. Red, white and blue bunting became rosettes for the bar and the balcony that ran around the three side walls, as well as drapes and valances for windows that had never known a shade.

Pennants hung everywhere, as numerous as icicles outdoors. It was spectacular, but garish. It outdid anything anyone had ever thought up for the Fourth of July, but it served its purpose. The Nugget was no longer a barroom.

"How's that?" Griz exulted, sweeping an arm clear around Mary. "How's that for the rooting-tootingest, son-of-a-gun from Arizona, Ragtime Cowboy Joe job of decorating you ever saw? Terr-rr-rific, huh?"

This was certainly the old Grizzly again! The Griz of that night in June and of the Sunday closing. The Griz who thrived on doing something that people admired and applauded.

"It's pure Griz for my money," Mary chuckled. "And you have a birthday cake for her?"

"One as big as your kitchen table," he boasted.

"Then you're all set. Have fun tonight." She sighed. "I only wish I could come, too."

He smiled with understanding, even as he shook his head. Then he winked. "Nobody will pay any attention to you if you just happen to stick your head in this back door again tonight and take a peek. But don't get caught at it!"

Bert and Mary had an early supper that night because Griz had asked the mayor to introduce the Redhead by her real name, Mary Armittage, from New Orleans. After supper, when Bert started to bundle up against the fierce winds outside,

Mary said quietly, "I'm going to walk down to the boardwalk with you."

"Oh, no you aren't!" he said emphatically.

"But I only want to share vicariously in the excitement of the crowd on their way to the party, Bert. That's why I got such a kick out of the night of Sunday closing—just being there when it happened. After all, I had so much to do in creating the setting, I ought at least to have this reward. You tell me you're coming right home after you introduce her and she opens her presents."

"That's right."

"I promise you I'll go straight to the Argonaut the minute you leave me. I'll be waiting there for you." She wrinkled her nose plaintively. "I don't want to stay home alone."

His pursed lips suggested the odds were in her favor.

"Is that too much to ask, Bert?"

"No," he admitted slowly, "just so you don't hang around after I go inside. But you must bundle up. I'm sure it's down near zero. This is a chance to wear your new sealskin coat."

"Oh, no!" She was horrified. "That's only for best. It would be awful if I fell on an icy spot and damaged it. No, I'll wear what I always do in weather like this—my old mackinaw and a couple of sweaters underneath. And a wool scarf around my neck."

"Okay," said Bert. "Get ready. Time to go."

They parted on the boardwalk opposite the Nugget. The walk was alive again with droves of men, heavily bundled with extra scarves over their faces. She was fascinated with the kaleidoscopic picture they created: skittering . . . sliding . . . slipping sideways . . . anything but standing up straight. In a hurry to get there; giving vent to anticipation of the treat in store for them . . . hooting . . . cat-calling . . . or just talking their heads off and sending up white, icy plumes of breath.

"This is wonderful!" Mary gloated. "Thank you so much for letting me come, Bert." She squeezed the hand wrapped around one of her arms. "How long do you think you will be?"

"Hard to tell. Maybe an hour or so." He gave her a parting pat on the back. "Now you run along and I'll come for you as soon as I can politely do so."

The Argonaut's lounge was deserted when she entered and curled up in a comfortable chair. The sound of clicking balls in the billiard room said there was some activity there. Otherwise she was safe from meeting someone she knew. "So far, so good," she said to herself nervously. She had no intention of staying in the club more than ten minutes. She had only promised Bert she would be there when he came for her. There was never any doubt in her mind that she would wind up at the back door of the Nugget in time to see at least a part of Red's birthday party.

When her watch showed ten minutes to eight, the witching hour for the start of festivities, she quietly left the club, keeping her head down and her scarf up to her eyes to foil recognition.

The scurrying to the Nugget had slowed to a trickle, and she had no trouble slipping across the boardwalk and reaching the Nugget's back door to find a fellow conspirator there—Parson Leckenby.

He bowed. "We meet again."

"For the same reason, no doubt."

"Precisely."

"The first night of Sunday closing."

"I remember well."

He remarked that he understood she had a great deal to do with the tactical success of that operation.

It was her turn to dip her head slightly to acknowledge the implied compliment. "That's why I'm at this door tonight," she added. "Griz and I created the setting. We stood here this morning to give it a final okay."

"You opened the door at the time?"

"Certainly. Just a couple of inches."

"I don't think we'd better do that now—at least to hold it ajar steadily. Men are standing four and five deep inside, except for the mandatory open space for a fire exit. They would be sure to feel a draft and slam it in our faces."

"What do you suggest?"

"That we quietly slip inside, working our way along the wall, until you find a spot that gives you a crack of light between the people ahead of you, so you can see something. I'll stand back of you. I can at least see over the heads of most of these men and I'll keep you advised as to what's going on."

She grabbed his elbow. "But in no case let them pull me up front, ahead of them, because of my size. My husband is the mayor, you know, and it is imperative that I not be recognized."

"I understand."

By eight o'clock that night the Nugget was quivering from the shattering effect of a Pandora's box full of ear-splitting noise: yelling, jabbering and whistling . . . catcalls and lonesome coyote howls . . . cowbells and sleighbells ringing wildly . . . whiskey mugs setting up an impatient clatter on the pine tables . . . and the calked heels of miner and lumberjack leather boots stomping out the cadence of the ragtime band's music.

Nobody cared that the icy wind shrieked outside or the windows were already opaque with frost. The body heat of two hundred men alone, fortified with all they wanted to drink of the Grizzly's hot toddies, packed buttocks to buttocks around the bar, in the aisles and around the tables, and standing five deep along the walls, was enough to heat the Nugget comfortably without any help from the two pot-bellied stoves in service.

However, those two twin stoves—already glowing cherry-red, choked to the flue outlets with blazing cordwood, keeping huge kettles of water on the lids at a boil—were escalating the temperature to near-shirtsleeve conditions.

Griz had decided to toast the Redhead with hot toddy— whiskey cut with boiling water, which meant there had to be gallons of boiling water on tap throughout the evening. There was no other drink. Whiskey was free for the asking at the bar, compliments of the Grizzly.

Meantime, long before the stroke of eight, a steady stream of men had created lines to both stoves. Each man waited his turn to ladle boiling water into his mug; then, at the bar, he spiked the pure spring water with the essence of John Barleycorn.

Griz made an observation to Bert Ascher, when he reported in for his part in the program, that he thought the men were "stoking their stomachs with more boiling water than whiskey."

"That's all to the good," Bert chuckled. "Then you won't have so many drunks on your hand."

"Think again!" Griz retorted. "The water is being ladled off so fast it's keeping three men working furiously, trying to keep those pot-bellies stoked with cordwood and the water boiling! I never counted on anything like this!" He was mopping the back of his neck and his forehead repeatedly. "Is it hot in here?"

Bert looked at him in surprise. "Coming in fresh from the outside," he said with a twinkle, "I find it exhilarating!"

Griz cocked his arm, as if to swing at Bert, when someone yelled, "Bring on the Redhead!" Quickly the cry echoed back and forth within the room until it became a measured chant, accompanied by a thunderous stomping of calked boots.

The Grizzly's hand was being forced. Waving both hands high, trying to silence them, he shouted: "Wait. I'm going up now to fetch her if you let me introduce your master of ceremonies."

He gave Bert Ascher a hand up on the band platform, turned to the band for a musical flourish, then said: "I give you the Honorable Ethelbert Ascher, mayor of Cracker Creek."

A roar of approval and applause welcomed the mayor.

Griz tarried only long enough to give the signal for three men to carry in an enormous white cake and place it on a table in front of the bar. Whereupon he said to the mayor, "Take it away, Bert; you're on your own," and threaded his way through the packed crowd to the stairs leading up to the balcony quarters of the women employees.

The mayor reached into an inside pocket, drew out a sheet of paper, and began reading: "Unaccustomed as I am to public speaking . . . "

He got no farther before a storm of boos caused him to look up in surprise, glance at the sheet again, scowl . . . and then grin. "Heck, that's a political speech from the last election. My apologies." He crumpled it up and tossed it into the crowd.

The man who caught it opened it up, took one look and shouted back at him, "Hey, Bert, this is nothing but a blank sheet of paper."

"That's right, Jim. That's why I never gave that speech." He waited for the snickering to die down. "Anyway, that gave you all a chance to get the muffins out of your systems." He gestured to the huge cake in front of the bar. "Has anybody got an idea what that is?"

"A birthday cake," shouted a short, whiskered man near him

before anyone else could get a word in.

"Now wait a minute," Bert cauthioned him. 'It may look like a birthday cake, but how can you be sure?"

He looked up quickly to make sure he had everyone's attention.

"Anyway, it looks like a birthday cake," the man insisted.

"That's just the point! Lookalikes don't count when the bets are down. For all you know it may be nothing more than wood, put together by a carpenter and frosted and decorated by a baker to look like a birthday cake, because a real cake this big might crack wide open and fall apart when it's hauled in here."

The man peered around, seeing everyone eyeing him for answers, confused as to what to say or do.

"Put your finger in to find out," someone yelled.

"Now that's a good suggestion," Bert was saying, when two or three men jumped up to test it with their own fingers. Bert had to shout, "NO!" with such authority they hesitated. "That shall be this man's sole privilege because he was the first to answer my original question. Come," he said to the little man and led him to the table.

"Where shall I put my finger in?"

"On second thought," the mayor decided after a moment's hesitation, "it might be better if you used a candle, lest you risk getting a splinter in your finger. A finger's better for finger licking when you get a piece."This thought got a great laugh, followed by applause for the little man after he took the yellow candle handed him by Tim, the bartender, stuck it in the cake where the mayor pointed, and brought it out, covered with telltale frosting.

"You get to keep that one as a souvenir," Bert told him. One might have thought he had been kissed by Red instead, his face flushed so brightly red under all his whiskers.

Now the mayor said: "Let's get down to the ground rules for what's to come. First, don't ask Red to sing when she comes down now with Griz, all dressed up as a New Orleans belle, which she was, under her real name of Mary Armittage. That comes later when she comes back in her tights as the Redhead."

Next he asked for twelve men to screen the cake until she was almost upon it. And he reminded them to sing it "Happy

Birthday, dear *Mary*, " rather than Red or the Redhead.

Meantime Griz had climbed the stairs to the balcony and had stopped momentarily to look down on how the festive crowd was shaping up under Bert Ascher. Satisfied that everything was going well, he turned to knock on the Redhead's door, only to find that she had anticipated him and was standing in the open door. He stood immobile, hand still raised to knock, speechless, as if he were a wax museum statue, until she dazzled him with a smile and the gorgeous look of her.

She was all in white, from tip to toe—full-skirted muslin adorned with lace inserts, sleeves slightly puffed, and a decorous high neck held in place by celluloid stays. A white flower set off the copper in her hair.

For a moment Griz thought to himself, "Parson Leckenby ought to see her now!"

"I can't believe it!" he gasped finally. "I came to escort Mary Armittage to the party below . . . "

"This is Mary Armittage," she said with a haughty toss of her head. "That's who the party's for, isn't it?"

"Yes," he agreed, kissing her. "I wish I'd seen more of her before tonight."

"Make the most of it tonight. Nobody around here has ever seen me in this outfit before and I'm not sure they ever will again. This belongs to Mary Armittage, not the Redhead."

"It becomes you, Mary," he said with great affection.

She squeezed his arm nervously. "I suppose we ought to go down now."

He looked at her sharply. "You're not nervous, are you?"

She gave a little laugh. "Mary is. Red never gets that way. It makes a difference which hat you wear."

"Before we go down," he said, fumbling in his pockets, "I want to give you something."

He produced a cameo brooch, as large as a silver dollar, its lacy gold setting tarnished with age. Her eyes opened wide as he laid it in her hand. She held it out and turned it every way, trying to see it in the best light.

"Your wife's?" she asked, lifting her eyes.

"Yes. My mother's originally."

"You're sure you want me to have it?"

"Quite sure."

She kissed him quickly, almost shyly. This was a situation quite different from those they usually shared.

"This is the nicest thing you could have done for me, Griz."

She pinned it over her heart. "This belongs now *only* to Mary Armittage. You must never expect me to wear it as the Redhead."

She took a deep, deep breath before asking him to give her his arm. "I'm ready to go down now."

They descended the stairs from the balcony with all the eclat of a royal couple, to the accompaniment of an accolade in brass and the Blue Mountain men's favorite paean to women they admired, the mournful howling of a lovesick coyote.

* * *

Just inside the back door of the Nugget, among the standees, a heavily muffled figure no bigger than a boy and a very tall man in a woodsman's mackinaw and visored fur cap gasped when they first caught sight of the Redhead in all her breath-taking elegance.

"O-o-o-h!" murmured Mary Ascher. "She's gorgeous!"

Parson Leckenby exulted: "All in white! Like I always said, she's the perfect Mary Magdalen!"

* * *

From the moment Red came downstairs until she went back up, she was Mary Armittage to the hilt. She tried to make this horde of men from the mines and lumber camps feel they were back home again, at a birthday party for the girls they left behind. She clapped her hands in glee when the twelve men chosen to hide her view of the birthday cake stood aside, to reveal candles lighted and flickering gaily, singing "Happy Birthday, dear Mary; happy birthday to you."

Griz turned to Mary to remark: "Bert crossed me up, I guess. Instead of any twelve men nearest the bar, he picks three quartets. How's that for class?"

Mary complimented them, adding: "I would have loved to have sung it with you, but of course that's a no-no in the circumstances," and shook hands with each of them.

She cut the cake in man-sized pieces with a butcher knife,

then called for a blanket to be spread in a cleared space on the band's raised platform so everyone could see her unwrap the gifts which a wheelbarrow dumped on the blanket. (Griz had posted notices that, if there were gifts, they must *not* be tied up or wrapped—just tagged.)

She put her head back and guffawed when one gift turned out to be an outsize pair of bloomers. She tossed them gaily into the crowd, where they were torn into bits in thirty seconds, to become mementos of the party.

But she slid the gift of a pair of spangled, Alice-blue garters up her forearms and held them up to be admired.

"Hey, Red . . . I mean Mary," a man yelled. "That's not where you wear 'em."

She rolled them higher, over an elbow.

"No! No! No!" came cries from all over the house.

She snickered, "I'll bet there's not a man here who'd not wear them on *his* sleeve," then tossed them to the coyotes, one at a time. The scramble for them was a battle royal.

There were fur skins, too, freshly trapped.

Logging Camp No. 2, Bear Gulch, gave her a bearskin rug.

Mary spun around, pretending to look wildly for Griz—a sly reminder that, though his real name was Quigley, he had long been dubbed the Grizzly because he had a mattress of brown fur from his eyeballs to the pit of his stomach.

Griz chuckled. "You thought they got me, huh?'"

"It could have been your brother," she grinned.

"Naw. That bear hasn't enough hair on his chest."

There were little bags of nuggets, too, but the gift she cherished most came from Mary Ascher. The mayor handed her a sofa pillow, embroidered with daisies. "From my wife," Bert hollered to the throng.

Mary Too held it aloft. "Memories of the Fourth of July," she said, "when you picked daisies for two Marys in the canyon!"

There were tears in her eyes as she hugged the pillow to her bosom. It was the only present given her that night by a woman, other than those who worked in the Nugget.

The gift-giving completed, there was an instant demand for her to sing, but she waved them off firmly. They had toasted her roundly—"for she's a jolly good fellow, which nobody can deny"—and expected her to reciprocate with a ballad that matched their affection for her.

"Not until I change back into the Redhead's flounces and frills," she shouted. "Can't sing in these duds—too dressed up! But I'll get back into my working clothes and sing anything your hearts desire."

Griz kidded her. "You weren't fooling anybody with that phony excuse."

Her eyes snapped in a rare show of determination. "I'm *not* singing in *this* dress in any *barroom*—not even for you!"

She was already gathering the gifts into her arms.

"Need any help lugging them up there?" he offered.

"No, I can get them all except the bearskin. Hang it over the bar for now—to remind them of you!"

She giggled and made a run for the stairs. Passing the musicians, she told them: "Give them something hot and smoky, to get the cricks out of their joints."

"How about 'A Hot Time in the Old Town'? "

"Perfect." She skipped up the stairs and out of sight.

* * *

Mary Ascher looked up at the parson from their standee spot against the wall near the Nugget's back door. "I guess I'd better scoot," she whispered.

"Me, too," he smiled knowingly. "I don't want to be caught here either."

Out front again, he looked up and down the boardwalk and reported: "Coast is clear."

She never hesitated, keeping her muffled head down, except for one quick sideways peek up the boardwalk. Her heart missed a couple of beats as she thought she recognized Monte Willcox, still some distance away, slipping and sliding, his arms outstretched like wings, on the icy walk.

She skittered fast from that point until she reached the Argonaut and collapsed into a comfortable chair in the lounge, completely exhausted. But at least she had beaten Bert, who arrived five minutes later, bubbling with excitement over how the birthday party had come off, anxious to regale her with all the details which she had seen for herself!

* * *

A bundled figure, repeatedly slipping sideways, bumped into Parson Leckenby as he left the Nugget.

"Sorry," said the man, trying to peer at Leckenby over a high, turned-up overcoat collar. "Hey! I didn't recognize you at first." It was Monte Willcox, one of seven male boarders at Mrs. Swenson's. His eyebrows were white with frost. "I could use a little of your hellfire to keep warm tonight."

"So could I," the parson admitted. "You'll find it warmer inside."

"Don't tell me you've been sampling it!" Monte exclaimed.

"Yes." Just the one word, head turned away.

Monte was mystified. "Was it pretty bad?"

"No, not at all. Just the opposite. I'm a little stunned by my reaction. If I . . . "

Monte laughed, slapping his mittens together to warm his hands. "If I didn't know you for an evangelical zealot, Parson, I'd say you'd just discovered that gal is quite a woman!"

"She could have delivered a sermon to them in there tonight. And they would have listened to every word. She was all in white."

"Have I missed her?" Monte hurried over to look inside.

"Yes, she's gone upstairs to change."

"Damn," said Monte. "Don't tell me I've missed all the fun. Griz said nine o'clock."

The parson told him the party started at eight o'clock. "She was the very essence of the Magdalen tonight." He shook his head. "Yes, the very essence . . . " His voice trailed off.

The birthday party was over, but there was still plenty of hot toddy to be consumed and spirits were high. The band was making the walls of the Nugget quiver with Mary Armittage's suggestion to give them something hot and smoky while she shed her dream of a dress, but their choice of music at that moment would always be recalled in the Creek as uncannily prophetic.

> There'll be a hot time
> In the old town tonight.
> Fire! Fire! Fire!

Thus ran the closing lines of the refrain. They sang it, and shouted it, with gusto, because they were free to start tapping the steaming kettles again to make hot toddy.

"Fire 'em up again!" Griz bellowed, pointing to the stoves. Fresh cordwood was stuffed into each dampered-down firebox and soon the pot-bellies were glowing blood-red again, right up to the dampers.

Now the ragtime band broke into the "March of the Wooden Soldiers," which had been the hit tune in town ever since Cara and the King twins had introduced it at the shivaree in June.

At once it seemed half the men in the Nugget were on the move, ostensibly to pour boiling water into their mugs. But restless energy was at work, too, and the Victor Herbert march provided a good excuse to give it free rein. At first by twos and threes, then in increasing numbers, single file, they began giving a burlesque imitation of toy soldiers on parade.

In these close quarters, with chairs and tables in the way, it was inevitable that they were bumping into each other all over the place. And squeezing past standees in line became a precarious accomplishment, if both were waving mugs freshly filled with boiling water.

The rag-tag column of mock paraders bore down on the knot of men waiting their turn at one of the kettles of boiling water. Bull-like, the paraders made the waiting men give ground or get run over. Unfortunately, a man with a full ladle of boiling water, which he was trying to pour into his whiskey, got sharply jostled and the man who bumped him got scalded. Blind with anger and crazed with excruciating pain, the scalded man spotted who now had an empty ladle and launched a fierce butt to the pit of his tormentor's stomach, sending him reeling backward into one of the stoves with such force that it rocked on its legs.

What everyone missed in the excitement that followed was the stovepipe becoming disjointed at its upper elbow when the stove rocked on its legs. Wires from the rafters still held the pipe in place, but there was now an open gap at the joint. Hot gases began escaping through the break with the ferocity of a blowtorch, raising to the kindling point all the crepe paper and bunting suspended there.

For hours now, hot air in the overheated room had been trapped against the rafters, building up a steady increase in temperature, but flammable only if an outside agent were suddenly introduced to superheat it. The hot gases that spewed into the web of decorations did this.

A crepe paper streamer began to smoke and eventually caught fire. Then a second . . . and a third.

The next moment there was a terrific flash as the upper air reached the kindling point and exploded—burning off all its oxygen in one tremendous burst of flame. Thereafter, it was only a question of time before the Nugget became an inferno.

* * *

This much is known, from interviews with the survivors, about first reactions to the holocaust in the Nugget. It was every man for himself. The pixilated were trampled under in a mad surge for the two doors. Not a helping hand was extended to anyone who had fallen. He was one less to fight in the scramble to escape alive.

The Grizzly was one of a score whose bodies were carried out and laid in the snow when the horrifying exodus had ended. He was alive, but unconscious. Eight others were not so lucky. They died from being trampled or suffocated.

* * *

Monte and Parson Leckenby found the Grizzly in a grotesque heap at the foot of the stairs leading to the Redhead's rooms. Monte gave one tentative look at the landing on the balcony above and shook his head. It hadn't begun to burn briskly there yet, but the smoke was frightening.

"Don't get ideas," Monte warned Leckenby. "You'd never make it." Monte looked around desperately for something to put under Griz to carry him outside. He was sure to be dead weight. There wasn't a bench which might be used as a makeshift stretcher, but the bearskin given the Redhead was still draped over the bar. It was beginning to singe, but it would do. They worked it under him with the help of two volunteer firemen and carried him out.

The parson stripped off his mackinaw, covering Griz with it, for want of a blanket; then dropped to one knee to put an ear to his chest. "He's still breathing!" he said quickly.

Examining a bloody patch of Griz's hair on the back of his head, Monte said, "A nasty blow here. Might be a concussion."

Griz stirred, trying to escape Monte's probing fingers. His eyes were tightly closed, but his lips twisted in agony as he sought to speak. All that came out at first were moans and one muffled word, repeated again and again, until Monte finally recognized that he was calling for "Mary."

Leckenby knew instantly which Mary he meant when Monte looked up at the flames pouring out of the Redhead's windows. At once the parson stripped off his shirt and tore it into wide strips, which he soaked in the snow.

"What do you think you're doing?" Monte snapped.

"I'm going to look for her."

"You're crazy, man! Remember, we looked up there when we were trying to find something to lug Griz out, and we both shook our heads." He stood up and tried to restrain the parson.

"I remember, " Leckenby admitted, "but at least I can try." He pointed to the prostrate Grizzly. "Tell him. If nothing else, I can bring her body out before it is consumed."

He wound the wet strips of shirt around his mouth and nose. Then he was gone. He was never seen alive again.

* * *

Until the roof fell in at the Nugget, the volunteer firemen had not seriously considered the posssiblity of a general conflagration. In fact, they had been delayed in fighting the fire itself by the need for rescuing the injured first and then carrying out the dead.

A ladder had been raised to the Redhead's outside windows, but nothing but flames were to be seen inside. "If she opened her door right after that first explosion," the volunteer fire chief said, "her lungs would have been seared by the first breath she took."

Its roof gone, the Nugget became a flue to spread havoc. The bitterly cold wind did the rest, blowing the soaring sheet of flame in every direction. Half a block away, the high false front of Buxton's Hardware Store began to smoke along its eaves, then caught fire in a dozen places.

* * *

158

Mary and Bert Ascher, stunned on coming out of the Argonaut and seeing the Nugget the focus of the explosion and fire, came running to the boardwalk, the mayor intent on rallying all of the town employees to aid the volunteer fire fighters in keeping the fire from spreading.

Thus they found the Grizzly lying in the snow, with Monte on his hands and knees, bending over him, apparently trying to make up his mind what he could do for him. Mary waved Bert on to what he must do as the only responsible town officer yet in sight. Then she dropped to her knees beside Monte.

"Is he badly hurt?" she wanted to know, giving way to a burst of tears as she listened for a heart beat.

Monte shook his head. "I don't think so, but he has this caked blood in his hair back here." He touched the spot. Griz, still with his eyes closed, shook him off, mouthing profanities.

"Hush your mouth!" She touched his lips lightly.

Monte told her about finding him at the foot of the stairs, apparently knocked out, either by a fall or by being caught in the stampede for the doors after the explosion.

Only then did Griz open his eyes and turn his head, hearing the crackle of fire, to see the flames fanning out wildly in every direction from the Nugget's roof and the Redhead's windows upstairs.

"Oh my god," Griz cried aloud, no longer in muffled words. Suddenly his whole body shook, as from a chill, with the shattering realization that he had, in effect, sent Red to her death. "If I had not given her a birthday party—all because I wanted to get back at Amelia Prentice for denigrating her— she would be alive this minute," he wailed helplessly to Mary as he tried to get up.

"And if I had not suggested that you make the Nugget festive with crepe paper and doodads," Mary moaned, "there might have been no fire."

"But it was I who asked you what I should do to make it look like a birthday party," Griz protested. "No, Mary, nobody else is to blame but myself. Everything was against me and Red tonight. I switched from straight whiskey to hot toddy at the last minute."

He looked up, his jaw quivering. "Help me, Mary!"

She cradled his head in her arms and tried to comfort him.

"Don't crucify yourself," she said tenderly. "If we could do it all over again, it would have been better if we had not met that night in June. That's when it all began. We were fated."

She swayed gently from side to side, as she would one day do, rocking to sleep the baby now growing inside her, and ticked off the succession of happenings which seemed to have made this night's tragedy inevitable.

"If it had not been for the stuffing of bed pillows being dumped on us that night on the boardwalk, we might never have met . . . or stopped to listen to Red singing and got pushed inside, where I got to know her and have loved her ever since."

"I know, I know," he agreed, his voice muffled by her cradling arm.

"I could go on and on. The shivaree . . . the baseball excursion and picking daisies in the Canyon for Red . . . Sunday closing . . . Labor Day and your hollow victory in the rock drilling . . . the dredge . . . and finally Thanksgiving Day and the wonderful time the four of us had together after the parson gave her her finest moment with the gift of his Bible. Don't blame yourself, Griz. It all added up to tonight. She went out as she would have wanted to—as Mary Armittage!"

He said it again: "But if I had never given her this party, she would be alive now, Mary.'"

He might have kept on saying it over and over again if she had not reminded him that Parson Leckenby had gone back into the blazing shell to be with her if he could not save her.

"For both of them," she said softly, "that was their destiny . . . their *kismet!*"

"And I did nothing for her!" The words were gall in his mouth. But he knew what he must do. His strength was coming back. He felt he could navigate again. Something told him this could develop into a great fire like those in Chicago and Seattle in the last century. He must find Marshal Abe Long and expiate for what he had done against Cracker Creek and the Redhead, by doing whatever need be done to keep this fire from spreading.

"Help me up, will you, Mary?" he asked.

That was no easy task. He was a big man, both in size and weight. And she was, by her own words, a little runt, and half frozen from sitting in the snow, consoling him. Most of all, the

foo⌄ing on the boardwalk was treacherous. But with her help he made it to his feet.

Only then did he realize Monte was no longer with them. He asked what happened to him.

"I'm not sure." She was honest about it. "One minute he was standing over us, intent on whether I thought you should see a doctor, and the next time I looked up he was gone. I guess he heard us arguing about who was most responsible for what happened and decided he'd better go and see Bert to ask if there was anything he could do to help."

"That's what I'm going to do, too," Griz said, "only I'm going to find Abe Long first. I'm still Deputy Marshal."

She tried to restrain him. "Wait until you get your bearings first," she pleaded. But he brushed her off and she fell. He did not even turn to help her up. She put her hands over her abdomen quickly, fearful she might have hurt her child; then scrambled to her feet and hurried after him, crying out: "Bert told me to stick with you."

* * *

No longer were there four or five isolated fires. They were linking up and creating a more powerful draft; the icy wind, barreling down the mountainside, was acting as a bellows to envelop a score more buildings.

Mimicking a forest fire racing from treetop to treetop, these fiery fingers skipped from roof to roof, leaving their victims to burn steadily down to the snow-covered boardwalk. If these roofs had not been so steeply pitched, built that way deliberately to shed snow, their shingles might have been wet enough to hamper or at least cut the speed of the fire's spreading front.

Only the boardwalk, hard-packed with snow and ice since Thanksgiving, could do that now.

* * *

Ever since Saturday night suppers had been cancelled, most Argonauts went to bed early on the Sabbath eve, for want of anything better to do. Among these were Constance and Howard Nichols. Constance sat up in bed the minute she heard the fire bell. "Hope that's not the smelter," she said.

161

Nichols hit the floor with one bounce out of bed. "The smelter, you said?" Already he was pulling on his trousers.

"No! No! N-o-o-o! I only said I hoped it wasn't your baby."

"God! That's a hell of a way to scare a man out of a sound sleep." Grumbling, he crawled back into bed.

"Aren't you going to find out where it is?" she asked.

"You take a look. It's too damn cold out for me."

She slipped into a flannel bathrobe and pattered down to the landing where their exquisite colored glass window commanded a view of the entire valley and the town below. On sunny days it was fascinating to view the scene below through each of the colored squares that surrounded the large clear glass center.

Constance quickly placed the fire downtown. Anyway, it wasn't the Argonaut Club—as if that mattered, now that it had split into two irreconcilable factions.

"Howard," she called up to the bedroom, "you must come down and look at the effect through the different colors. It's positively uncanny."

"Come back to bed," he growled. "I'm cold."

* * *

About this time, Marshal Abe Long decided he wasn't going to wait for the town to burn down before he started evacuating people. He stepped up to the nearest telephone and gave the crank a couple of vicious turns.

"Effie!" he shouted when the telephone girl answered. "I want you to take no more calls—"

"Just a minute, Marshal," she snapped right back at him. "This is a private company and you got no right—"

"Now you listen to me, Effie. As of this minute, this town is under martial law and you're working for me!"

"If you say so."

"I say so! Now you ring every party line and tell everybody to bundle up to his eyebrows and get ready to move up the hill to safety if we don't stop this thing pretty soon. Mind you, I said don't take any calls and don't let anyone ask questions. Just tell 'em to listen and do what I said."

"How'll I know it's you ringing, if you want to call me?"

"Effie, the way things look now, there ain't going to be any

phones around here to call from. "

* * *

One of the better known prostitutes in town came up to Marshal Long. "There's six of us burned out," she said. "Got no place to sleep tonight."

"That's a switch," he guffawed with unconcealed sarcasm.

"Where do we go? We got nothing but the clothes on our backs, and we're freezing to death."

"Tried knocking on doors?"

"You know any more jokes?" She opened her furskin coat. She was wearing nothing but a negligee and overshoes. "We didn't take it seriously until it was too late."

"Greedy to the last for a buck!" he snorted. "Well, you might try Swenson's up the hill. Looks like it's going to ride this one out."

The six trudged up Schoolhouse Hill, bucking the icy wind that for the moment was blowing in their faces.

Answering their knock, Mrs. Swenson opened the door only a crack. "What do *you* want?" she snapped at them.

"Marshal Long said you'd give us a bed for the night."

"Oh, he did, eh? Well, we've got no beds for the likes of you. We're full up." she tried to shut the door, but there were several feet blocking it.

"Please, Mrs. Swenson. We're freezing."

"Couldn't some of the men double up?" another said.

The boarding house owner's eyes flashed. "You didn't think I'd let you sleep with them, did you?"

"Even one. We could take turns."

Mrs. Swenson's eyes shifted from one to another as they begged. She looked mostly into their eyes and was surprised to find they were like those of any other women in deep trouble. She thought for a long time, and she knew she was going to hate herself for what she was about to do; but, after all, they were women sorely in need of help.

"Okay," she said. "Get in there"—she pointed to the parlor—"until I can fix it for some of the boys to double up. I'll get you two rooms, *but*"—she shook her finger at them vehemently—"don't you dare stick your noses out of those rooms till I say you can in the morning, not even to go to

163

the bathroom. Use the chamber pots."

They could hear her grumbling to herself all the way to the stairs.

* * *

It is quite possible a good many people were not convinced the town would burn down until they saw the Opera House collapse in a fiery heap. These were the dedicated men who manned the hopelessly inadequate hoselines and organized bucket brigades.

The Opera House's demise symbolized the collapse of hope as well. It was hard to believe that, only a few hours earlier, the place had been jumping with lively music and only the bouncy two-step of a hundred prancing couples could have then threatened to bring the house down.

Deserted and dark, the Argonaut Club died quietly in its sleep. It is doubtful if more than a handful of its feuding members even noticed that it burned slowly and with decent restraint, as was befitting its position in the community.

* * *

Homer Prentice had asked Monte Willcox to give him a lift at the bank, hauling currency, cash and books from the vault to the Prentice home up the hill. Howard Nichols came in steaming and protesting. "why didn't you call me, Homer?"

"Phone doesn't ring," said Prentice.

"The hell it doesn't! That damned Effie blasted me out of bed to say, 'Run for your lives!' or something crazy like that. Came down here instead and ran into Monte loaded with books. I guess it's serious, isn't it?"

" 'Fraid so."

"You're going to let me help, aren't you?"

"Yes, if you like."

"You know the Argonaut is gone next door?"

Prentice stopped for just a moment, shaking his head. "I never had a chance to check." A sickly smile crossed his lips. "Too bad about the Argonaut. It was great while it lasted. I'm so glad we made up before it was too late."

They had been the prime opponents in the stalemate.

"Me, too," said Nichols warmly, offering his hand to shake

on it, which Prentice took avidly, then turned to give him an armful of books. "I hope you don't mind," he grinned.

"Of course not. Just like old times."

* * *

Homer Prentice's bank held out longest against the fiery onslaught. Its brick walls naturally couldn't burn, but its window frames did, releasing the three huge plate glass windows to crash both inside and out, leaving three gaping holes in the facade that looked down on the rock-drilling platform, for the wind-driven flames from elsewhere to gain entry.

That once proud building became an oven which baked its interior to the kindling point, awaiting only a match, or its equivalent. Within moments, like the rest of Cracker Creek, it finally exploded into one tremendous burst of flames.

* * *

Prentice stood at a safe distance, unable to accept what was happening. He had been told the building would last fifty years. Now it was dead in ten. It was literally the cornerstone of Cracker Creek, the only permanent structure around which to build an enduring city, not just a mining camp.

Why was it, he wondered, that a brick building always seemed to die such a horrible death in a fire? The inside could be a roaring inferno, as his bank was now, but the walls still stood intact, silhouetted by the gaps in their facade where once there were eyes.

And from time to time, he thought he could still see the bank's steel vault, blackened but untouched, like a man's heart that refused to give up the ghost.

Homer was going to miss his roll-top desk most. He had never had any other. He had brought it with him when he came to the Creek. It was as dear to him as a child might have been to him and Amelia. He knew every pull-out drawer and pigeon-hole in it, and what was filed or stored there. In losing it, he was giving up half of himself. "How does one re-create what is irreplaceable?" he asked Bert Ascher, who had been standing near him, but apart, lest he intrude on his desolation.

"He doesn't," Bert told him, "but cherish the memory."

Homer shook his head and turned away. All of a sudden he felt very old.

It was there Griz and Mary finally found the mayor, after what seemed hours in seeking him everywhere. Bert squeezed Mary's hand affectionately and shook Griz's, but a finger to his lips told them not to disturb Prentice, who was talking to himself in a muffled monotone.

"You should come right home with me," Mary scolded Bert. "You look awful. You have big circles under your eyes and your jowls are sagging. Please, Bert. Come home now before you collapse from exhaustion."

He shook his head. "I can't, Mary. Wish I could, but I can't. There's nobody to take over for me. Not a single councilman has shown his face around here. Guess they're all looking out for yours truly, not giving a damn what happens to anyone else. But I want you to go right home yourself." He turned to Griz. "Will you see that she does? Go with her, Griz. She needs rest more than I do. She's in a family way, you know."

"No, I didn't." But Griz broke a big grin and pumped Bert's hand vigorously. "I'm so glad for both of you."

Mary was embarrassed. (Why should she be embarrassed? she asked herself. But there it was—she *was* embarrassed.) She turned away quickly to look at Homer Prentice. He had gone back into his shell again—dazed, mute, unable to accept what was happening to all he cherished, except for Amelia.

She was vaguely conscious at that moment of a dull thud behind her, but turned only when Griz called to her. He was bending over Bert Ascher, peeling off his mackinaw to put it under Bert's head, which was in the snow.

"Bert!" Mary screamed, falling at his side to minister to him, as she had done once before this night for Griz.

Griz had his ear to Bert's chest and his fingers on his pulse. Mary knew before he looked up and said anything that it was useless. Bert was gone just like that.

Mary collapsed on his chest, crying softly for the man whom she had just begun to love, the husband of two short months who was giving her a child. Perhaps, if he had to go, it was best that it should be so unexpected and so final. She sobbed most of all for the fact that he would never know what they might have made of their marriage. Thank God they had had such a fine start. At least she had not disappointed him.

She heard Griz say to Prentice: "I want you to take Mary home to Amelia. She must not stay alone the rest of this night. I've got to stay here to take care of Bert."

Her instinct said, "No. I don't want to go home. I can't go home. I must be strong, but I cannot be strong lying in bed thinking of all the things that might have been, had Bert been spared.

"Dear God," she prayed, "let me stay here and help those who need help tonight, like those prostitutes Mrs. Swenson took in. Let me keep busy, doing in his place and in his name what Bert would have done."

She sat up on hearing Griz prodding Prentice anew to take her to his home and Amelia. Homer was still comatose. He seemed utterly unable to comprehend or accept the misfortune which had not touched him personally. She could have cried out, "Why, Homer? Only ten minutes you were babbling to Bert about the desk you had lost, as if it were as precious to you as Bert has been to me!

"No!" she cried suddenly, with anger, scrambling to her feet. "No! We don't need your help, Homer. We shall take care of Bert ourselves. And then," she cried, her big eyes burning into Griz, "you and I are going to carry on for Bert! *They* killed him, Griz—the people like Homer here who, Bert told us, were only thinking about looking after themselves and what they owned, rather than pitching in to help this town from being wiped out. That's what Bert was trying to tell us. This town needs leadership tonight and he was trying to do it all alone. Now we must do it for him."

Griz shook his head in impulsive awe of, and great admiration for, her courage and desire at such a moment of personal loss. "But he told me to take you home," he said firmly. "That I well remember and I'm going to see that you go."

"Oh, no you're not, Mr. Grizzly! Not even if you carry me. Now you go and get help. I want to stay here with Bert until somebody besides us is willing to take care of him for tonight."

When that was being done, she and Griz looked at each other as if to say, "What now?"

Then her explosive mind began to percolate.

"Griz," she reminded him, "you and I have been all around

this downtown area tonight since the fire started. Has it occurred to you that all anybody is doing is trying to put out fires and nothing about stopping them from continuing to spread?"

He agreed. "But what can you expect? Our volunteer fire department is trained only to put out fires, not how to deal with something of these proportions."

"Exactly what I'm getting at!"

He could see she was thinking hard, blinking her eyes at flames only a block away that shot higher every minute.

"This is like a forest fire, Griz. Isn't it? How do they keep a forest fire from spreading?"

"They backfire."

"*That's* the word I've been trying to remember! Why don't we backfire before we have a conflagration?"

"We already have a conflagration on our hands."

"Then why don't we backfire? Do you know any better way to keep the whole town from burning down?"

"Good question. Who's going to order it done?"

"You are!" she said without hesitation.

He gasped. "Me?"

"Yes, you! Who else is there?"

"Bill Saxon, I suppose. He's chairman of the council."

"But have you seen him anywhere around tonight?"

Griz shook his head.

"Or any of the other councilmen? 'Probably looking after yours truly,' Bert said. He was disgusted with them. That leaves only Abe Long," she concluded.

"And he's a good cop," Griz said, "but that's all. Not an idea man or organizer. You remember I had to pull his irons out of the fire the first night of Sunday closing—and with your suggestion for the march down Schoolhouse Hill."

"Which reminds me," she said, "if we have to take the responsibility for doing something to stop the spread of this fire, only you and I and the man who took Bert away know what happened to him. So we can say to anyone who challenges our right to speak for him that he appointed you to be deputy mayor, to carry out his plans, and me to assist you in seeing that what you order is done. Agreed?"

"If you say so!" Griz looked with wonder on this mere slip

of a woman, with the figure of a twelve-year-old boy, unmarried until thirty-one and widowed within two months, standing ten feet tall at the moment. Despite the sorrow in her heart, she had *desire*, the greatest driving force any man or woman could possess. She was so determined that something must be done to save Cracker Creek—and Bert Ascher should get credit for it—that there was no longer any doubt in his mind it could be accomplished.

"What are your orders, Mrs. Mayor?" he said with an affectionate grin.

"No orders, just ideas. It was that way, too, back in August on the first night of Sunday closing of the bars and taverns."

She suggested they should try first to persuade the volunteer firemen to stop fighting hopeless boardwalk fires and go out among the homes on the lower hillside instead, helping put out little roof fires that were being started everywhere by flaming pieces of wood, blown far and wide by the vacillating north wind.

They went first into the fire zone and cornered the fire chief with this idea. A skeptical Marshal Abe Long listened in on the argument that a fireman's first job, said the chief, was to put out the big fire.

Mary spoke up quickly. "Your mayor said to tell you that people have to have shelter before they can go back to rebuilding what has been lost by fire."

"They can live in tents," the chief said.

"That's what they did in Seattle in 1889," Long recalled.

"Not in weather like this," Mary shot back at them. "The Seattle fire was in midsummer. Just you let these people lose their homes while you try to save the stores and bars along the boardwalk and scores of them will take the next train out and never come back."

Griz broke in: "What's it to be? Stores and bars and cat houses or people's homes and their belongings? Which do you want to live with in the aftermath of this night?

The chief and marshal looked at each other and shrugged.

Griz turned to Abe Long. "You know when I set out to get something done, I don't quit until it's done. You appointed me your deputy on the Fourth of July when you had a big hot spot at the depot and I cooled it off. And again in August when I had to make sure every one of those bars and taverns was locked up at the stroke of midnight. And they were!"

Mary told them, "My husband, the mayor, has had a heart attack and he appointed Griz to be deputy mayor to carry out his wishes, especially with respect to saving people's homes."

"How are you going to do it?" the chief asked.

"I'm going to start a backfire, just like you do in a forest fire." Griz barked out the words to give them the ring of authority.

"Where are you going to get the men to do it?" the chief asked, a smirk on his face.

"I've got scores of friends among the miners and lumberjacks who were in town tonight at the Redhead's birthday party. Just you tell me you have no objections and I'll see it's done."

The marshal said, "As far as I'm concerned, you're on your own, Griz." He waved goodbye as he turned away.

He chuckled as the chief agreed. "That includes me, too. I never heard you say nothing." But he added, out of the corner of his mouth, that he would pull most of his men off the boardwalk fires and try to stop the fires from spreading up the hillside among the homes.

What a job Griz and Mary did from that moment on, recruiting miners and lumberjacks and rounding up axes and dynamite to create a firebreak! Some homes were leveled in the process. Dynamite was used to do it on the theory that a pile of "jackstrawed" lumber is not likely to ignite as easily as a roof. And they chopped down and hauled away some trees that would have provided more fuses to set the whole hillside afire.

By morning, Griz and Mary were ready to drop from exhaustion, but high on their accomplishment. Cracker Creek had been saved from extinction by the men who had feted the Redhead. That, at least, was a measure of satisfaction.

Griz had to put an arm around Mary to keep her from collapsing as they slogged their way up the hill to their separate homes.

Mary looked up to Griz with tears in her eyes. "Remember how you saw me to my door the day I told you I was going to marry Bert?"

He dipped his head in agreement, as much in salute to her unbelievable stamina in carrying on, only hours after losing Bert, as in reply to her question.

"Thank you for what you did in his name tonight. That's why you did it, wasn't it?"

"Sure thing—and for you, too!"

"I knew you wouldn't let me down." Her face glowed in the morning light with the affection she still bore him.

He gave a little laugh, then kissed her lightly on the forehead and sent her on her separate way.

With the coming of daylight, it was clear there was nothing left downtown but remnants of the boardwalk and the brick shell of Homer Prentice's bank. Fire had leveled everything else down to the depot. But most everyone still had his home.

In the stillness that followed this night of terror, only one sound rent the morning air. From far off, muted but inexorable, came the Stygian clamor of the monster known as the dredge.

"Business as usual," Griz grimaced to himself as he got up after two hours' sleep to go to work.

12

Mary Ascher had not slept more than four hours before she was awake and thinking. She no longer had the comfort and love of a kindly man who had made a woman out of her. And the tragedy of it was he had not lived to enjoy the fruits of their love.

What could she do now to bridge the gap in her life? She had given up teaching with her marriage. There might not be another opening in the grades for a year or two. And there would be no clerking jobs downtown until it was rebuilt. Without a job she simply could not face the prospect of keeping house for herself alone.

The irony of her situation was that she had always hated housework, but she had loved doing it for Bert. It made a difference when she was washing and mending *his* socks, or getting the right amount of starch in the collar before ironing *his* shirts, or making sure she did not break the yolks when doing *his* eggs "over and easy."

She had not realized that these were the little things which made a marriage satisfying. She wept quietly for the dream of what might have been, then gave her head a toss and flounced out of bed, determined to find something to do quickly.

"Something to do!" these words were a command to put an end to feeling sorry for herself and to get with it. Recalling the terrifying night's best story—six prostitutes in search of a bedroom—she wondered how many other folk, normally disdainful of asking for help, might be incapable of getting their bearings this morning. Who but she and Griz, both having lost the one person closest to them, were better qualified to help those who had only lost a home or place of business?

She went to the phone to call Griz, but it rang in her ear as she lifted the receiver. "They found the bodies of Red and Leckenby this morning," he said quickly.

"Oh, Griz!" Her voice broke.

"I thought you'd want to know. She lay in his arms, as if he had been carrying her."

"Oh, I hope she didn't suffer," Mary prayed.

"The coroner said she was most likely dead when he reached her."

Mary could no longer hold back her tears. "But at least he did find her and take her in his arms before he died. Isn't that wonderful?"

'I don't know," Griz hedged. "I was wondering why it had to be Mary Armittage on the night of her finest hour, unless it was ordained *up there* that he should give her his Bible on Thanksgiving Day."

"Maybe," Mary said, "but I can't forget how he tore his shirt in strips and soaked them in snow, then wrapped them around his nose and mouth. I think he chose to die, rather than never be able to worship her again."

Griz hesitated. "I'm not sure I would have made the same sacrifice."

He told her the town's ministers had arranged for them to be buried that afternoon in the little cemetery high on the hillside above town. He offered to drive her up there for the service.

Mary next heard from Mrs. Swenson, who was at her door within the hour. Since the landlady never made a call on anyone for any reason whatever, Mary feared she was going to hear that the prostitutes had made a shambles of morale at the boarding house. Even before Mrs. Swenson could speak, Mary asked: "Did those women make a sucker out of you in taking them in?"

"No," was the amused answer. "They behaved like ladies. They even made their beds before they left—with fresh sheets!"

Mary heaved a sigh of relief.

Mrs. Swenson said, "I came to ask you to dinner, but what I really wanted to say was, 'Move back with us until you get your bearings.' "

Mary put her arms around her old friend. "You're sweet, Mrs. Swenson, but . . . " She shook her head. "Leave Bert's house and all it means to me?"

"I know," Mrs. Swenson comforted her. "You don't want to

let down. That's good. But what you need most of all now is family around you. We have been your family a long time, Mary. Come back to us until you know what you want to do."

Mary opened her mouth to say she wanted most of all to work with Griz, helping people in trouble because of the fire, but she held her tongue, remembering Mrs. Swenson's dislike of him. Yet she felt she ought to tell her Red's body had been found.

"Oh, that's too bad," Mrs. Swenson said, quite sincerely. "Bring Mr. Quigley to dinner with you."

Mary looked up quickly, openly surprised he should be included. She dared not ask why, but Mrs. Swenson, as serious as ever, explained: "Men take it harder than women, that's why. He needs company today more than you do. Bring him."

Which Mary did. And Mrs. Swenson surprised everyone by complimenting Griz for what he had done to stop the fire.

"You did more than a lot of people around here who think they are God almighty," she said, looking straight at Bill Saxon, who had a reputation for being the most outspoken town councilman. "You and Mary both. You were the only folks in town who lost more than what they owned."

"Hear, hear!" exclaimed Saxon, ever the politician, leading the handclapping around the table.

The feeling of being caught in a vacuum came over her as she and Griz drove home from services for Red and Leckenby. She began crying softly, tears which had been held back at Red's grave, knowing that she would not be able to stem them on the morrow when Bert was buried nearby.

"Griz," she cried, "what am I going to do now? It was so wonderful last night having something to do for others when I needed to forget my sorrow. I don't want to stop now and think, Griz. I want to start doing something to keep my mind occupied. Don't you feel the same way today?"

"Maybe," he grunted laconically. He had gone into his shell at the Redhead's grave.

She babbled on. She thought he was being aggravating, just mumbling answers. She needed to talk about anything and everything, just so she could keep her mind off herself.

"Mrs. Swenson wants me to come live with her again for

a week or two," she told him.

"I think you should," he agreed.

"But I'll go crazy just sitting around the boarding house, doing nothing between meals except sewing and reading books. What are you going to do, now that there is no more Nugget?"

"Maybe I'll stay at the dredge until it's time to go home to bed."

"That's it!" she cried. "We both need something to take our minds off our sorrow. Isn't there anything we can do together, like we did last night?"

"What people need most now is money." He spread his hands significantly. "What can *we* do about that?"

"Get the money out of the dredge!"

"I don't think they have that kind of money."

"I'll bet Monte's bank would give people the money if the dredge stood behind them."

"You mean guarantee their loans? Yes, Utah Mining and Dredge might do that."

"Let's ask Mr. Trench," she bubbled. "Right now when the iron's hot!"

Griz was amazed at the way she was bouncing back. If people only had half her get up and go, he was certain the Creek would be on its feet again in a matter of weeks.

"Okay," he said. "We will go see Trench right now."

Impulsively she hugged his arm as she always did in the old days. "I knew you wouldn't let me down!"

The tart-faced manager of the dredge listened to their proposition impassively, then remarked, "Might make us liked a little better around here. I'll get a telegram off at once."

Approval by the company came the next day.

"Get the word around," Trench told Griz. "I want to see all who lost a business here at three this afternoon."

"That's the time the mayor is being buried," Griz said.

"So it is. Make it ten tomorrow morning. I want Mrs. Ascher here especially." He grinned. "She'd light a fire under a mule. Take the day off and look after her."

Griz found Mary in Mrs. Swenson's parlor as that good lady was fitting her with a small bonnet and starting to drape it with widow's weeds. She was surrounded by yards and yards of black veiling. He stood, open-mouthed in his astonishment.

"It's only fitting she should be dressed in proper weeds for the funeral," Mrs. Swenson said emphatically.

Griz realized this was no time to tell Mary of the good news from Trench. He stood back to take a good look at the effect Mrs. Swenson was creating. Poor Mary, her dark eyes clouded now, was peering through the black netting like a caged bird. Crinkled veiling streamed over her shoulders and down her back almost to the floor, accentuating her tiny frame and childlike face.

Mary was clasping and unclasping her hands and looking plaintively to Griz for help. "Could I just wear the bonnet and face veil and forget the rest?" she asked Mrs. Swenson.

Griz came over and gently turned back the veil from Mary's face. "There now," he said softly, as if reassuring a child, "that's better. Let's take this heavy stuff off her back, too," deftly unfastening the great length of black veiling.

Mary looked at him gratefully.

"Now that is real nice," Mrs. Swenson agreed after studying the effect. "She's now dressed as becomes the mayor's widow, yet she still looks like our Mary."

The two of them jumped at the same time to catch Mary as she grabbed a chair and hung on tightly, eyes closed and swaying perilously from dizziness.

Mrs. Swenson hurried off to get smelling salts while Griz picked Mary up and would have laid her on the couch if she had not demanded he put her down.

"I'll be all right now," she insisted, waving the smelling salts away. "I just felt faint for a moment and had to hang onto something. It has passed now. Don't baby me." She turned to Mrs. Swenson. "I suppose you've guessed by now I'm pregnant."

"I noticed you were a little pale but didn't want to say anything."

Griz looked at his watch. "Time to get going, Mary."

She looked up quickly at him with such simple devotion he blinked in surprise. She wanted to tell him she didn't know what she would do without him, but was afraid Mrs. Swenson would be scandalized if she did. She only meant to say he was, in a way, all the family she now had to lean on. Her folks were too far away in the dead of winter.

Cracker Creek gave Bert Ascher a funeral befitting the love

and respect most everybody had for him. "He would have been humbled, but deeply moved, by it," said Mary.

"You loved him, that's why," said Griz simply.

"And that's why we must do what he would have done had he lived," she vowed.

Then he told her of the "go ahead" answer from the dredge. "You don't mean it!" She shrieked her joy, then buried her face in her hands, letting her head sway from side to side until the ecstasy of the moment had passed.

"Trench said to make sure you would be at the meeting tomorrow morning," Griz added.

"I'll *be* there," she grinned. But she was not prepared to be asked to sit up front alongside Griz while Trench spelled out the details of his company's offer.

"I have asked the widow of the late mayor to join us," he said, "because she and Quigley came to me Sunday morning to ask if U M & D would underwrite rebuilding the boardwalk area. I remember especially the way she put it, in words which went something like this:

" 'Cracker Creek still has a heart, Mr. Trench, but no body. Its workaday world has been burned out. Its heart, its desire to keep on living, will die, too, if fresh blood, in the form of money, is not pumped into its veins immediately.'

"I was so impressed I got on the wire at once with my company in Ogden. This is the answer U M & D makes to Mary Ascher, in memory of her late husband, for whom I had great respect: 'To put Cracker Creek back in business quickly, we will guarantee the notes of responsible business men, not exceeding one-quarter of a million dollars in the aggregate, provided they use the money to replace a going business lost in the fire and convince Quigley and Mrs. Ascher they have an intense desire to make a go of it again.'

"Furthermore, I am authorized to offer the use of dredge personnel to help clean up downtown debris at no cost either to the town or to you individually. You just tell me how many men you need and we'll do the rest."

The response was inspiring. They crowded around Trench to thank him and to present their needs. He waved them away. "Don't thank me. Talk to Quigley and Mrs. Ascher. It's their idea, not mine. You tell them just what you need and how much it will cost. When you've had your say, I'll get together with them and we'll determine who gets what."

Mary could not believe it. Trench had named her to work with Griz evaluating requests for U M & D backing on bank loans. She turned to Griz, humility written all over her face. "Why me?" she asked, seeming to dissolve into a little girl again, whose hunched shoulders and anxious hand at the throat said this was a gift more precious than anything she had ever dreamed of possessing. "Why me?" she asked again, barely above a whisper.

"Because I asked for you," he laughed, tipping her chin up affectionately. "We got into this together and we're going to see it through as a team!"

"As a team!" She seemed to be enchanted by the words.

"Enough of that! Now let's get busy!" he said brusquely. "You're better at that than dreaming about it." He handed her a tablet and pencil and seated her beside him at a table.

"Who's first?" he said to the men lining up for interviews. One by one they seated themselves opposite Griz and Mary to state their cases and needs. Griz emphasized to each this was only a preliminary listing of names and money needed; that they would be called back later for extensive interviews.

Worn out with listening and probing for initial answers, but exhilarated by a sense of accomplishment under way, they looked at each other at day's end and fell into an exhausted embrace, slapping each other on the back.

"Your face is flushed," Griz told her.

"So's yours," Mary giggled, collapsing back into her chair. "But, oh! hasn't it been exciting? Except I don't know yet what I'm supposed to be contributing."

"If you've got it all down in writing, you're worth all the money you're not being paid."

"But seriously, Griz. I'm no secretary."

"Of course, you aren't. If I wanted a secretary, I'd have called in the girl in the next office. I wanted you because you have a gift for being able to read people. I'll bet you can give me a rundown on every one of those we interviewed today. And their wives, too."

She nodded. "Pretty much so."

"That's important. Trench is counting on you and me to say

who is good for the money he borrows and who is not. And whether or not any of them is asking for too much.."

"How would we know that?"

"Because I'm an engineer for one thing. I know costs. But what is far more important is knowing they are good at playing poker."

"I don't know anything about playing poker."

"He shook his head at her naivete." "You're one of the best poker players I know."

"I never played it in my life," she insisted.

"I don't mean with cards. You, and every woman worth her salt, plays it every day of her life with a word or a gesture, a change in her mood or the look in her eyes"—he grinned because he knew this hit home—"whenever any given moment will get her what she wants. She's the one who will say to the husbands we've been seeing today: 'Ask for five or ten thousand extra so you'll get what we want.' I want to spot the man whose wife is good at that game. I'm going to lean heavily on your instinct and judgment in dealing with these people."

One of the best poker players he knew? She zinged with delight in the implied tribute. She guessed this was a man's way of doffing his hat to her without putting it in words. But she blushed, too, because this most likely meant he was wise to her making a great play for his love the past summer.

But now she must play a different sort of poker. She was a matron and a widow, with a child in her womb, and it ill behooved her to let her old feelings for him run rampant again. She must steel herself against him. More than ever they were vulnerable to each other now, a pair newly bereaved, in need of love. A dangerous combination when thrown together like this, day after day.

But she suspected it was a losing game they were now playing. Day after day they found they had to work into the night to complete their recommendations to Trench. She apologized to Mrs. Swenson for bringing Griz to so many suppers. "I could move back to my home and start getting meals again."

"No!" Mrs. Swenson put her foot down. "It is better this way." She had given them the use of her private parlor evenings.

"Otherwise people might talk," she said.

Yes, Mary admitted, there was the rub. They dared not go off by themselves, especially on these long winter nights. The work was exhausting, but exciting. Interviews, conferences and still more talks, poring over plans for rebuilding and estimates for restocking. They wound up many a night washed out completely.

It was then she sensed they had a growing need for each other; that she realized what the Redhead had meant to Griz and Bert to her. Red and Bert were the even-tempered ones. She and Griz were the fire horses, the ones who needed love and all its rewards as much as they needed meat and potatoes. Now they needed it most at day's end when they were jaded and irritable and their resistance was low. At those moments she knew she only had to put a sympathetic hand on Griz's arm and he would have swept her into his arms at once, hungry for the love that Red had given him when he was at low ebb. The very thought that this might happen panicked her.

More so because, fight it as she did with every bit of will power, she had to admit she was falling in love with Griz all over again. And for entirely different reasons. His appeal was to her respect now, as well as to her heart. He had become a personage in his own right, not just a physically attractive, fun-loving, sometimes crude outdoorsman. She could be proud of him in any company. He no longer wore corduroy jackets and britches with leather boots on all occasions. He was quite handsome in a business suit and kept his beard neatly trimmed at all times.

Most of all, she would never have believed he could be so dedicated about making sure that money backed by U M & D got into the right hands. Working side by side with him these last three weeks, she had never ceased to marvel at the way he cut through instantly to the heart of a problem and wasted no time coming to a decision. This decisiveness impressed her. It had taken a job with the dredge and a calamitous fire to bring the best out of him. Where had she and Red failed him in the past?

Then a committee of three town councilmen put an end to appreciation of his capabilities. She hardly gave them a second glance when they called at the dredge and asked to speak to him privately. He was closeted with them no more than fifteen minutes before he came out to tell her they had asked him to succeed Bert Ascher as mayor.

"What do you think of that!" he rejoiced, slapping her desk in his excitement. "How does that sound—Mayor Quigley?"

It was good for his new ego that he had been asked, but she knew instinctively that he should not accept. She squirmed in her chair miserably.

"You don't like it!" he barked at her in sudden anger. "Why not?" He had taken to pacing the floor, waving his arms about to emphasize his fury.

"Oh, Griz, you should be flattered, of course, but not mayor!"

He leaned over her desk, spitting out the bitter words. "I suppose you're trying to tell me I'm not good enough to be mayor, that I'm not a Bert Ascher. Let me tell you, young lady, that husband of yours wasn't so wonderful that he can't be replaced."

She thought for a moment he was going to grab her shoulders and shake the life out of her. But, with a toss of his head, he strode toward the door, smacking his fist into the palm of his left hand.

"Come back here," she called sharply to him, knowing that the only people he respected were those who spoke up to him. When he complied, she said: "Now look at me! You know me better than to think I'd belittle you. I'm only thinking of you and your future. Being mayor was just perfect for Bert. He was middle-aged and going nowhere. But you, Griz, are young and ambitious. So much of your life still lies ahead. Don't get mired in small town politics. It's a dead end."

"But it's everything I want at the moment," he pleaded. "Remember how long I have been tossed about in this town? So I can be cock of the walk now! The old biddies who'd never invite me to their homes would have to lump it and like it now! And I could tell Bill Saxon to go to hell. . . ."

Mary shook her head sorrowfully. "You would be trading a great future for the fleeting enjoyment of getting even with no more than a few people, Griz." She threw up her hands. "But who am I to try to influence you? Only the Redhead was good at that."

Instantly he was angry again. He bounded to his feet. "You leave Red out of this. My relationship with her was our affair. And," raising his voice higher with each word, "she never tried to *dictate* to me!"

"Nor have I," Mary said quietly. Too quietly, in fact, because he missed her answer in his haste to close the door on further discussion. "Just see that you remember," was his parting shot.

"Very well, Griz. Thank you for putting me in my place."

She took the black cuffs off her forearms, gathered up her papers and put them in the drawer. She was sick at heart for having failed to convince him he was destined for greater achievements. Disheartened, too, because she had begun to dream that, with the Redhead no longer around to comfort him, he might eventually turn to her. But she would never marry him if he became mayor of Cracker Creek. This was final.

When she put on her galoshes and reached for her coat, Griz relented. "Going home early?" he asked.

She nodded. Nothing more.

"I'm sorry I popped off," he said, a bit sheepish. "I know you feel this way because you care, and it means a lot to me that you *do* care. But I must just get it out of my system."

Putting on her mittens, she asked, "Did you tell them you would take the job?"

"Not exactly. But I'll tell them Monday."

She looked up at him with tears in her eyes. He was so startled by the effect he almost missed what she was saying.

"I ought to tell you, Griz, that if you become mayor, you and I part company. I shall leave the Creek."

"But I was going to appoint you my secretary."

"I mean it, Griz. I'm not going to stay here to see you go downhill once more."

"Oh, come off it, Mary. I'm going to be a good mayor. I'll make you proud of me. I'm going to do everything Bert would have done."

"I'm sure you will," she said, reaching up to pull his head down for a quick kiss on the cheek. "That's to remember me by."

She was long gone before the words came back to him.

She went straight home to the boarding house, quickly

packed an overnight bag, and told Mrs. Swenson she was taking the four o'clock to Baker for a few days.

"Do you good to get away from everything for a week or two," Mrs. Swenson agreed.

Mary never let her see the tears in her eyes. This was for good. She would send for the rest of her things when she finally decided where she would settle down.

Griz did not know Mary had walked out on him until two days later, after Cracker Creek had been all but snowed under over the weekend. He did not telephone her on Sunday because he was still miffed with her, but he broke down when he had such a terrible time getting to work on Monday because of the depth of the snow. He rang the boarding house to tell her not to try to come in.

He was stunned when Mrs. Swenson told him Mary had taken the afternoon train to Baker on Saturday. ("Only two hours after she left me," he muttered to himself, unable to believe it.)

"Didn't she tell you she was going?"

"Well . . . " he hesitated. "Yes and no. But I didn't know she was leaving right away."

Now he knew what she meant when she said, "This is to remember me by." When he hung up, he was furious. He railed against her out loud, pacing the floor. "Of all the dad-blasted, contemptible things to do to a guy!"

He stomped to the phone and asked Central to get him Cara on the line in Baker.

"Sorry, Mr. Quigley," she informed him, "the line to Baker is down. We don't know when it will be fixed."

Then he'd use the telegraph. He waded through snow and drifts, sometimes up to his hips, to the railway depot, to be further astounded by finding Old Pluto sitting on its haunches, quietly snoozing, with its fires banked to keep the boilers from freezing.

"What's that train doing here this hour of the morning?" he demanded of Jillson, the stationmaster.

"Trying to make up its mind whether it can get back to Baker," Jillson said. "Been here since yesterday P.M. Canyon's blocked until they get there with snowplows."

Griz snorted. "Telegraph still working?"

"Sure enough."

Griz handed him the message for Cara. It read: "MARY LEFT HERE SATURDAY. HAVE YOU SEEN HER? RUSH REPLY."

He had an answer within the hour: "ANSWER IS NO. SHOULD WE HAVE SEEN HER?"

"Any reply to that?" Jillson asked over the phone.

"No. Forget it." Griz crumpled the paper on which he had written down the message and fired it across the room. But he was no longer as angry as he was worried. What if she had gone and done something desperate? He couldn't believe it of her, but her parting words were beginning to haunt him. *"This is to remember me by!"* A kiss on the cheek and she was gone from his life. For how long? God only knew.

He stuck his hands in his pockets and stepped outside to think. He stood under the overhang of the roof, gazing forlornly at a frozen world, swirling with snow being blown about by the same cruel wind which had half buried Cracker Creek. The streets were deserted, the only sounds to be heard being the occasional scraping of a snow shovel and the whining of a freezing dog.

Suddenly he felt very lonely and forgotten.

More than anything else he needed someone to tell him where to turn now. His training and experience as an engineer were of no help now in solving the human experience. With Mary and the Redhead gone, who was there left to turn to?

He could think of only one person who would be as honest with him as Red and Mary had been. He called Amelia Prentice to ask if she would see him.

"Troubles?" she asked.

"Very much so."

"Come ahead, but I would have thought I would be the last person you would want to tell your troubles to."

She listened to his story carefully, then asked shrewdly, "Are you in love with her, Griz?"

He gasped. "You called me 'Griz,' instead of 'Quigley.' " He was completely astounded by her unexpected warmth.

"I'm not going to apologize for the past," she explained, "but I think you have earned the right to be called by whatever name you choose. Now answer my question."

He hesitated, running a hand over his whiskers, scratching the back of his neck.

"You are taking too much time to think," she objected. She snapped her fingers. "You should answer just like that."

"It's not a matter of a simple yes or no," he said. "I haven't let myself think about her that way because it wouldn't be proper, so soon after Bert's death."

"Fiddlesticks!" Amelia scoffed. "She was married only a couple of months. That was not long enough to go into deep mourning. Except for that?" She waited.

"I'm afraid we were getting deeply attached to each other every day, Amelia."

"That's another name for love, Griz."

"Yes, I know."

"And you are missing her like fury now?"

"I can't work. I can't even think straight today. We had suddenly become a team, Amelia."

"Like man and wife?"

"I guess you're right. I need her and I'm worrying myself crazy, afraid something has happened to her."

"Which would you rather have?" she asked. "To have Mary come back or be mayor?"

He grinned. "Both, if you ask me to be honest. But I guess she won't have it that way, so I'll take Mary."

"If you can find her. She's got the right idea, Griz. With what you have shown us you can do since the fire, don't settle for politics."

"Where do I look for her, Amelia? Where would she go?"

"Have you ever thought she might go home to her family?"

He laughed. "It never occurred to me. I guess that proves I'm in love, Amelia. I miss her like hell."

"That's a pretty good test," she smiled, patting him on the hand. "Now go find her quickly."

The problem was to find out where her parents lived. He remembered she had once said they lived on a farm between Pendleton and Hermiston, on the Umatilla River, one hundred fifty miles away. One look at the map said this was a huge area, miles from any important town except those two.

"Whew!" he whistled to himself, "if they are snowed in like we are here, finding their farm will be nearly impossible."

185

He spent a useless day in Pendleton, getting no clue to a family named Meakin, but some worthwile advice. Forget postmasters, he was told. Check grain elevators and feed dealers. If anyone knows where a farmer lives, they do.

Next day he moved on to Hermiston, again by train, and quickly learned there was a Meakin farm down by the Umatilla River, some ten miles back off the main road to Pendleton, on a county road that involved a couple of left and right turns at crossroads. By midday he was on his way in a hired sleigh.

This was a fantastically different sort of country from that to which he had become accustomed. It was like a laundry washboard, undulating higher and higher in wave on wave of open prairie. He imagined it must be unbelievably beautiful when the wheat was golden brown and rippling in errant breezes that never seemed to cease blowing.

Now it was a wonderland of drifts carved by the gusts into weird curlycues and patches of brown earth blown clear of snow. Trailing sheafs of the filmy stuff danced tiptoe over the fields like a ballet dancer. But it was tough going, even in a sleigh. Only a fence here and there marked where the road *might* be. The next minute it might be buried under a drift up to his elbows and he would have to get out to break trail for the horse.

Eventually he came to a mailbox marked "Meakin." He thanked someone for that shoveled path from the mailbox to the farmhouse door. A kindly woman answered his knock.

"Is Mary here, Mrs. Meakin?" he asked.

She studied him closely, even looked around him to see how he had gotten there, in the middle of nowhere.

"Who are you?" she asked finally, unsmiling.

"Who's there?" a man said, coming up behind her to look over her shoulder. Griz assumed this was Mr. Meakin.

"I'm a friend of Mary's. From Cracker Creek. She would have called me 'Griz' if she ever mentioned me in her letters."

"Are you the one she's come home about?" Mrs. Meakin asked.

He could have kissed her on the spot. She had told him all he needed to know. At least he had found Mary. The cold fear that had been paralyzing him was at an end.

"I don't know what it's all about," the mother continued, "and

186

it's none of my business anyway, but if you're the one, I wish you would do something to straighten her out."

Shaking his head, he said, "I'm the one who needs straightening out, Mrs. Meakin. That's why I've come, to tell her she's right. I've been three days trying to find her. She never told anyone where she was going. Just lit out. We had to guess where she might be."

The words rattled off his tongue, he was so excited about finding her.

Mrs. Meakin turned to Pa. "Shall we tell him?"

"You the fellow they want to elect mayor?" Pa asked.

"Yes, sir, but that's all over now."

The last thing he did before leaving the Creek was to call one of the councilmen to say, regretfully, he could not accept.

"Then we'd better tell him," Meakin said to his wife.

She pointed a finger. "See those footsteps leading to that clump of trees yonder, down by the river?"

Griz nodded.

"Follow them and you'll find her." She was smiling now. "But I wish you'd come in first and get dried out." She stood aside to let him enter, but he shook his head. "I want to see Mary first."

He struck out at once, lifting his feet one at a time and setting them down in the holes made in the snow by her galoshes. In some places they were two feet deep. He had trouble several times keeping his balance because she had taken such short steps, but nothing could induce him to strike out on his own in virgin snow. This was a game he had been good at when he was a child and he meant to show her he was not a . . . what did she call it that night at Riverside Park? Oh, yes! A "nincompoop!"

While he was still quite a distance away, he saw that she was sitting on a log, down by the river. Even though she had her back to him, the sight of her, alone and hunched over in that cold and desolate spot, roused all his pent-up feelings. He stumbled forward, driven by an urge to smother her in his arms and to make amends for all the heartaches he had caused her, beginning with that night in the park.

He had felt it in his heart that night that she was to be his destiny, but he had put her ruthlessly out of mind because he was not yet ready to become involved with any woman after his late wife, Alice.

"Oh, the waste of all the months since that night of the shivaree!" he said to himself bitterly. "Both Red and Bert Ascher might still be alive if I had not put Mary out of mind!"

Mary had come to the scene of her most cherished childhood memories to resolve the doubts and regrets which had been destroying her ever since she walked out on Griz. Whenever, as a child, she got in bad with Mother and Pa, all she had to do was come down here, sit on the same log, take off her shoes and stockings, and dabble her toes in the Umatilla and all her troubles would be washed away.

Of course, she could not dip her toes today in a swimming hole covered with thick ice, but it was the exquisite stillness of the place which had finally given her peace. She had thought that just coming home would do this for her, but she should have known better. As always, she had brought her problems to her parents, when all she wanted was the peaceful isolation of the farm.

At first, it was just as she had hoped to find it. All was cozy in Mama's kitchen. Pa was resting from arduous, everyday chores, smoking his pipe, his chair tipped back comfortably near the stove. He reminded her of Bert, and Mama of Mrs. Swenson. It was all very pleasant until they began to draw her out about why she had come home.

They made her tell the story of the fire over and over and what she had been doing to help rebuild the town. They hungered to hear all about her marriage and Bert's funeral. She wished she might tell them about Griz, other than he had been asked to be mayor and she had quit her job because he was going to say yes. She could only shrug when they asked why he should not take it, because she could picture their shocked faces if she had replied, "Because I'm in love with him and he would rather be mayor, even if that means I won't marry him."

Today she had finally told them about the baby. Bert had died so soon after she knew for sure, she had put off writing about it until she knew what was going to happen to her.

Mama's reaction to the good news wavered between joy over

the prospect of becoming a grandmother and anxiety over how Mary was going to support herself and look after a child. Now it was going to be embarrassing to have to admit she had been hoping to marry Griz before she had Bert's baby.

Eventually she simply *had* to get completely away from family for a few hours every day. She had two choices: To go to her room and read or down to her beloved swimming hole. When the weather was nice, there was no contest. She didn't mind breaking trail. That made it more exciting. But Mama had a conniption fit. "In your condition, dear? You know you mustn't!"

"Nonsense! I've been doing it before you knew about the baby, so what's different?"

She felt better at once, getting out into the crisp, clear air; listening to the gurgling river out where it ran too swiftly to freeze over, and swirling against shore ice where this swimming hole had been created centuries ago.

She could hear again the cry that panicked every child as they tried to shed their clothes in jig time:

"Last one in is a nincompoop!
Last one in is a nincompoop!"

Then she must have dozed for a moment. Now she heard a new sound, distinctly above the river slapping fringe ice. Crunch of steps in the snow behind her. Instantly alert, she refused to turn to see who it was. None but Griz would satisfy her now. She was lost if he had not come seeking her. She shivered as the crunching came nearer. Then a voice she would never forget said: "Last one in is a nincompoop!" and his rough hands caressed her shoulders, and she was instantly on her feet, shrieking his name and whirling around to be engulfed in a mighty bear hug.

"Oh, Griz! If you had not come I would have died. How did you know where to find me?"

But he had no time yet for answers. He was kissing her again and again, as if he could never satisfy his hunger for her. His whiskers, all frosted over by his breath, were scratching her face, but she loved it because he had never kissed her like this before.

"I thought I might never see you again," he whispered in her ear.

She took his head between her mittened palms and carressed his face. "It's so cold! And your nose is—oh, my!" She wanted to cry, and did, silently, but they were tears of joy. "You cared enough to find me! That's all that counts!"

"Mary, I've been such an ass. I didn't realize until you left me that I couldn't go on without you. Can you ever forgive me?"

She put a finger on his lips to show he had no need of being forgiven, but he brushed it aside. "That's not all I have to tell you," he said. "Before I left the Creek I told the council I would not under any circumstances take the job of mayor."

"Oh, but you must!"

"Not while you're my wife," he said sternly.

"But you haven't asked me yet," she countered.

He frowned briefly before fixing her with steely eyes. "Consider it said."

She cocked her head expectantly. "No more than that? Just three words?"

"No more! I mean to be the boss in this family, on my *say-so* and *acting on your judgment* in whatever the matter be."

On which note, they fell again into each other's arms, laughing their heads off with such vigor she would have fallen backwards off the log, onto the ice of the swimming hole, if he had not been holding her tightly.

"Now who," he asked with a twinkle in his eyes, "would have been the nincompoop this time if I had let go?"

They told no one but Mrs. Swenson about their plans on their return to the Creek. "I'd say it was about time!" that estimable lady remarked in giving them her blessing. She favored them with one of her rare smiles.

"We are not telling anyone else now," Mary said, "until about my sixth month. Meantime we shall continue to work as a team at the dredge, putting together the details for U M & D to guarantee loans restoring business on the boardwalk. That way everyone will get used to seeing us together all the time and whatever we do eventually won't come as a surprise."

"But we want to be married before she has her baby," Griz added, "so I can give it my name."

"That's gracious of you," Mrs. Swenson commented with a

warmth she had never shown him before. Turning to Mary, she asked, "I suppose this means you won't be needing your room here any more?"

"No. I want to get my house fixed up so it will be ready for both Griz and the baby to move in. And I've got to learn how to cook and keep house all over again."

"In that case, Griz," said Mrs. Swenson, blushing as she used his familiar name for the second time, "perhaps you'd like to take over her room when she moves out."

"Just give me the key," he said with a big grin.

Mary hugged Griz with newfound exhilaration. "Do you realize what this means? At last you *are one of us* here!" Not the least embarrassed by Mrs. Swenson's presence, she held up her face to be kissed and Griz obliged with gusto!